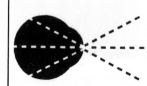

This Large Print Book carries the
Seal of Approval of N.A.V.H.

AN UNDERCOVER DISH MYSTERY

THE BIG CHILI

JULIA BUCKLEY

WHEELER PUBLISHING
A part of Gale, Cengage Learning

GALE
CENGAGE Learning

Farmington Hills, Mich • San Francisco • New York • Waterville, Maine
Meriden, Conn • Mason, Ohio • Chicago

LIBRARY OF CONGRESS CATALOGING-IN-PUBLICATION DATA

Names: Buckley, Julia, 1964– author.
Title: The big chili / by Julia Buckley.
Description: Large print edition. | Waterville, Maine : Wheeler Publishing, 2016. | © 2015 | Series: An undercover dish mystery | Series: Wheeler Publishing large print cozy mystery
Identifiers: LCCN 2016012202 | ISBN 9781410489630 (softcover) | ISBN 1410489639 (softcover)
Subjects: LCSH: Murder—Investigation—Fiction. | Large type books. | GSAFD: Mystery fiction.
Classification: LCC PS3602.U2648 B54 2016 | DDC 813/.6—dc23
LC record available at http://lccn.loc.gov/2016012202

Published in 2016 by arrangement with The Berkley Publishing Group, an imprint of Penguin Publishing Group, a division of Penguin Random House LLC

Printed in the United States of America
1 2 3 4 5 6 7 20 19 18 17 16

*To my husband, Jeff,
who makes the best chili.*

ACKNOWLEDGMENTS

Thank you to my super agent, Kim Lionetti, who sold this book in less than a week. Thank you also to my Berkley Prime Crime editors Michelle Vega and Bethany Blair, and to the wonderful art department who brought Mick to life.

I am grateful to my writing group, with whom I have worked for almost fifteen years and who have become my good friends: Martha Whitehead, Cynthia Quam, and Elizabeth Diskin. Big thanks to Kathi Baron, who is always willing to read and critique a manuscript despite her own busy writing schedule, and whose literary breakfasts and lunches always reenergize my writing spirit.

Thank you to the MWA, who supported me when I was an orphaned author and gave me scholarship money, which helped me obtain my MA in English.

For their friendship and super support of my efforts in the publishing world, big thanks to Sue Ann Jaffarian, Sheila Connolly, Anne Frasier, and John Dandola.

Thanks to everyone in my family, starting with my mom and dad, Bill and Kate Rohaly, and extending to my siblings and all of their children. Thanks to my English Department colleagues for their daily inspirations in the discipline I love: Terese Black, Rose Crnkovich, Linda Harrington, Maggie McNair, Margaret Metzger, and Kathleen Maloney. Thanks to all of my students, past and present, for inspiring me to a deeper love of language and literature.

Much appreciation to my husband, Jeff, and sons, Ian and Graham, for providing answers to all my random questions about guns, realistic dialogue, music, and poison.

Thanks to all the great musical artists who provide the sound track in Lilah's head.

Thanks to all booksellers and librarians for being the coolest people around, especially librarians Molly Klowden and Sue Tindall, and bookseller Augie Aleksy of Centuries and Sleuths bookstore.

Next to music there is nothing that lifts the spirits and strengthens the soul more than a good bowl of chili.
> — HARRY JAMES, band leader
> and trumpeter

Whenever I meet someone who does not consider chili a favorite dish, then I've usually found someone who has never tasted good chili.
> — JAN BUTEL, author of
> *Chili Madness*

Some enchanted evening
You may see a stranger . . .
> — EMILE DE BECQUE,
> "Some Enchanted Evening"
> from Rodgers and Hammerstein's
> *South Pacific*

CHAPTER ONE

My chocolate Labrador watched me as I parked my previously loved Volvo wagon and took my covered pan out of the backseat; the autumn wind buffeted my face and made a mess of my hair. "I'll be right back, Mick," I said. "I know that pot in the back smells good, but I'm counting on you to behave and wait for your treat."

He nodded at me. Mick was a remarkable dog for many reasons, but one of his best talents was that he had trained himself to nod while I was talking. He was my dream companion: a handsome male who listened attentively and never interrupted or condescended. He also made me feel safe when I did my clandestine duties all over Pine Haven.

I shut the car door and moved up the walkway of Ellie Parker's house. She usually kept the door unlocked, though I had begged her to reconsider that idea. We had an agreement; if she wasn't there, or if she was out back puttering around in her garden, I could just leave the casserole on the table and take the money she left out for me. I charged fifty dollars, which included the price of ingredients. Ellie said I could charge more, but for now this little sideline of a job was helping me pay the bills, and that was good enough.

"Ellie?" I called. I went into her kitchen, where I'd been several times before, and found it neat, as always; Ellie was not inside. Disappointed, I left the dish on her scrubbed wooden table. I had made a lovely mac and cheese casserole with a twist: finely sliced onion and prosciutto baked in with three different cheeses for a show-stopping event of a main course. It was delicious and very close to the way Ellie prepared it before her arthritis had made it too difficult to cook for her visiting friends and family. She didn't want her loved ones to know this, which was where I came in. We'd had an agreement for almost a year, and it served us both well.

She knew how long to bake the dish, so I didn't bother with writing down any directions. Normally she would invite Mick in, and she and I would have some tea and shoot the breeze while my canine lounged under the table, but today, for whatever reason, she had made other plans. She hadn't set out the money, either, so I went to the cookie jar where she had told me to find my payment in the past: a ceramic cylinder in the shape of a chubby monkey. I claimed my money and turned around to find a man looming in the doorway.

"Ah!" I screamed, clutching the cash in front of my waist like a weird bouquet.

"Hello," he said, his eyes narrowed. "May I ask who you are?"

"I'm a friend of Ellie's. Who are you?" I fired back. Ellie had never suggested that a man — a sort of good-looking, youngish man — would appear in her house. For all I knew he could be a burglar.

"I am Ellie's son. Jay Parker." He wore reading glasses, and he peered at me over these like a stern teacher. It was a good look for him. "And I didn't expect to find a strange woman dipping into Mom's cash jar while she wasn't in the house."

A little bead of perspiration worked its way down my back. "First of all, I am not a strange woman. In any sense. Ellie and I are friends, and I —"

I what? What could I tell him? My little covered-dish business was an under-the-table operation, and the people who ordered my food wanted it to appear that they had made it themselves. That, and the deliciousness of my cooking, was what they paid me for. "I did a job for her, and she told me to take payment."

"Is that so?" He leaned against the door frame, a man with all the time in the world. All he needed was a piece of hay to chew on. "And what *job* did you do for her?" He clearly didn't believe me. With a pang I realized that this man thought I was a thief.

"I mowed her lawn," I blurted. We both turned to look out the window at Ellie's remarkably high grass. "Wow. That really was not a good choice," I murmured.

Now his face grew alert, wary, as though he were ready to employ some sort of martial art if necessary. I may as well have been facing a cop. "What exactly is your relationship to my mother? And how did you even get in here, if my mom isn't home?"

At least I could tell the truth about that. "I'm Lilah Drake. Ellie left the door unlocked for me because she was expecting me. As I said, we are friends."

This did not please him. "I think she was actually expecting *me,*" he said. "So you could potentially have just gotten lucky when you tried the doorknob."

"Oh my God!" My face felt hot with embarrassment. "I'm not stealing Ellie's money. She and I have an — arrangement. I can't actually discuss it with you. Maybe if you asked your mother . . . ?" Ellie was creative; she could come up with a good lie for her son, and he'd *have* to believe her.

There was a silence, as though he were weighing evidence. It felt condescending and weirdly terrifying. "Listen, I have to get going. My dog is waiting —"

He brightened for the first time. "That's your dog, huh? I figured. He's pretty awesome. What is he, a chocolate Lab?"

"Yes, he is." I shifted on my feet, not sure how to extricate myself from the situation. My brother said I had a knack for getting into weird predicaments.

I sighed, and he said, "So what do we do now?" He patted his shirt pocket, as though looking for a pack of cigarettes, then grimaced and produced a piece of gum. He unwrapped it while still watching me. His glasses had slid down even farther on his nose, and I felt like plucking them off. He popped the gum into his mouth and took off the glasses himself, then beamed a blue gaze at me. Wow. "How about if we just wait here together and see what my mom has to say? She's probably out back in the garden, picking pumpkins or harvesting the last of her tomatoes."

I put the money on Ellie's table. "You know what? Ellie can pay me later. I won't have you — casting aspersions on my character."

"Fancy words," said Ellie's son. He moved a little closer to me, until I could smell spearmint on his breath. "I still think you should hang around."

I put my hands on my hips, the way my mother used to do when Cam or I forgot to do the dishes. "I have things to do. Please tell Ellie I said hello."

I whisked past him, out to my car, where Mick sat waiting, a picture of patience. I climbed in and started confiding. "Do you believe that guy? Now I'm going to have to come back here later to get paid. I don't have time for this, Mick!"

Mick nodded with what seemed like sympathy.

I reversed out of Ellie's driveway, still fuming. But halfway home, encouraged by Mick's stolid support, and enjoying the *Mary Poppins* sound track in my CD player, I calmed down slightly. These things could happen in the business world, I told myself. There was no need to give another thought to tall Jay Parker and his accusations and his blue eyes.

I began to sing along with the music, assuring Mick melodically that I would find the perfect nanny. Something in the look he gave me made me respond aloud. "And another thing. I'm a grown woman. I'm twenty-seven years old, Mick. I don't need some condescending man treating me like a child. Am I right?"

Mick was distracted by a Chihuahua on the sidewalk, so I didn't get a nod.

"Huh. She's pretty cute, right?"

No response. I sighed and went back to my singing, flicking forward on the CD and testing my upper range with "Feed the Birds." I started squeaking by the time I reached the middle. "It's tricky, Mick. It starts low, and then you get nailed on the refrain. We can't all be Julie Andrews." Mick's expression was benevolent.

I drove to Caldwell Street and St. Bartholomew Church, where I headed to the back parking lot behind the rectory. I took out my phone and texted I'm here to Pet Grandy, a member of St. Bart's Altar and Rosary Guild, a scion of the church, and a go-to person for church social events. Pet was popular, and she had a burning desire to be all things to all people. This included her wish to make food for every church

19

event — good food that earned her praise and adulation. Since Pet was actually a terrible cook, I was the answer to her prayers. I had made a lot of money off Pet Grandy in the last year.

"She'll be out here within thirty seconds," I told Mick, and sure enough, he had barely started nodding before Pet burst out of the back door of the church social hall and made a beeline for the adjoining rectory lot. Pet's full name was Perpetua; her mother had named her for some nun who had once taught at the parish school. Pet basically lived at the church; she was always running one event or another, and Father Schmidt was her gangly other half. They made a hilarious duo: he, tall and thin in his priestly black, and she, short and plump as a tomato and sporting one of her many velour sweat suits — often in offensively bright colors. In fall, you could often spot them tending to the autumnal flower beds outside St. Bart's. At Christmastime, one of them would hold the ladder while the other swayed in front of the giant pine outside the church, clutching strings of white Christmas lights. Pet was utterly devoted to Father Schmidt; they were like a platonic married couple.

As she marched toward my car, I studied her. Today's ensemble, also velour, was a bright orange number that made her look like a calendar-appropriate pumpkin. Her cheeks were rosy in the cold, and her dark silver-flecked hair was cut short and no-nonsense. Pet was not a frilly person.

She approached my vehicle, as always, with an almost sinister expression, as if she were buying drugs. Pet was very careful that no one should know what we were doing or why. On the rare occasions that someone witnessed the food handoff, Pet pretended that I was just driving it over from her house. Today she had ordered a huge Crock-Pot full of chili for the bingo event in the church hall. Everyone was bringing food, but Pet's (my) chili had become a favorite.

I rolled down my window, and Pet looked both ways before leaning in. Her eyes darted constantly, like those of someone marked for assassination. "Hello, Lilah. Is it light enough for me to carry?"

"It's pretty heavy, Pet. Do you want me to —"

"No, no. I have a dolly in the vestibule. I'll just run and get it. Here's the money." She thrust an envelope through the window at me with her left hand, her body turned sideways and her right hand scratching her face in an attempt to look casual. Pet was so practiced at clandestine maneuvers that I thought she might actually make a good criminal. I watched her rapid-walk back to the church and marveled that she wasn't thin as a reed, since she was always moving. Pet, however, had the Achilles' heel of a sweet addiction: she loved it all, she had told me once. Donuts, cookies, cake, pie, ice cream. "I probably have sweets three times a day. My doctor told me I'm lucky I don't have diabetes. But I crave it all the time!"

Pet reappeared and I pretended that I was about to get out of my car to help her. I did this every time, just to tease her, and every time she took the bait. "No," she shouted, her hand up as though to ward off a bullet aimed at her heart. "Stay there! Someone might see you!"

"Okay, Pet." She opened my back hatch and I spoke to her over my shoulder. "It's the big Crock-Pot there. Ignore the box in the corner — that's for someone else."

"Fine, fine. Thank you, Lilah. I'm sure it will be delicious, as always." She hauled it out of the car, grunting slightly, and placed it on her dolly. Then, loudly, for whatever sprites might be listening, she said, "Thank you so much for driving this from my house! It's a real time-saver!"

I rolled my eyes at Mick, and he nodded.

Mick totally gets it.

I waved to Pet, who ignored me, and drove away while she was still wheeling her prize back to the church hall. My mother played bingo there sometimes and probably would tonight. We were church members, but we were neither as devout nor as involved as was Pet. My mother called us "lapsed Catholics," and said we would probably have to wait at the back of the line on our way to heaven, at which point my father would snort and say that he could name five perfect Catholics who were having affairs.

Then they would launch into one of their marital spats and I would tune them out or escape to my own home, which was where I headed now.

My parents are Realtors, and I work for them during the day. I mostly either answer phones at the office or sit at showings, dreaming of recipes while answering questions about hardwood floors, modernized baths, and stainless steel kitchens. It isn't a difficult task, but I do lust after those kitchens more than is healthy. I have visions of starting my own catering business, experimenting with spices at one of those amazing marble islands while a tall blue-eyed man occasionally wanders in to taste my concoctions.

Mick was staring at the side of my face with his intense look. I slapped my forehead. "Oh, buddy! I never gave you your treat, and you had to sit and smell that chili all through the ride!"

Mick nodded.

We pulled into the long driveway that led to our little house, which was actually an old caretaker's cottage behind a much larger residence. My parents had found it for me and gotten me a crazy deal on rent because they had sold the main house to Terry Randall, a rich eccentric who had taken a liking to my parents during the negotiations. Taking advantage of that, my parents had mentioned that their daughter would love to rent a cottage like the one behind his house, and Terry had agreed. My rent, which Terry didn't need but which my parents had insisted upon, was a steal. I'd been in the cottage for more than two years, and Terry and I had become good friends. I was often invited into the big house for the lavish parties that Terry and his girlfriend liked to throw on a regular basis.

I pulled a Tupperware container out of my tote bag — Mick's reward whenever he accompanied me on trips. "Who's my special boy?" I asked him as I popped off the lid.

Mick started munching, his expression

forgiving. He made quick work of the chili inside; I laughed and snapped his picture on my phone. "That's going on the refrigerator, boy," I said. It was true, I doted on Mick as if he were my child, but in my defense, Mick was a spectacular dog.

I belted out a few lines of "Jolly Holiday" before turning off the sound system and retrieving Mick's now-clean container. I checked my phone and found two text messages: one from my friend Jenny, who wanted me to come for dinner soon, and one from my brother, who wanted me to meet his girlfriend. I'd met lots of Cam's girlfriends over time, but this one was special to him, I could tell, because she was Italian. My brother and I, thanks to a wonderfully enthusiastic junior high Italian teacher, had developed a mutual love of Italian culture before we even got to high school. We immersed ourselves in Italian art, music, sports, and film. We both took Italian in high school, and Cam went on to get his PhD in Italian, which he now taught at Loyola, my alma mater. We were Italophiles from way back, but Cam had never met an Italian woman. It was I who had won the distinction of dating an Italian first, and that hadn't ended well. But sometimes, even now, when I found myself humming

"Danza, danza fanciulla gentile," I could hear Miss Abbandonato saying, *"Ciao,* Lilah, *splendido!"*

She had told us, in the early days of our classes, that her family name meant "forsaken," and I had remembered it when I, too, was betrayed. *Abbandonato.* How forsaken I had felt back then.

I turned off my phone and smiled at Mick, who was still licking his chops. We climbed out of the car and made our way to the cozy little cottage with its green wood door and berry wreath. Home sweet home.

I grabbed my mail out of the tin box and unlocked the door, letting Mick and me into our kingdom. We had hardwood floors, too, at least a few feet of them in our little foyer. The living room was carpeted in an unfortunate brown shag, but it was clean, and there was a fireplace that made the whole first floor snug and welcoming.

My kitchen was tiny and clean, and between my little dining area and the living room was a spiral staircase that led up to a loft bedroom. Every night I thanked God for Terry Randall and his generous heart (and for my savvy parents, who had talked him into renting me my dollhouse cottage).

As I set my things down, my phone rang.

"Hello?"

"Hi, honey." It was my mother. I could hear her doing something in the background — probably putting away groceries. "Are you going to bingo with me tonight?"

"Mom. Bingo is so loud and annoying, and those crazy women with their multiple cards and highlighters . . ."

"Are what? Our good friends and fellow parishioners?"

I groaned. "Don't judge me, Mom. Just because I get tired of Trixie Frith and Theresa Scardini and their braying voices —"

"Lilah Veronica! What has gotten into you?"

"I don't know."

"Sweetie, you have to get out. Dad thinks you have agoraphobia."

"I don't have agoraphobia. I just happen to like my house and my dog."

"What song is in your head right now?"

My mother knew this odd little fact: I always had a song in my head. There was one in there when I woke up each morning — often something really obscure, like a commercial jingle from the nineties, when I was a kid — and one in my head when I went to bed at night. It was not always a conscious thing, but it was always there, like a sound track to my life. My mother had used it as a way to gauge my mood when I

27

was little. If I was happy it was always something like "I Could Have Danced All Night" (I loved musicals) or some fun Raffi song. If she heard me humming "It's Not Easy Being Green," she knew I needed cheering up. Nowadays my musical moods could swing from Adele to Abba in a matter of hours. "I don't know. I think I was humming Simon and Garfunkel a minute ago."

"Hmm — that could go either way."

"Don't worry about it, Mom."

"You haven't spent much time with young people lately. You need to get out on the town with Jenny, like in the old days when you two were in college."

"I'm planning just that next week. We've been texting about it. But, Mom, I'm not in college anymore. And neither is Jenny. She's busy with her job, I'm busy with my jobs — plural. And if you are subtly implying that you want me to meet men, I am not ready for that, either."

My mother sighed dramatically in my ear. "One bad relationship doesn't mean you can't find something good."

"No. It just means I'm not *interested* in finding a man right now. I think I'm a loner. I like being alone."

"I think you're hiding."

"Mom, stop the pop psychology. I have a

great life: a growing business, a nice house, a loving family, and a devoted dog. People who saw my life would wish they were me."

"Except no one sees your life, because you hide away from the world in your little house behind a house."

"Right. With my agoraphobia," I said, choosing to find my mother's words amusing instead of annoying. She had found me this house, after all.

"Come with me tonight. I heard that Pet will be making her chili. It's my favorite," said my mother, who was one of only three people who knew my secret.

"I guess I'll go," I said. "But only because I'm hoping your crazy luck will rub off on me and I'll win the jackpot."

My mother had won two thousand dollars at bingo six months earlier. She came home beaming, and my father groused about the fact that she went at all. Then she pulled out twenty hundred-dollar bills and set them in his lap. Now he didn't say much about bingo, especially since they'd used the money to buy him a state-of-the-art recliner.

What I could do with two thousand dollars. . . . I gazed around the kitchen and indulged a brief lust for gourmet tools, an updated countertop, or even a new stainless steel refrigerator — the wide kind that accommodated large pans.

"Great!" said my mother. "Do you want to come over now and we'll hang out together before we go? I have a couple of Netflix movies. One is a Doris Day. Remember how we used to watch her when you were little, and have our tea parties?"

I laughed. "I do remember. And as I recall, you developed quite a crush on Cary Grant after watching *That Touch of Mink.*"

"Oh yes," my mother said. "My secret crush."

"It's not secret. Dad knows about it and hates it."

She giggled. "Your father is attractive when he's jealous."

"*Anyway.* I have to pass on the movies — I need to walk Mick. I have one last delivery, and then I'll be there for our bingo date."

"Okay." Her voice had brightened since I'd agreed to go. My mother was an innately cheerful person.

I grabbed a water bottle from my fridge and hooked Mick's leash to his collar. We went outside, through Terry's amazing backyard, with its plush furniture and giant stone birdbath, down his driveway, and out onto Dickens Street, where we walked at a leisurely pace and admired the Halloween decorations. The evening was cold and dark, yet somehow cozy because of all the glowing yellow and orange lights, and the occasional jack-o'-lantern lighting up a storefront window. The air smelled like woodsmoke and winter, and Mick kept pausing to sniff it. My brain was playing a song that my dad had once sung to me when I was little — something by Don Henley with the name *Lilah* in it. The melody was a pretty blend of love song and lullaby, and my father said he had started singing it to me almost the moment I was born. So I walked along hearing the refrain of my own name, which was both comforting and disconcerting. We went around the block and returned home, where Mick ambled to his basket beside the fireplace for a little evening nap.

"Okay, buddy. I'm going out for a while, but I'll see you after bingo, okay?"

Mick gave a half nod because he was already dozing.

I went out and locked my door behind me. I returned to the car, where I had a Mexican casserole waiting, keeping chilled in the October air. This one was for Danielle Prentiss, who hosted poker parties at her house on Saturday nights. I drove to the outskirts of town, to Jamison Woods, a little forest preserve where Mick and I would sometimes go on a weekend morning to watch wildlife and enjoy nature. In Mick's case this often meant chasing things, and once it had even involved pursuing a young deer. He stayed on its tail as far as the tree line, and then they both paused, looking at each other. Mick finally peered back at me, confused. He wasn't sure what in the world he was supposed to do with this animal. I laughed and took pictures on my phone; eventually the deer ambled off, no longer afraid of my big soft-hearted puppy.

I pulled into the empty parking lot; no hikers were visible on this particular day. Dani showed up in her station wagon with the wood-look sides, seeming as always like a throwback from the seventies. She climbed out of her car and met me at the back of mine. "Hey, Lilah. Thanks for meeting me at our little rendezvous point." She grinned at me and blew out some smoke; only then did I notice the cigarette in her hand, although I shouldn't have been surprised — Dani was a two-pack-a-day smoker, and her raspy voice told the tale.

"Sure. I made this one with some extra onion and cheese, as your patrons requested," I said, pulling out the box that contained the glass baking pan. "I think you'll like it even better than last time. I put in a new and wonderful spice."

"What?"

"Just a little cumin. Not enough to change anything — just to enhance it."

She looked at me, dubious. "I really liked it the old way."

"You'll love it. Have I ever given you anything bad?"

She shook her head. "No. I love your cooking." She grinned at me. "And my poker pals love mine!"

"That's right. And when they ask you why it's so extra delicious, say it's cumin."

I set the box in her arms and slammed my door.

"Money's in my jacket, hon," said Dani, sniffing the box.

A little white envelope jutted out of her pocket. I took it out; it smelled like smoke.

"Thanks, Dani. Just e-mail me when you need another dish."

"You got it, hon. Hey, your hair looks pretty. I like it in a braid like that. It's so thick." She sighed. "I always wanted blonde hair, like a Disney princess. Instead I got boring brown, and then it turned gray. What're you gonna do?" she asked, and laughed.

I laughed, too. "Thanks, Dani. For the job

and the compliment. See you soon!"

I climbed into my car and sighed deeply. My day's work was done, and now I could relax. With my mother. At St. Bart's bingo.

Some Saturday nights were more exciting than others.

CHAPTER TWO

When my mother and I got to St. Bart's, the parking lot was already full. People loved bingo; these were serious gamblers who figured the odds were much better here than in the lottery, and they meant business. Sure, there was some socializing, but when Father Schmidt called those numbers, people who were smart knew to sit down and shut up. I told my mom about the Lilah song, and we started singing it together as we walked toward the entrance. Then she laughed one of those nostalgic laughs. "Ah, I can still see Daddy rocking you in your little carrier and singing that song. And you would look at him so solemnly, with your big wide eyes, as if you didn't want to go to sleep and miss part of the melody."

I laughed, too, and we walked through the entrance. Things hadn't started yet, but the room was bustling with activity. Mom and I purchased our cards (a modest three each) and found a table. Barb Hadley and her husband, Mel, whom we knew only slightly, had already taped down their thirty cards and were lining up their big pink daubers. They were no-nonsense about winning, and they barely spared us a glance. Mel was telling his wife that when the buffet line opened, she should grab him a bowl of chili before it ran out. My face warmed with the unexpected compliment.

In the kitchen on the north side of the hall, we could hear chatter and laughter as various cooks prepared their dishes. Pet's chili pot already sat on a side table, the one labeled "may contain nut products." I had never revealed my secret ingredients to Pet, but there was a nut-based ingredient in the chili, so it had to be separated from the non-nut food in these days of terrible allergies. The "nut products" table was quite full, with all sorts of other appetizers and main dishes. Across from it was an equally long table of nut-free dishes. The food smelled good, and I realized that I was hungry.

I waved at some people I knew: the three Grandy sisters, Pet, Angelica, and Harmonia; Trixie and Theresa, the inseparable "church ladies"; Shelby Jansen, a teenager from the parish and a family friend; Father Schmidt and Mary Breen, the housekeeper at the rectory. Bert Spielman, our town librarian and a bingo lover mostly because he enjoyed socializing with the St. Bart's crowd, many of whom were his patrons, stared down at his two cards with an intelligent gaze, as though he were finding significance in the random numbers.

"Isn't this fun?" my mother asked. "Mother and daughter on the town."

"I could think of other ways to be on the town," I murmured.

My mother waited until I locked eyes with her. She looked pretty; her brown eyes were wide and bright, and she wore a lavender dress that brought out their color. "What I mean is that it's nice to spend time with you. We haven't done anything lately, just you and me. What takes up all your time?"

"Nothing," I said glumly. "Just Mick and my jobs. You know the drill. And I read a lot of books and listen to music and stuff."

Clearly she wasn't finished with her agoraphobia theme. "You should get out more," she said brightly. "And not just with me. Terry's having another party next week. Are you going?"

"He invited me, yeah."

"You should bring a boy with you."

"A boy? Like a six-year-old?"

My mother sighed. "A man, then. Are you

seeing anyone?"

"Not since Angelo." We both shuddered. Angelo, true to his name, had once seemed sent from heaven; that had proved to be an illusion. My brother Cameron said that men named for angels probably felt compelled to be bad.

"I see Pet is in her element," my mother said, leaning closer and lowering her voice. "I'll bet she's jealous that Alice Dixon is the one who gets to start off the festivities and do her little tasting ritual. So weird, really."

Alice was the president of St. Bart's Altar and Rosary Guild, which helped to run bingo nights. While Pet tended to slave away on the setup for events, Alice was the face — and the voice — of authority. Generally on bingo nights she would signal that the buffet was open by tasting a main dish — usually Pet's chili, because Pet had earned this honor with all her labor — and telling everyone how delicious it was, and that they should join her in the buffet line.

Alice was a tall woman with dark hair, artfully graying at the temples. She had dark eyes and wore elegant clothing, and generally she was considered a trendsetter among the St. Bart's congregation. I imagined her age to be anywhere between forty and fifty — it was hard to tell with people like Alice, who probably used expensive products that preserved a certain youthfulness in her appearance. She seldom smiled, and I had always suspected it was her way of trying to minimize mouth wrinkles.

"Well, Alice was elected fair and square," I said. "I don't see why Pet doesn't run for president."

My mother nodded, watching Perpetua as she scuttled toward the food table with a basket of rolls. Behind her were two of her seven sisters, Angelica and Harmonia. Pet and these two were the last of the Grandys to stay in Pine Haven, probably because they were the three who had not married. They all looked similar to one another, except Pet's sisters were light-haired and not yet graying. They tended to follow Pet as a matter of course, supporting her in all of her endeavors and often seemingly reading her mind. Now Angelica marched after Pet with a dish of butter, and Harmonia with a pile of napkins.

"Oh, those Grandy girls," my mother said with a sigh. "They're like a throwback to the sixties with their nun names and their servitude. They need to find a hobby, or travel outside this town."

"They're not *girls*, Mom. They're probably in their fifties."

"Well, anyway. Oh, good — here's Alice. I'm starving!"

Alice Dixon approached the microphone that Father Schmidt had set up a few moments earlier. She looked perfect, as usual, with her dark sweep of hair and her stylish blue-gray dress. I didn't know Alice Dixon well, but I had never liked her. My feelings were based not on one event but on various things I'd noted over the years: Alice's tendency to wear a superior expression when she was around Pet or one of the other women who toiled around the church; her usual excessive use of a very unpleasant perfume; her snappish answers when people asked her questions. Once I had seen her give a sarcastic response to two little children who were helping with Christmas decorations around the altar. They'd asked her something, in voices barely audible, and she had snarled at them.

In public, though, and in front of a microphone, Alice was all smiles and loveliness. Her ex-husband Hank sat in one corner with his bingo cards and his new girlfriend, Tammy, and he barely looked up when Alice began to speak.

"Good evening, everyone. I'm Alice Dixon, and I'm the president of St. Bart's Altar and Rosary Guild. Thanks for coming out to support St. Bart's bingo night!"

Some scattered applause.

"Tonight's big jackpot is two thousand, five hundred dollars!"

That got bigger applause. People really were greedy, I reflected. But then again, I'd been wondering how many bingo jackpots would allow me to enlarge the kitchen in Terry's little guesthouse. . . .

Alice smiled again and picked up a bowl of chili from the table next to her. "Pet has made her delicious chili for us tonight, and many other cooks have brought delicacies to our table so that we won't go hungry while we listen to those numbers!"

Applause and some laughter.

Alice took a big bite of chili. I hoped she hadn't let it get cold. "Pet's chili is delicious, as always — and I think you've added something new, haven't you, Pet? Something sweet. It provides an interesting counterpoint to the flavor." Pet shot a look at me and I shook my head. Nothing new in the chili. Alice took another bite and set the dish down. "Anyway, this officially starts our evening's festivities; I hope that — oh my!" She swayed slightly before us, looking distressed. Her right hand flew to her forehead, her left to her abdomen. "I think that — something's wrong. With the chili."

41

Then she fell like a stone, and we heard her head hit the floor.

A chorus of screams and groans rose in the crowd; several people ran to Alice where she lay unmoving, including my mother, Alice's ex-husband Hank, and Brad Witherspoon, who was a doctor. I made my way to the front, too, and went to the chili pot. Surely I couldn't have used bad ingredients? I always checked expiration dates and smelled the food before I cooked it. This had been a fine batch — a delicious batch. I lifted the lid and inhaled. Oh, there was something wrong with the chili, all right. Someone had tampered with it, and it did not smell right.

I turned to Father Schmidt, who stood near me. "Don't let anyone eat this," I said. "And I think you should call the police."

"We've already called an ambulance," Father Schmidt said, his face pale.

"Call the police, too, Father," I said gently. "Something's wrong about this."

I moved to the doorway, where Pet stood wringing her hands. "What should I do?" she said.

"Do you want me to tell them? When the police come? Should I tell them I made it?" I whispered.

Pet looked surprisingly defiant. "Well, no

— because after Alice gets better I'm still going to want to make food for events. Everyone loves my food," she said, tears spiking her eyes.

"It's okay, Pet. Maybe one of the ladies thought she was being helpful and added something to it in the kitchen. But it smells strange now."

"So if they ask me — ?"

"Just say that someone tampered with your chili. Go lift the lid — you'll see what I mean."

The ambulance arrived, and the attendants rushed in to Alice, who was surrounded now on the floor. Pet went over to the chili and opened the lid; her brows creased in surprise. Then she returned. "I'll tell them that. So I don't want you to say anything, Lilah. This is mine and I made it. Okay?"

"I just don't want you to be blamed for anything —"

"I won't, because I didn't do anything wrong." Her plump little body was rigid and stubborn as a child's. She wore jeans and a sweatshirt that said London in white letters on a black background.

"I know, Pet." I tried not to look at the cluster of people around Alice. "How many

people had access to that kitchen tonight?"
I asked.

Pet sighed a quivering sigh. "Oh Lord, everyone and her brother. There were some high school kids helping us for a service project. Me and my sisters, of course. Alice and some of the Rosary Guild ladies. Hank and his girlfriend, who made a dessert. Father Schmidt. Trixie and Theresa. Mary, the rectory housekeeper. Bert Spielman came in to sniff things. Some more people, probably."

She trembled as they carried Alice out on a stretcher, her arm connected to an IV. The ambulance attendants were running. The brief glimpse I caught of Alice must have been an optical illusion, because her skin looked weirdly pink.

"Oh God," I murmured.

Father Schmidt had started a group prayer, and most of the people in the room had joined in.

A moment later some uniformed officers showed up at the door and glanced around; they spied Father Schmidt and went to him, their various tools of the trade clicking and jingling on their belts. He stopped praying and conferred with the officers in low tones. Then he went to the microphone and lifted it with shaking hands.

44

"The police have just informed me that they would like everyone to stay here for the time being." He cleared his throat. "They have also informed me that our dear friend Alice Dixon — has just died."

A wail of distress and fear rose in the small crowd.

Father Schmidt wiped away a tear and said, "And the ladies have told me that no one else should eat the chili."

Chapter Three

Pet was sitting on a folding chair near a window, taking deep breaths and accepting comfort from her sisters. My mother, who had CPR training and had tried to help Alice, was looking pale and shell-shocked. I was scanning faces, trying to imagine what could have happened, what horrible accident had somehow caused Alice Dixon's death.

The police had been questioning people and taking notes; now a new group of police officers appeared in the doorway, and more of them flowed into the scene, including a man in a shirt and tie and a woman in a blue suit. The man looked familiar — my stomach lurched. It was the man from Ellie's house: the one who had accused me of being a thief. He looked different because he didn't have his glasses on, but it was the same guy, all right. Now I was at the scene of a death, and I had made the food that might potentially have killed the woman in question.

As if sensing my fear, the man in the suit looked my way and seemed to recognize me; his brows went up and his body moved forward, toward me. Then he was there, tall and intense, his mouth a serious line. "Hello again."

"Hello. Did your mother verify that I was not a criminal?"

He nodded, smiling briefly as he scanned the room over my head. "What brings you here tonight?"

"Bingo. I mean, my mom wanted to play, so I came along. We were just waiting for the event to start, and Alice did this thing she always does, which is to eat some food in order to encourage people to start heading toward the buffet. And it seemed to make her sick. Are you a cop, or what?"

He pulled out a badge. It said *Detective Inspector Jacob Parker, Pine Haven PD.*

"Oh boy," I murmured.

"Excuse me?"

"Listen, there's something you should know. Pet's chili is always delicious, and — it's made with great care. I've eaten it many times. But tonight, after Alice ate the chili, I went to the pot and smelled the batch, and it's not right."

"So you think she might have gotten food poisoning?"

I shook my head. "Food poisoning doesn't manifest itself that quickly. She took a bite and she was almost instantly ill."

His brows rose. "Where is this chili?"

I led him to my big, beautiful Crock-Pot, and he lifted the lid. He leaned in and inhaled, then quickly covered the pot again. "Simmons!" he yelled, and a man jogged over. "I want this taken into evidence." He turned to me. "Excuse us for a moment, will you?"

I stepped away, but I kept watching them as they spoke in low voices. Then they wrapped the entire pot in some sort of crime lab cellophane and carried it out of the room.

The police were ordering that all of the windows be opened.

Parker came back to me. "Listen — Lilah, right?"

"Yes."

"Go into the nearest lavatory and wash your face."

"What?"

"Wash your eyes, too. If this is the poison I think it is, then you'll want to wash off any trace of vapor before it can affect you. Just to be on the safe side. Did anyone else inhale it?"

I gestured toward Pet, and he sent some-one to her with the same message.

"Did you say *poison*?" I said.

He pointed. "Go wash."

I ran to the bathroom and washed, sud-denly terrified that I was dying. Pet was at the opposite sink, splashing away at her face and crying. "What in the world is happen-ing?" she asked, burbling into the water.

"I have no idea." But I did. Parker thought there was poison in that chili. I certainly hadn't put it there, and I was sure Pet hadn't either, which meant that someone in this familiar little church hall had put it there — and committed murder. On a sud-den impulse I took out my phone and Googled "poison that smells like almonds." Several links popped up, and they all shared one word in common: cyanide. I stared at the little screen while my stomach did nervous somersaults. Outside of an Agatha Christie novel, who really poisoned people? How could this possibly be happening?

Pet and I returned to the main room, damp and nervous, and Parker loomed again. I looked at Pet, nodded at her, and then said, "Detective Parker, you need to know — regarding the chili — I mean, if you're investigating it and how it was made —"

"Then you can talk to me," said Pet, extending her hand. "I'm Perpetua Grandy, and I made the chili. I'm kind of famous for it around here."

I looked at her, shocked. "Pet, I think —"

Pet sent me a rather intense look. "I am very proud of my chili, Detective Parker. It's — it's quite a tradition here at St. Bart's." Her eyes had grown moist. I sighed, staring at the Big Ben image on her London shirt.

"Lilah? Did you have something to add?" asked Parker.

"No. Just that Pet is right, and her chili is beloved by all. Hopefully this — event — won't dissuade people from eating it in the future." Parker nodded, thanked us, and moved away.

Pet grabbed my arm in a fierce grip. "Thank you," she hissed. "It will be fine, I swear." I nodded without speaking, and she wandered off toward the kitchen.

I found my mother and explained everything that had happened. "I feel weird not telling them that it's mine," I said in a low voice. "But this means everything to Pet. She was crying when she said that people loved her food."

My mother touched my hand. "It won't matter. You're innocent and so is Pet, and they'll find whoever did this. God, I can't believe it." And then she added, "Your father will never let me go to bingo again."

They finally released us at about ten that evening, after they had taken a statement from everyone and bagged up all of the food. My mother asked if I wanted to come home with her. "You'll feel safer with Dad and me," she said, which was probably true, but I also craved solitude.

"I'll be okay. Just drop me off at the gatehouse. Thanks for the offer, though."

My mother drove to Terry's place, a big gray stone building sitting in dignified splendor on the corner of Dickens Street. I kissed her on the cheek, jumped out, and waved as she drove away. Then I made a beeline for the path that led past Terry's house and straight to mine. I was trying to figure out which Norah Jones song was in my head, but I had only narrowed it down to a bluesy, breathy, sexy something with lots of brushing of the snare drum.

A car door slammed behind me. "Lilah?" said a man's voice.

I turned, frightened, and saw Detective Jacob Parker standing in front of his car.

51

"God, you scared me. What's going on?"

"I'm sorry about your friend," he said, warming his hands in his pockets.

"She wasn't my friend. I didn't even like her, but I still feel terrible about what happened to her."

He nodded. "I wanted to talk to you. Do you have a minute?"

"Sure."

"You're shivering. Can we go in your house?"

I hesitated and he said, "Perhaps you'd like to invite someone else to join us? I realize it's an odd thing to ask this late at night."

I looked at Terry's place. I didn't see lights, which probably meant he wasn't home. He and Britt often went to Chicago social events until the wee hours.

This man was Ellie's son, and a police officer. He looked about as wrung-out as I felt. I decided that it was okay, with Mick by my side. "Sure. I live in the back." I led the way to my door, which I unlocked to the accompaniment of Mick's energetic barking.

"I forgot about your dog. What's his name?" Parker asked.

"Mick." Then we were inside, and Mick was greeting not me but Parker, leaping all over him and licking every available bit of skin. "He's a great guard dog, as you can see."

Parker laughed. "I have a cat. He probably smells Winston."

I whisked to the shadowy corners and flicked on the Tiffany lamps I had bought at a garage sale. They lit up my little room with a cozy, multicolored radiance. I turned on my electric fireplace, and faux flames began to dance behind the screen. Then I turned to him; he had sat down in one of my stuffed green chairs and begun to massage Mick's head. Mick, that traitor, had apparently forgotten my existence. He smiled up at Parker, his eyes slitted with pleasure. "Maybe I should leave you two alone," I joked.

Parker laughed. Then he looked at me with those blue eyes. "Listen, I'm here because I owe you an apology."

I had not expected this. I dropped into the other chair and said, "What?"

"This morning. I was rude to you, and I still haven't heard the end of it from my mother. She insisted that I deliver your payment in person so that I could apologize — which I was going to do before I got called to the church."

"Oh, okay. God, this morning seems like a

thousand years ago."

"Yes."

"Well, it's not a big deal."

"It is. I guess I've just become so cynical in my job that I tend to be suspicious of everyone, and there you were —"

I nodded. "When I think about it now, it's kind of funny. Me there pinching money and then telling you I mowed the lawn." I laughed, and he did, too, and finally I wiped tears out of my eyes. "Did your mother — uh —"

"No. She said it was none of my business, and that she owed you fifty dollars. So here I am, with my tail between my legs and my mother's scolding ringing in my ears." He took out his wallet and removed the money, which he set on the table beside him. "Again, I apologize."

I smiled at him. "Your mom is a good friend of mine. She's a great lady."

"I agree." We kept eye contact in the silent room, and I found it oddly comfortable to look into his eyes. Normally this would have been beyond awkward.

I stood up. "I never did get dinner tonight, and I'm starving. Can I persuade you to share a little something with me? Usually I just have Mick as my dining companion. I'm guessing you didn't eat, either?"

"As a matter of fact, I did not. I was just going to wait until morning at this point, but now that you've mentioned food, my stomach has awakened."

I led the way into my tiny kitchen, with its blue tile walls and shining white tile floor. In an alcove above the stove was a picture my parents had enlarged for me as a gift on my last birthday: me at ten years old, wearing a red apron and making dinner for our family. I was grinning at the camera and holding a wooden spoon; my blonde hair, down to my waist back then, was tied into two silky pigtails.

"This is you?" asked Parker, peering at it while I went to the refrigerator.

"Yes. I love to cook."

"And is that what you do? Is that your job?"

This was getting a little too close to his mother's secret. "Oh no. I work at the Pine Haven Realty offices by day. At night I weave fantasies of one day being a caterer while I make dinner for myself and Mick."

"Sounds lonely," he said, shooting me a blue gaze that was intense even in my dim kitchen. I had the sudden sense that if this man ever looked at me in bright sunshine I would faint.

"Sometimes. But I'm okay with aloneness, for the most part." I had saved a small pan of Dani's Mexican casserole; I did this with most of the things that I made, so that I could taste them and determine what I would change or add the next time. I put the dish into the microwave and set the timer for three minutes.

Then I got out two plates. "Can I offer you something to drink? I have Diet Coke, water, and one bottle of red wine."

"What are we eating?"

"It's a little casserole I invented. I call it Fiesta."

"Ahh. That sounds like a good red wine meal, but I should probably stick with Diet Coke so I can drive myself home. As you pointed out, it's been a long day."

"Yes." Again, a moment of eye contact. Then the timer beeped and I turned to retrieve our meal and serve it out onto plates. The kitchen was too small to hold a table, but it did have a little counter built into the wall separating it from the living room. In front of this counter I had placed two high bar stools, and we perched on these now with our sodas and our hot meals, and neither of us stood on ceremony before digging in. The stools were necessarily close together, and our arms bumped now and then.

"God, this is good," he said, staring at his food.

"Thanks. I like to experiment. Uh — after a long day at the realty office," I added.

"You're a Realtor?"

"My parents are. I just help out with office work and showings. It pays fairly well."

He smiled at me and ate some more.

Then something dawned on me. "Hey — isn't it like, illegal for you to talk to me? Because of Alice and everything?"

He shook his head. "You're not on my list. You are not in the pool of suspects."

"Why is that?"

"We've noted everyone who had access to the kitchen this evening. Several of the people we spoke to admitted to tasting the chili before Alice Dixon did — some of them hours earlier. At that point the chili was fine, which means there was only a short window of time — and a finite number of suspects. You are not a part of that group, according to several witnesses, so that rules you out."

I was tempted again to tell him. To beg him to keep Pet's secret, and to let him know that it wasn't quite true. I hadn't really had access to the tampered-with food, but I'd made it. It was on the tip of my tongue.

Then he said, "It's good to know that some people are what they seem to be. You can get a little jaded in my line of work."

"Ugh," I said. It was meant to sound like agreement, but came out more like the sound one makes after being punched in the stomach. We had both finished eating, so I got up and took our plates to the sink.

"Lilah?" he said.

"Hmm?"

"Not to beat a dead horse, but would you please tell me now why my mother owes you fifty dollars?"

I whirled around. If he weren't so good-looking I might be tempted to yell at him, the way his mother had.

Then I put on a humble face. "Okay, you asked for it. Sometimes, for a little extra money — I clean people's houses. I think your mom felt sorry for me, actually, and so she hired me even though she's perfectly capable of cleaning her own place. I cleaned her first floor, and that was the price we agreed upon."

His pale brows lifted. "Well — that seems like a lot of work for only fifty dollars."

"It was a fair price," I insisted. Would I ever be able to stop lying to this man?

He shook his head. "That was nice of Mom to think she was helping you out, but

I know what house cleaners charge, and you did a great job. I saw how the floors glowed. I'm going to add some money here." He took some bills out of his wallet and put them on my tiny counter. Who walked around with that much money? I had about three singles in my wallet at all times.

"Jay, really —" It was the first time I had called him by his name; not Jacob, but Jay, which was what he had called himself. He looked surprised.

"No. And I won't say a word to Mom. Your secret is safe with me."

"Oh boy," I said.

"Why do you sound so miserable? I should be, because I treated you so badly this morning. And you were just trying to protect Mom's privacy." He paused for a moment, then said, "Well, I should get going."

I walked him to the door, and at the threshold I had a crisis of conscience.

"Jay," I said.

"Hmm?" He turned, smiling, and I folded my arms against myself.

"Nothing. Have a good night."

"I'll be seeing you, Lilah."

He left and I locked the door after him. Then I let Mick out the back to do his evening business; I watched him through the window as he wandered through the cold grass, in search of exciting smells.

After a few minutes he trotted back up to the door, and I let him in, clicking the lock in place. I picked up the money Jay Parker had set on my counter: five twenties. A hundred dollars. Was that really what house cleaners earned? I felt weird about the fact that he'd left piles of money all over my house. I retrieved the other one, too, the fifty dollars I actually deserved. My parents said that I had a tendency to undervalue myself, and that was becoming clear now, as I contemplated the cash. If I could have figured out a way to give it back without exposing my own lie, I would have done so. I would have to tell Ellie tomorrow about the lie I'd had to invent and what her son had done. She could figure out a way to give the money back to him. Yeah — it would be Ellie's problem.

I sighed and went to my little bathroom to get ready for bed. I emerged wearing a pair of long underwear and a Hogwarts T-shirt. I turned off the fire and the lamps, did one last check of my locks, and said a brief prayer for Alice Dixon. In my mind Alison Krauss was singing "Amazing Grace."

Then I climbed the circular staircase which led to my bedchamber, Mick pawing carefully behind me; finally, there was my bed, with its big lavender duvet and its multitude of pillows. I threw back the covers and dove inside, and that was the last thing I remembered until morning.

Chapter Four

The next day, Sunday, I had an open house for one of my parents' listings. It was a huge, beautiful house in the wealthier part of town, offered at four hundred thousand dollars. I pulled into the brick driveway half an hour early, wearing my professional navy Realtor suit with the little green chiffon neck scarf and the pin that said *Pine Haven Realty.* Humming a peppy Hall and Oates tune about dreams coming true, I turned on the lights, slid my store-bought cookie dough squares into the oven, and put out my brochures on the chic kitchen island — a Milanese model in antique white, with soft-close European hinges and hand-painted ceramic knobs. The surface was polished maple. I ran my hand across it and whispered, "Someday, my lovely."

Then I heard the first knock at the door. "It's open," I called, and my visitors came in — an older man and woman who, I could tell from experience, were here out of curiosity, not because they were looking to buy. They probably lived on the same street and had always wanted a peek into their neighbors' place. That happened all the time. "Feel free to look around, and let me know if you have questions," I said brightly. "I have brochures here with all the pertinent information."

They each took one, then wandered upstairs.

Another couple came in, and to my surprise, I recognized this one. It was Hank Dixon, Alice's ex-husband, and his girlfriend, Tammy, whose strawberry-blonde hair was pulled into a casual and graceful ponytail and whose shoes looked like they had cost more than my monthly rent. She wore a brown skirt with a little matching jacket, and her gaze was focused not on the house but on her boyfriend's face. She seemed genuinely smitten with Hank.

Dixon himself was a relatively handsome man, although he was clearly too old for Tammy, who couldn't have been more than thirty. Dixon was closer to fifty, and today his face looked lined and tired. I wondered why they were even here while he was still reeling from the shock of his ex-wife's death.

Then again, I had been at the bingo night,

and I was here. Perhaps Tammy had her heart set on this house.

"Hello," I said, moving forward and extending my hand. "I'm Lilah. I'll be happy to answer any questions you have about the house today."

Tammy looked at me and gasped. "Oh my gosh! Weren't you there last night, at the bingo thing?"

I nodded. "Yes. I'm sorry for your loss." I directed this at both of them, although that felt weird. Tammy, despite her little-girl appearance, proved to have good manners.

"Thank you, Lilah. Hank is taking it pretty hard, but he was sweet enough to bring me here today because he knows I've had my eye on this place."

Trained by my savvy parents, I knew an opportunity when I saw one. "Perhaps a distraction is the best thing, and this place is a beautiful distraction. You have to check out the master bedroom — it has a walk-in closet, a Jacuzzi, and a skylight. And the whole place has far more closet space than the average home around here."

Hank Dixon nodded, looking around. His hand sat on Tammy's shoulder, and his fingers played nervously with her silky hair. "New roof?" he asked.

"Yes — two years ago. And you'll note the

lovely hardwood floors throughout, natural wood trim, art glass windows — it's a piece of art in itself."

Dixon nodded again. "Go ahead and look at the master bedroom, honey. I'll be up in a minute."

Tammy went prancing off in her high heels, and Dixon gave me an intense look. "You were there last night. Did anything seem funny to you?"

I stared, not sure how to answer. Of course something had seemed funny.

He shook his head. "I mean, *before* Alice ate the food. Anyone acting weird or skulking around?"

I shook my head. "Not that I recall, Mr. Dixon."

"Hank."

"Hank. I got there just before the event was supposed to start — my mother and I did. We looked around the room and everyone seemed to be in good spirits — including the ladies who were preparing the food and filling the tables. Father Schmidt was cracking his jokes, as always. And Alice —"

His eyes were weary and regretful. "Yes?"

"She seemed happy with the way things were going and — very healthy. That's what I thought later: that she had seemed healthy and strong until she tasted that food."

65

He nodded, leaning eagerly forward. "That woman was as strong as an ox. We may not have kept our marriage together, but, well, she was my friend. And I don't believe for a second that she died of natural causes."

"I don't think the police believe that, either, Hank. I think they're on it, and they'll determine what happened very soon."

He nodded again, and then asked, man-like, where the circuit box was. I directed him to the finished basement, and he disappeared. Curious, I wandered upstairs to find Tammy looking at herself in a three-way mirror. She was quite pretty; I could see why a man like Dixon would take the plunge with a younger woman if that younger woman was Tammy.

She spied me and said, "Oh God, this place is perfect. It's got such clean lines, such elegance. I want to throw parties in this house!"

I thought of her boyfriend's tired face. Then I noted an engagement ring on her left hand. "Oh, congratulations," I said, pointing. "I didn't realize you two were engaged."

She nodded. "For about a month now." She looked behind me to see if anyone was in hearing distance, then lowered her voice. "Alice was quite a bitch about it when she heard we got engaged. She said Hank was being an old fool and that I was a money-hungry climber."

Tammy's face still reflected the hurt she had felt at hearing those words. "Which, if you think about it, is an insult to Hank — as if I couldn't find anything appealing about him but his money. Hank is a real catch. He's got a beautiful soul." She looked back at the mirror for a minute and removed a smudge of lipstick from the corner of her mouth. "Besides, Hank isn't rich. He's just well-to-do. And I didn't know that when I started going out with him. I didn't even know that he was in banking."

"I'm sure she was just shocked. Speaking out of jealousy or something."

Tammy sniffed. "She had her chance with him and made his life a living hell. I could tell you stories. . . ."

I sort of wanted to hear them, but I heard the bell jingling downstairs, signaling another arrival. "Oh, shoot," I said. "I've got more company."

She shrugged. "Well, another time I'll tell you all about the precious Alice and what she was really like. To be honest, I dreaded the effect she was going to have on our marriage. She was always calling Hank, day and night, to ask advice, or get him to fix something at her house, or chat with him about some moldy old memory."

"Sounds a little excessive."

"Thank you!" she said, her green eyes wide. "The woman called practically every day. I told Hank she was trying to get him back, and he laughed and said that was ridiculous. Which it was, because Hank is in love with me."

And yet relationships could be very, very complicated. I knew from experience. . . .

Tammy read my mind. "Oh, I know they had a history. But Alice was a witch." She lowered her voice again and leaned toward me. "I'll tell you, I know it's a sin to be glad that someone dropped dead, but —"

"Miss? Do you work here?" said a young man with a burst of blond hair and tanning-salon skin in telltale orange.

"Yes — oh — I'll catch up with you later, Tammy."

She waved and headed toward the walk-in closet.

I led the new visitor downstairs to my brochure pile and answered his questions; his companion, whose skin was an even deeper shade of orange, asked me if there was a deck for tanning and if there were tanning salons in the area — clearly the two questions that concern every prospective buyer. I led them out to the deck and left them to pace around, imagining future sunning sessions.

By two o'clock my high heels were starting to pinch my toes, and I could feel some of the hair oozing out of the sweep I'd invented that morning, aiming for elegance. I slipped into one of the four bathrooms (two with bath) to repair my hairdo in front of the mirror. I patted it into place and re-clipped it, then smiled at myself for encouragement. Two more hours.

Back in the kitchen I handed out a couple more brochures and placed the cookies that had been cooling on the stove on a serving platter, which I set on the kitchen island. You can always tell the sugar lovers, because no matter where they are, they seem to sense that chocolate is available nearby. A few of them drifted into the kitchen now, pretending to be examining the cabinetry.

"Please, help yourself to a cookie," I said. They all did, and then they disappeared, validating my theory.

I smiled, and the bell jangled, and there was Jay Parker, tall and dark, his blue eyes shining under the foyer skylight. My mouth opened in surprise, and I walked toward him.

"Uh — hello," I said.

He looked surprised, too. "Oh — Lilah. You did say you worked in real estate, didn't you?" His eyes were distracted, scanning the room before they came back to me.

"Yes, I did. What a surprise to find you here."

A little smile escaped him. "You look good in that outfit. Sort of like a stewardess from the seventies."

I ignored this, although the heat in my face meant that I was blushing, which made me sort of angry at Jay Parker. "Did you want a brochure?"

His face turned cop-like again. "I want Hank Dixon. Is he here?"

"Oh yes — he and Tammy. He went to look at the circuit board and the finished basement."

"Point me to the basement, please?"

I pointed, and Parker went, leaving a trace of his scent — soap and sandalwood.

By the time Tammy wandered back downstairs, Jay Parker was leading Hank Dixon toward the door. Dixon called up to her. "Tam — take the keys. I need you to drive the car home, okay? They want to ask me some questions at the station."

Tammy stomped down the stairs and marched up to Parker, her eyes sparking. "What is this all about? If you have questions for Hank, you can ask them with our attorney present. And I do not believe he has to go with you — unless you are, in fact, charging him with a crime?"

Parker raised his eyebrows at her, as did many of the people milling around the room. "No, ma'am, we are not charging him with a crime. But we would like to speak with him at the station, and you can certainly have your lawyer there if you wish."

Tammy's hands trembled with anger — or some other emotion — as she retrieved her wallet from her purse and selected a white business card. "I will be calling her right now. And you can bet your sweet bippy that she will be furious with the way you have conducted yourself here."

Hank Dixon, to my surprise, was laughing. "Okay, Tam, calm down." He turned to Parker. "She's a little spitfire."

"It would seem so," said Jay Parker. "I'll go start the car." He sent an intense blue gaze in my direction and then walked out.

Tammy kissed Dixon as though he were being taken to the electric chair, and the moment he was out of the house she burst into tears. I went to her and patted her arm.

"Tammy, it's okay. I'm pretty sure they just want to talk to him. I mean, they have to eliminate all of the obvious suspects, and he's the ex-husband."

I kept my voice calm, and she nodded, wiping at her nose with one well-manicured hand. "I know. I'm sorry I made a scene." She glared around at the people who were still staring, then sighed raggedly. "I guess I'd better get home. I'll — I'll see you around, Lilah."

"Okay."

I watched her walk forlornly to her car, a cell phone pressed against her ear. She certainly seemed devoted to her fiancé. I wondered if that meant that she would kill for him.

Where had that thought come from? How silly to suspect a girl like Tammy — okay, a *woman* like Tammy — would poison someone to death. The whole affair had made me paranoid.

Someone tapped my arm and said, "Is there a washer and dryer?"

"Oh yes — state-of-the-art. Let me show you."

Over four hours, I had twenty-four visitors, at least six of whom seemed truly interested in the house. I'd been humming "Cowboy,

Take Me Away" for about three of those hours. I wondered what emotional cues my mother would get from a Dixie Chicks song.

I drove to the office and turned in my yard sign and sign-in sheet to the receptionist. I had marked the names of the people who showed interest in buying — including Hank Dixon and his betrothed.

"Thanks, Lilah. Oh, I see your mom and dad are back, too."

My parents had been working their own open houses today, and they trudged rather wearily up the steps but brightened when they saw me. "Hey, cupcake!" said my father, the only man who was allowed to call me that. He ran a hand through his thick peppery hair (he was a man who would never go bald) and smoothed his unruly eyebrows. "You look awfully pretty today."

I gave him a hug, then offered one to my mom. We are a huggy family. At holidays and birthdays, when we can lure my brother, Cam, away from his city job and his string of sexy girlfriends, greetings sometimes take five full minutes, as we all stand at the door and take turns embracing one another.

"How did it go today?" my mom asked.

"I gave the sheet to Becca. Lots of visitors, six prospectives."

"Great! I'll make some calls," my mother said. She was a good and conscientious Realtor, and she had more of a nose for fresh blood than my father did. My father was the glad-hander. He loved meeting people and chatting with them, but my mother liked to whisk through introductions and get out the paperwork.

"You want to go have dinner somewhere, honey?" my father asked. I could hear his stomach growling from two feet away.

"No, thanks, I have to take Mick for a walk and ask Terry something. But you two go — feed him, Mom. He's obviously starving."

My mother pursed her lips. "He's always starving." Then she patted my father's belly. It wasn't huge, but it was there, and my mother was always patting it.

My father scowled at her. "And I'm not having a salad, either!"

I gave them each a quick peck on the cheek and waved, since they were warming up to one of their favorite arguments. It would be good-natured, and my father, this time, would win, because my mother, despite all her talk about being healthy and working out and eating salads, was a secret feeder. Cam had once confessed to me that he had been relieved to finally move out of the family home because he feared our mother would fatten him up beyond the point of luring girlfriends.

Homeward bound at last, I turned on the radio in time to hear a Beatles song. My father was a huge Beatles fan, and so Cam and I had grown up being Beatles fans, as well. Now I sang along with "Eleanor Rigby" at the top of my lungs, appreciating the sunny fall day.

When I finally pulled into the long driveway, I stopped near Terry's entrance door and hopped out. I moved down his cement walkway, lined with pots of marigolds and little pumpkins that had words scrawled on them in dramatic black. As you walked, the pumpkin-revealed message said "Beware . . . of . . . ghouls . . . and . . . goblins . . . and . . . witches . . . and . . . salesmen!"

This was typical of Terry's sense of humor, and his girlfriend, Britt, had probably done all the artwork, since she was an actual artist, with her own gallery on Breville Road. She sold prints of her work in the shop and online and made scads of money at it. She and Terry, although both artistic in temperament, were also unexpectedly good businesspeople. Terry had started out in Internet sales, then developed his own company, called Sterling Stars, which sold, as he put it, "quality sterling silver jewelry and collectibles for unbelievable prices." This business had done so well that Terry eventually sold it for a profit. Now he worked his own hours, functioning as a "broker," which he told me meant "helping rich people find things to waste their money on." Terry, of course, got a percentage of every wasted penny.

I rang Terry's bell and peeked through the window into his foyer. He and Britt had wonderful taste, and their house was sophisticated yet fun, packed with all sorts of interesting pieces that somehow went together because of the stylish arrangement. It looked as if a Hammacher Schlemmer catalogue had exploded all over the lovely pinewood floors.

My favorite piece was right there in the foyer, and I could see it glowing on the nights when I came home in the dark. It was a Wurlitzer jukebox — a big one — fully functional and filled with an amazing array of songs. It glowed with blue, green, and yellow lights that chased one another around the rectangular surface. One of the greatest things about Terry's parties — aside from the hilarious stories told by Terry and Britt about one of their many, many adventures — was the fact that you could wander over to the jukebox and choose any song from the 1960s to the present. Many a jocular battle had been fought in Terry's foyer, as people loudly defended their choice of music to someone else who thought it was horrible.

I was still gazing at the lovely jukebox when Terry wandered into sight, holding a beer. He was of medium height, but fit and healthy-looking, with a perpetually optimistic expression and a well-trimmed blond beard about which he was incredibly vain. He had a shock of blond hair, too, which made him look like a stereotypical surfer dude. Britt, by contrast, was cool and dark, with silky black hair that hung in sheets on either side of her face in a perfect '20s-style bob. Britt admired the '20s and the art deco style, and she would have fit right into the jazz age. She favored long skirts and long necklaces against low necklines (scandalously low, my mother insisted), which I thought all combined to make her look beautiful.

The door opened, and Terry waved. "Hey, Lilah. What's up? You want to come in and join us for some dinner?"

"No, thanks, Terry. But that's so sweet of you to offer. I have to take Mick for a walk, and I owe him a kind of long one."

"That's cool." He stroked his beard with one hand, looking pleased with life.

"I was just wondering — regarding the party this Friday —"

His expression grew dark. "Do NOT tell me you're not coming! I wanted to have an eighties singing-fest with you!"

Terry and I liked '80s music, and sometimes, with a bit of wine-inspired courage, we would sing together on his karaoke machine. We both loved singing and were good enough that we'd gotten requests from returning party guests.

"No, I'll be there. I just wondered if I should bring something."

Terry shook his head. "Nah — got it covered. Britt hired that caterer she loves."

"Ah." Britt's caterer was wonderful. In my dreams I worked for someone like them — but I had heard they were a family operation.

"Okay, well, I'll see you then."

"You bringing a date?" asked Terry with a twinkle in his eye.

"Nope. Not this time. Dates cramp my style," I joked.

"Good. I'm glad you're not still with that guy from last year. He was bad news."

"We've already had this discussion." I could feel myself blushing. I did not like to think of my history with Angelo.

Terry brightened and leaned toward me. "Can you stay long enough to sing a song? Britt loves to hear you sing."

"No — maybe Friday," I said. "Now I have a reproachful dog to walk."

"You got it. I've already got a song picked out for a duet. You and me!" Terry yelled, smacking his chest like an ape.

"Weird, Terry."

"You'll love it. See you Friday!"

He was still laughing when he closed his big oaken door.

I went back to my car, feeling depressed. Terry had made me think, if only briefly, of the worst failure of a relationship I'd ever had. It had been tempestuous and exciting, yes, but ultimately ugly and demoralizing. Love affairs could devolve that way.

As I predicted, Mick was ready for me with his baleful look. I usually got this one if I was gone for more than about three hours.

"Hey, buddy," I said. "You do know I have to work for a living, right? It keeps you in dog food."

This did not please him.

"You want a walk?" I asked.

Mick could not hold out against this particular bribe. His chocolate tail pumped back and forth, and he gave me a toothy smile.

"Okay, that's my boy. Go get your leash."

He did, dragging it back to me within seconds. I grabbed a couple of plastic bags for the necessary pickup job, and we went back into the night. There were even more Halloween decorations now, putting me in a holiday mood. The big event was on Friday night, and I couldn't wait to see what Terry and Britt would do for Halloween decor. They wanted people to come in costume, but I planned to cop out and just put some silver glitter in my hair, maybe do some crazy eye makeup and call myself Elvira.

We walked down to Main Street and once again admired the store window displays, all Halloweeny and glowing with holiday fun. I liked Halloween, as a rule, and Cam and I had come up with amazing costumes every year, often dressing as a duo (my brother was cool that way). The best was probably when we were Luke and Leia from *Star Wars,* although I'd also been fond of our retro Starsky and Hutch costumes, which had required me to wear a wig of tight black curls that was not flattering but looked good with the multipatterned Starsky sweater.

We crossed the street and came down the

other side of the block, pausing often so that Mick could sniff and I could look in the windows of the florist (lots of pumpkins and autumnal garlands), the dry cleaner (with a surprisingly cool haunted-house display), and Bettina's Hair Palace, which sported a skeleton holding its own head. "Fun, Mick," I said. Mick looked up and nodded.

We also passed an Italian restaurant owned by my former boyfriend. I avoided looking into this window.

Then we ambled back home, taking deep healthy breaths of cool air. I started humming "Hazy Shade of Winter," and Mick's paws seemed to keep rhythm to my beat.

When we finally strolled down Terry's driveway, Mick slowed down. I saw the hackles rising on his neck before I heard him growling. I went for the keys in my pocket, weaving them between my fingers in eyeball-stabbing position.

"Who's there?" I yelled.

Pet Grandy stepped out of the shadows, and she didn't look happy.

Chapter Five

"Perpetua, you scared me," I said sternly. "What are you doing here this late, anyway?"

Pet looked at her watch. "It's only six o'clock," she said. "We were taking a walk, and I said I wanted to come and talk to you."

Then I realized that her sisters were there, too, standing in the shadow of my porch and looking at a phone that one of them carried. "Hi, Angelica. Hi, Harmonia."

Angelica looked up and nodded; she wore little black reading glasses, and her reddish-blonde hair was covered by a red babushka. "Pet was really eager to talk to you, Lilah. We've been trying to calm her down, and we thought a walk would help, but then she got it into her head that she had to see you. You'll have to forgive her — she's obviously still upset."

Harmonia stepped forward, the phone still

in her hand. She was dressed for winter in a shapeless green parka with a fake-fur-trimmed hood. "I was trying to see if there was a movie playing tonight at the Old-Time Theater. Something fun that would take her mind off things. But — it's not — quite what we were looking for. Oh, look at the sweetheart!" She knelt and began to pet Mick with enthusiasm.

I knew what was playing at the Old-Time Theater: *Dial M for Murder.*

"Well — do you guys want to come in? I can make some hot chocolate or something."

Pet looked at her sisters. "Could you two just walk once around the block? I want to talk to Lilah — it's about real estate — some questions about Mom and Dad's house. Just give me five minutes, okay?"

Harmonia stood up and exchanged a glance with Angelica. The sisters looked like they'd had just about enough of Pet's weirdness for one day, but they sighed and marched back down the sidewalk, like cute little salt-and-pepper-shaker people. I remembered something my father had once said, in a moment of rudeness, while observing the Grandy family at a church function. "There's something weirdly big about each of them," he'd whispered to me. "Angelica's got big feet, Harmonia has huge hands, and Pet has a big head."

It was true. Pet's head was large and round, although it had seemed proportional to the rest of her body until my father made me realize it was a bit — extra. My mother had once said that most celebrities had larger-than-average heads, which ended up looking just right on movie and television screens. I didn't know if that was true, but I had always vaguely wondered if Pet would end up being a celebrity. In any case, the Grandy girls had clearly inherited their large features from their father, Morton Grandy, who was six foot eight and had the largest Adam's apple I had ever seen on a man. He had always frightened me in church, while he belted out hymns and swayed in his pew, as though he were an uprooted tree about to fall with a mighty crash onto some unsuspecting parishioner. Morton and his wife, Peggy, had retired to Florida two years ago, but I still recalled them both clearly.

"What's going on, Pet?"

Pet waited until her sisters reached the bottom of the driveway. Then she turned to me, her face crumpling with agitation. "You're the only one I can talk to. The only one who knows the truth! Did you say anything to the police?"

"No. And I'm having second thoughts about that, Pet —"

"Don't worry. You won't have to say anything. They told me that they believe my story and they haven't determined any reason why I might want to hurt Alice Dixon. They also don't think that if I were going to poison her I would poison my own chili. But . . . they told me to be available for further questioning."

"Okay . . . so we probably won't have to worry about this much longer. They brought Hank Dixon in for questioning today."

Pet froze. "What?"

"Hank. Her ex. He was looking at the house I was showing, and the police came and got him. Tammy drove home alone."

"That is ridiculous. Hank is a good person and a loyal parishioner. He gave one thousand dollars to the Retired Sisters Fund last year!" Her face was indignant on his behalf. Women really seemed protective of Hank Dixon.

I shrugged. "I know it's hard to believe — but as far as we knew, everyone in that basement was a good person. So it's up to the police to look beneath the veneers and find the truth. Find a motive, I guess."

Pet sighed. "This is what upsets me, Lilah."

"What?"

"I — Well, I'm afraid people will say I had a motive."

"Come on!"

"No, it's true. People probably don't realize this, but I was — jealous of Alice. I sometimes felt as if she — showed off at church functions. To the point that the rest of us were left in her shadow."

"Well, that's not fair. You work very hard for the church, Pet."

"I know. And I'll admit I like my fair share of the attention. Well, *you* know that better than anyone." She gave me a humble look, and I realized this was a Perpetua I had never seen before. "But it wasn't just that. You know that I spend time with Father Schmidt. We have him over for dinner every Friday night, and he often comes over to play cards, or on Friday nights to watch *Bones.*"

I giggled. "He likes those gory special effects, does he?"

"Oh yes. We're all big fans." Pet's face was sweet and childlike. Then it grew hard. "But Alice had started suggesting that it wasn't appropriate for Father to come to our house. She suggested to me — and to Father — that he should stop coming over. This upset Father very much; he's sensitive to any accusations of impropriety, you understand."

"Of course." Poor Father Schmidt. It was hard to be a priest these days, even if you were a good and decent person.

Pet looked near tears; her eyes glinted in the dark. Mick rubbed against her leg and she patted his head absently. "The thing is — the Grandys have always hosted the priests at their home — going all the way back to the 1960s, when my mother was the first to invite Father Eisenbart for Thanksgiving dinner. After that all the ladies vied to have the priest over for dinner, but it was always sort of a Grandy tradition. And in the meantime, we've become good friends. We enjoy Father Schmidt's company, and he enjoys ours. I think it would be a very lonely life if he had to sit in the rectory all the time and never fraternize with his parishioners."

"Of course it would. And it's ridiculous to say it's inappropriate for him to have dinner with you or anyone else."

Pet sounded relieved. "Well, I thought that, too. Alice — in the last few days — was really campaigning about it, talking to other people in the community. And the thing is, I felt she did it not because she thought it was wrong but because she wanted to ruin something for me. Alice Dixon always wanted to ruin things. I don't know why."

She wiped at her eyes again. I leaned forward and squeezed her arm. "Pet, I'm sorry that Alice is dead, but I'm going to say this: she wasn't a nice person. I never thought so myself, and I've heard two different accounts today that verify that idea. It's not speaking ill of the dead to simply speak your mind. She wasn't a good person, and you're better off without her in your life."

Pet looked at me fearfully. "But that's exactly what I'm afraid the police will find out!"

I finally calmed her down, and her sisters reappeared. Once again I offered them hot chocolate, and once again they refused. "We promised Pet we'd make apple pancakes," said Harmonia with a wink while Mick licked her hand. "It's her favorite treat, and it will cheer her up."

"It sounds delicious," I said. "Can I get a recipe sometime?"

"Sure," said Angelica. "I'll write it down for you tonight. It was our mother's."

"That would be lovely. I keep a little notebook of my favorites. I'll be adding it

in. I'll call it Peg Grandy's Apple Pancakes."
They beamed at that, and I waved as they walked away.

Mick and I went inside and I checked the locks on all the doors and windows; an October wind had picked up in the last half hour, and now it was moaning against the panes of glass in my living room like a ghost demanding entrance. Mick whined and looked uncertainly at me.

"We're both a little bit nervous these days, aren't we, Mick?" I said.

Mick nodded.

I sat down and grabbed my television remote, then saw Parker's money lying on my side table. "Oh, shoot!" I yelled. I picked up the phone and dialed Ellie.

"Hello?" said Ellie in her hearty voice.

"Ellie. It's Lilah."

"Oh, Lilah! I've been meaning to call you. I'm so sorry for what happened with Jay. He did apologize to you, didn't he?"

"Yes — and it was almost as embarrassing as our morning meeting. Not only that, but I had to lie to him again."

Ellie sounded intrigued rather than annoyed. But that was Ellie; she liked stories and gossip, even, apparently, if they involved her own son. "Why is that?"

"Because he paid me and apologized, but

then he still wanted to know what I did for you."

"My goodness, that boy! He has always had such a type A personality. And he can't stand an unanswered question or a mystery. Hence his chosen profession. So he asked you again. And what creative story did you tell him?"

"I said that I cleaned your house."

Ellie's laughter rang in my ear, comforting me. "Oh, Lilah. You're priceless. Jay told me what you said about the lawn — you need to do a little research *before* you lie."

"Yeah, so I've learned. Anyway, he claimed that if I cleaned the house, you didn't pay me enough. He put a hundred dollars on my table, Ellie! And I couldn't think of a way to give it back to him!"

"Why don't you just keep it?" Ellie said. "You deserve a bonus, and he's paying a price for his endless curiosity."

"*Ellie.* I will bring it to you as soon as I get a chance, and you'll have to find some way to give it back. But listen — I'm really tired of telling him lies. I understand that old line about the tangled web. Who said that?"

"Walter Scott, dear. In *Marmion.* 'Oh, what a tangled web we weave, when first we practice to deceive.' " Ellie was a former schoolteacher, and as far as I could tell, she knew everything.

"Yup. That's the one. So now I'm stuck with your son's hundred dollars and a whole lot of other problems that I'm not going to divulge right now."

"Are you worrying about this dead woman? Jay told me she was in your parish."

"Not worried, no. But there have been some . . . mitigating circumstances . . . and I'm smack-dab in the middle of that web we speak of."

Ellie laughed again. "Lilah, ever since I met you I have been so entertained by the drama of your life. Especially because you don't go looking for it — the craziness just finds you."

"Glad to oblige," I said, my voice dry. "It seems to me that some recent drama could have been avoided if a certain person had been home when I dropped off a casserole."

Now she was repentant. "Oh, honey, I am so sorry! I knew Jay was going to come by, but I didn't know he'd be there that early, and so I thought I could run out to my shed and do a bit of harvesting. And somehow I missed you both."

"Somehow," I said.

"Come over soon," she said. "I'm sorry I missed you last time, and the casserole was wonderful, as always. We need to have one of our talks."

"Yes, we do. I'll call you when I have a free hour and see if you're available."

"Sounds good, Lilah." Ellie's good humor transferred itself to me. Mick looked more cheerful, too. Now we climbed the spiral stairs in a better state of mind, warmed by the reality of friendship.

But for some reason, right before I fell asleep, I remembered what Pet had said: "Alice Dixon always wanted to ruin things." I wondered if this tendency in Alice was the reason that she'd died.

CHAPTER SIX

The next night I went to Jenny Braidwell's place. Jenny had been my college roommate for four years, when we had challenged our intellects and our social lives on the Lake Shore campus of Loyola University. I majored in English but decided, in the end, that I didn't want to teach, and that was how I ended up doing secret catering and working at a real estate office, occasionally tutoring young people who didn't get *The Scarlet Letter* or *Moby-Dick.*

Jenny had majored in elementary education, and she was now a respectable third-grade teacher. She had a cute two-bedroom apartment in a twelve-story building in the center of town, and while I liked my space better, I did admire Jenny's sense of style. She had inherited some rustic-looking furniture, which she highlighted with little country accents like a whimsical goose wearing an apron and a wooden magazine rack with a dotted-swiss skirt.

When I walked in, I waved to Jenny, who was tying her sandy red hair into a ponytail in front of her hall mirror; we were distracted from our meeting by a dark-haired child, who launched himself at me and began patting my pockets. This was Henry, Jenny's nephew, who knew that I sometimes carried Baggies full of cookies on the off chance that I would encounter a small boy. Jenny babysat for Henry fairly often; his father sometimes had the night shift at the post office, and his mother, Jenny's sister, had an evening class twice a week.

I pried his hands from me and forced him to give me a proper hug. "Hello, Sir Henry of Pine Haven."

Henry shook his head. "I'm Sir Henry of *Weston.*"

This was true. Henry lived a town over. "I stand corrected, Sir Henry of Weston. And what are you seeking in my pockets?"

"You know," said Henry. "Stop tickling me."

"I'm not. I'm just brushing some dust off of your clothing. There's so *much,* Henry." He giggled and then screamed, so I finally let go of him and let him find the cookies. "Only two before dinner, or your parents will never let me see you again," I warned.

"You need Aunt Jenny's healthy dinner — What are we having, Aunt Jenny?"

"Hot dogs," Jenny said drily. "And frozen French fries."

"You need Aunt Jenny's *minimally* healthy dinner to stabilize you before you consume more sugar."

"Stabilize," said Henry, who liked learning words. He was newly six, but had the brain of an older child. "What's *stabilize*?"

"You know — to strengthen and balance you. Like the big blocks at the bottom help to stabilize those giant towers you like to build."

"Huh." Grasping his cookie bags in one hand, Henry took my hand in his other and led me to Jenny's rather cluttered dining room table, where she had cleared a corner for him and given him some Play-Doh. "Look," he said. He pointed at a strange blob of clay sitting on a base of tinfoil.

"It's kind of a hideous color, dude."

Henry laughed. "Hideous," he said.

I sent an apologetic look to Jenny, whose lips curled in disapproval. "How did you get that shade?"

Henry shrugged his little shoulders. "I mixed orange and brown."

"And what is that supposed to be?"

"A kind of monster guy."

"Well, he's pretty scary, Henry. You have done well. Now eat your cookies and never darken my door again. I need to speak with your aunt on official business."

Henry giggled and took out some more Play-Doh. Jenny and I moved into the kitchen, where I asked her for the latest news.

"There's always gossip at a school," she said. "I learned this week that one of the kids' mothers is leaving his dad for the father of a different kid in the same school. It's embarrassing, the things some people do," she said.

"Yeah. While they're telling their children to lead moral lives."

"Exactly." Jenny and I exchanged self-righteous expressions, and then I shrugged.

"I can't really judge anyone. I did something bad."

This got her interest. She had been prying apart frozen French fries to set on a baking sheet. Now she paused and looked me in the eye. "What happened?"

I told her the tale: Bingo. Alice Dixon. The chili. Detective Jay Parker. How the fact that I sometimes made food for her school events and allowed her to let on she had made it herself was actually something I did for a lot of people — and something I had done for Pet Grandy.

Jenny pursed her lips, finished her French fries, and put them in the oven. "So what's the big deal? You're clearly not a murderer. And you said the cops don't suspect your friend. So you're in the clear."

"But I lied, Jenn. To the police."

"You didn't *lie*. You just didn't tell them a detail, because it has no relevance."

I sighed. "See, you're just defending me now because you're my friend. But I have to tell them, don't I?"

She was working on the package of hot dogs now. The things some people ate. . . . "Well, clearly it's bugging you, Li. So why not go to the cops now and say you couldn't tell them because your friend's reputation would have been ruined, and could they please keep it under their hats."

"Yeah, I don't know if the police make promises like that."

"You should not tell," said Henry, standing in the doorway with a stern expression on his little face. He had a tiny chocolate mustache that made him look like a wise Poirot.

"Henry, kindly stop eavesdropping and go back to your clay."

"I'm not ebesdropping. I was just listening. And you wouldn't want to make that lady sad and lose all of her friends. They all like her because they think she's a good cooker, but they would all be mean to her if they found out she was pretending. This is like an episode of *Arthur*," he concluded.

I didn't watch *Arthur*, but it was disheartening to know that my life resembled the plot of a children's cartoon.

"It's not that simple, Henry."

He looked disappointed. Jenny started frying her hot dogs in a pan. How had I never noticed her minimal culinary skills when we lived together?

Jenny wanted to talk without her nephew around. She pointed away from us. "Hen, go look in the floor of my closet. I need one of the skeins of yarn from in there. It's blue. Oh, and there might be some old toys there that I was going to throw out. You can check them out, see if you want them."

Henry disappeared so quickly that I wondered if I had seen him at all. Then he was back, restoring my belief, holding two plastic-sealed action figures and *not* a skein of blue yarn. "These are brand-new Batmans," he said, breathless and mildly indignant. "Why would you throw dese guys away? I like guys like dese!"

Jenny shrugged. "Okay, okay. I guess they're yours, then, buddy. Maybe those two action guys would like to fight your blob monster."

This was clearly the best idea Henry had heard all day. I helped him open the ridiculous hard plastic packaging, and he carefully removed the Batman and the Robin toys, along with their plastic accessories, then disappeared into the dining room.

"Dinner in ten minutes, Henry," Jenny called.

There was no response, but we could hear distant sounds of battle, which were mainly a series of *Aaaaaaghhhhh* noises. I did hear one "That is hideous!" and a warning that someone should "never darken my door again." Henry learned fast.

Jenny snapped her fingers at me. "Hurry up; let's solve your problem before he comes back. And then we can talk about our latest crushes. I am assuming you must have one, even though Angelo ruined you for love."

"Fine. Solve my problem."

"Why not just send the cops an e-mail? Just word it carefully and apologize and say that it was a delicate situation." She brushed a stray red hair out of her face; her green eyes held no irony.

"That seems weird, though, like I'm avoiding a face-to-face meeting. Like I'm hiding something. You should see the looks on their faces when they ask you questions, Jenn. It's disconcerting, even for innocent people."

"Probably *only* for innocent people. If you have enough gall to murder someone, I'm guessing you're not bothered by a few questions. Ugh. These look gross. But they'll taste good, don't worry." She started putting the hot dogs into buns.

"And the thing is, the longer I wait, the harder it gets to do anything, because every day that goes by is another day I waited to tell them, which will also look weird."

She nodded. "I see your point. And what if coming forward starts to make you look suspicious? Like you crave attention or something? Don't criminals do that?"

"I don't know what criminals do. I just want this to be over so I can go back to my life."

"I'm with you. I would be freaked out to watch someone just drop dead in front of me."

We left things unresolved and joined Henry with our plates of dogs and fries. As Jenny predicted, they tasted good, despite the grease and salt. It was comfort food, which had been our specialty in college, the land of pizza and chocolate chip cookies.

While we ate I gazed at Henry's action

guys, whom he had left knee-deep in Play-Doh. They were frozen there, trapped until Henry decided to set them free. What amazing power children had, simply because of their imaginations. I felt imprisoned in a way similar to the plastic Batman: frozen with indecision and trapped by the choices I had already made.

Later, Jenny and I did the dishes while Henry played. She confided that she had liked a man at work and had dated him several times, but had recently broken it off. "Can you imagine?" she asked. "He asked me out, paid all this attention to me, took me out on dates, but never mentioned that he was married. I had to hear that from a coworker. It was more than embarrassing."

"What a jerk! Can't you get fired for something like that? Him, I mean — not you."

"I don't know. He's actually one of the administrators, which makes it worse."

"Ugh. I hope people realize that you had no idea."

Jenny nodded. "Some of my friends passed the word. But still. I turn red whenever someone looks at me. Thank God I didn't sleep with the man."

She sighed, putting away the last dried dish. "Henry never did bring my yarn, and

I need to start making snowflakes for our Christmas show."

"It's October."

"Yeah, which means Christmas is around the corner for teachers. We plan in advance, Li. These darn things take a long time to make, but they're really pretty, and the kids love to see them." Her face warmed at the idea of happy children.

"Great. So you'll be holed up in here making snowflakes by hand, and I'll be lying low, hiding from the police and making secret food for people. Maybe we *both* have agoraphobia."

She laughed. "We're not in college anymore. Maybe your parents just don't realize that we can act like adults. Henry!"

He appeared, a toy in each hand. "What?"

"Remember the other thing I needed from my closet?"

"Ah!" He darted away again in his warpspeed way. Then he returned with a skein of pale blue yarn. "Here ya go. Sorry about dat." He handed Jenny the yarn and began to retreat.

I grabbed him before he made it out the door and gave him a sound hugging, with a kiss on his messy hair. He wiggled and complained, which made it somehow more satisfying. "You're the best, Henry."

"Okay, okay," he said, shaking his head as he left the room.

"He loves it," Jenny whispered.

I left half an hour later; Jenny was disappointed, since we'd had a good conversation going, but I saw her eyeing the blue yarn. She was probably calculating just how many snowflakes she'd have to make per day to cover her classroom ceiling by December.

Henry saw me to the door. "Say hi to your dog for me," he said. "And thanks for the cookies."

"You're welcome, Sir Henry of Weston. Keep Pine Haven safe with Batman and Robin."

I held out my hand for a high five, and he slapped it incredibly hard. "Ouch, Henry."

"Sorry."

I gave him a crushing hug, waved again to Jenny, and left. Jenny and I, to my disappointment, had not solved my dilemma. At least it had distracted her from asking about my love life or commenting on my past with Angelo; but her idea of sending a personal e-mail to Jay Parker was oddly appealing.

As I drove home I saw flashing blue and red lights in my rearview mirror; heart beating rapidly, I began to pull over, but the car flew past me. I sat for a moment, recovering. The thought of meeting with the police, in that instant, had been terrifying. For a split second I had feared they suspected me and were coming to take me away.

I sighed and pulled back into traffic.

CHAPTER SEVEN

October 28 was a cold day — so cold that I had to put on a coat and mittens before I bundled Mick and my covered dish into the car and drove them to the home of Maura and Mike Sullivan. Maura and Mike were leaders of a Boy Scout troop — a job they'd been corralled into when their son Tommy joined — and they almost always felt overwhelmed. Today they were having some troop leaders over for breakfast, and they wanted to appear calm and in control. Or so Maura had told me once in the grocery store, where we had bonded over a surprising sale on chocolate chips.

I came across my secret clients in a variety of ways, and most of them, after hiring me once, tended to hire me again. This was the fourth meal I'd made for Maura and Mike. It was a lovely breakfast casserole based on quiche Lorraine, but with a few additions of my own, including blue cheese dressing. All they had to do was bake it for thirty minutes, and voilà — they'd have something fragrant and delicious.

The song in my head was "Baby, It's Cold Outside." Of the many covers of that song, I favored the one by Suzy Bogguss and Delbert McClinton, and it was their version that I hummed as I pulled into the Sullivan driveway on Crisp Street. Maura came running out, wearing her Troop 17 bandanna over a gray fleece jacket that matched her gray pixie haircut. The dish was concealed in a cardboard box, which I handed to her. "Here are those brochures you ordered, Maura."

She winked at me. "You're a lifesaver. Here — I'll toss the money on your front seat with your doggie. Now let me take that heavy box from you."

We made the exchange, and then Mike ran out to take it from Maura. "Thanks, Lilah," he called over his shoulder as he marched back in.

Maura stayed for a moment. "Cold, isn't it? But I love it. This is my weather, I'll tell you."

"Yeah — I do like fall," I agreed.

Suddenly Maura looked slightly conspiratorial. "You're a parishioner at St. Bart's, aren't you?"

"Yes."

"So — do you know anything about Alice Dixon? Did you hear what happened to her?"

There was no escaping the name *Alice Dixon* in this town. "I was actually there when it happened."

"Oh my God!" Maura's face was a mixture of horror and curiosity. "What did it look like? I mean, did she just drop dead, or did she say she'd been poisoned?"

"How did you know she was poisoned?"

She pointed behind her. "In the paper. There's a whole big story about it. The headline says 'Poisoned in the Parish.'"

"Oh geez."

"Yeah. But the article itself is well written, and kind of interesting. They say the police are pursuing leads."

"I guess they are. There were quite a few uniforms swarming around that night."

"Did they make you all stay in one room, like they do in the movies?"

"For a while. Then we all got to leave, after they had our information. How do you know Alice?"

Maura sighed. "She was our neighbor. That's her house." She pointed to a blue Cape Cod a couple of doors down — well kept but rather prim and Puritan-looking, unadorned by any decorative plants or pumpkins or wreaths. Prim and Puritan — two words that described the personality of Alice Dixon herself.

"Oh — well, it must have been unnerving to everyone on this block."

"Yeah. And now her husband has to figure out what to do with the house. It was hers, but she left it to him in the will, I've heard."

"Ah." That would certainly give Hank some capital to pay for the super-expensive house his wife-to-be wanted. "Well, I'd better get going, Maura. Just text or call if you need something again."

"You know I will — you're a treasure," she said, giving me a quick hug. "You take care, now. Brrr, it's cold."

She ran back into her house, and I got into my car, at which point I called Pet. Harmonia answered after the third ring — I knew it was her, because she had the most musical voice, and she made my name sound like a song she was singing. More than apropos, considering her name. "Oh, hello, Lilah. Yes, Pet's here. Hang on."

A clunk of the phone — the number was for their landline — and then Pet's voice. "Hi, Lilah. What can I do for you?"

I wasn't supposed to call Pet at home because of her intense secrecy about the covered dishes. I had asked her once how she fooled her sisters into believing the food was all hers, and she said that she told them she made it in the rectory kitchen, where there was more room, and that she always left samples for Father, so that he would have something to eat when helpful parishioners weren't around. This was an effective lie, because Pet spent a lot of time at the rectory: cleaning it, helping sort the mail, and doing any other odd jobs with which Father needed assistance.

"Listen, you don't have to say anything out loud, but I'm wondering if you know when I'll get my Crock-Pot back. That's the biggest one I have, and I need it for other jobs."

"That's a good point, Lilah. I see what you're saying," Pet said in a loud fake voice. "Let me think about it and text you if I have an idea."

I sighed and thanked her, then hung up. I rolled my eyes at Mick, and he nodded. I started my car and pulled out of the Sullivans' driveway, sparing one last glance for Alice Dixon's empty house. Then I screamed, because a face appeared in an upper window and scared the life out of me. The face resolved itself into the familiar countenance of Hank Dixon, who was frowning. I realized that Hank had gone through several of the top stressors in the last couple of years: divorce, a new relationship, moving, and death. That was one downer of a combination, I thought as I contemplated his long, sad face. He didn't see me, so I didn't bother to wave.

This day was getting a little too Halloween-y for me. My phone buzzed; I saw my mother's number on the screen. I clicked it on. "Hi, Mom."

"Hey, daughter. Just to let you know we won't need you at the office today. Mrs. Andrews is doing the filing and Dad has someone coming in to do the floors."

This was good news, except that I wouldn't get paid for my normal half-day hours. Still, I preferred freedom to the real estate office. "Okay, that's cool," I said, although I did think that I was better at the job than was Mrs. Andrews, who had worked in the place since about 1950 and wore her stark white hair piled high on her head like a giant ice cream sundae. She tended to dislike modern technology, which is why she still filed everything the old-fashioned way — in paper files and a file cabinet — while I made PDFs and preserved everything in Google Docs. I supposed that in the case of a solar flare or a zombie takeover, we would be glad that Mrs. Andrews had kept all of her 1950s files intact, labeled with such whimsical headings as *Client Filofax Info* and *Meeting Memorandums.* Working with Celia Andrews was like taking a vintage bicycle ride back in time. "I'll make new plans — thanks for letting me know, Mom. I have to go now because I'm driving."

"Sure, honey. See you soon!"

I hung up, but my phone buzzed again, so I pulled over under a maple tree farther down the block and looked at the screen while Mick studied the rustling leaves with his philosopher's face. It was a text from Pet:

Lla, Trxi sd sh wd lnd me th chrch pot in the bsmnt ktcn. You cd gt it instd nd sy its fr me.

Since I was used to Pet's annoying texts, I was able to translate this to mean that there was a big Crock-Pot in the church basement kitchen, and Trixie, who was sort of in charge down there, said that Pet could borrow it until hers was replaced. I could claim it instead, and if anyone stopped me, I would say I was bringing it to Pet as a favor.

This was a workable plan. I certainly

didn't want to ask the police when that Crock-Pot was coming back. "Mick, we're headed to the church," I said, and Mick agreed.

On the way there I stopped at McDonald's (I'm normally against fast food, but we all have cravings that go beyond logic) and picked up two Egg McMuffins. One went to my companion, who snarfed it up only slightly faster than Jay Parker had eaten his Mexican casserole. This made me smile to myself.

After we ate, I headed to the church lot. I hadn't been back here since Alice Dixon died, and I felt a little weird about it. I went to Mick's side of the car and he leaped out. I grabbed his leash and said, "You're my protector today."

We walked across the lot and down the steps that led to the basement entrance. A police officer met me at the door. "Hello — can I help you?"

"Oh — I was supposed to pick something up from Trixie's kitchen in there. Uh — is it open to parishioners again, or —"

Then I heard the loud, loud voice of Trixie Frith herself, a woman who I was convinced must be deaf because she said everything about five decibels above what her listeners could endure. "It's okay, Li! You can come on back. The cops are here, but they said it's okay for me to clean back here."

I nodded at the female officer, who wore a no-nonsense short brown haircut and an even-less-nonsense expression. "Thanks," I said. I let go of Mick's leash so that he could pad around the cement and act important. He immediately went to the cop, and she started petting him with a significantly softer mien. Then I darted to the back of the hall, where Trixie was scrubbing the kitchen floor.

"Hi, Trixie," I said. She looked up at me, her shaggy blonde hair glinting with silver strands. She wore a bright coral lipstick that was a bit overwhelming for daytime use (and for scrubbing a floor). She was a friendly person, though, and I had always gotten along with her. "Is this okay to do? I mean, aren't you — like — scrubbing away evidence?"

"They said they got all the evidence they needed. Cleared us to come back in just this morning." She sat back and took a breath; her face was perspiring from the effort of scouring. I was amazed by how much energy the women of this church were willing to expend just on cleaning things. I had never seen a man scrubbing a floor at St. Bart's — or anywhere.

"What brings you here, sweetheart?" Trixie boomed.

Trixie was about sixty years old and clearly remembered my toddler years; therefore, like many of the older parishioners, she persisted in talking to me as though I were a little girl.

"Well, I was helping out Pet, and she doesn't know when she'll get her big chili pot back —"

I watched Trixie take a big breath — she actually needed to pull air up from her lungs to get the kind of volume she wanted — before she bellowed at me. "Oh, right! I told her she could use the church Crock-Pot. Pet is usually the one who provides Crock-Pot meals, anyway. So she can borrow it as long as she wants — just sign it out on our little list, there, so we can see where things wander off to."

I went to the cabinet below the big silver sink. Some of the church stuff was hand-me-down junk, so I was happily surprised to see the Crock-Pot — it was indeed big and rectangular, and almost new. It was a Breville seven-quart slow-cooker with non-stick quantanium coating and a removable cooking well. "Oooh," I said.

Trixie yelled her approval. "Yeah, Pet will love it. I've told her she could just make her chili here, save her the trouble of moving it, but you know Pet! Everything's a secret about how she makes it. She's priceless!"

I pretended to be scratching my ear, but I was actually plugging the one closest to Trixie. If I were a good person I would take her to a doctor and get her a hearing exam. Instead I pulled out the box that held the pot and read about its features on the back panel.

Just then a new head peeked around the kitchen door. "Hey, Trix! No rest for the wicked, right?" It was Theresa Scardini, Trixie's best friend and constant companion. My mother always joked that Trixie's husband thanked God for Theresa every day, because a person could only take Trixie in small doses — even someone who had gone and married her. Theresa was divorced, so the two of them had plenty of time to spend hanging out, and often they did it at church events, or in the church itself. They were part of what my father called the *CAV,* or "constantly available volunteers."

Theresa came all the way in. She was a tiny woman who got tinier every year. My mother remembered a time when Theresa was about five foot five, but now she was closer to four eleven. She shopped in the girls' section at Kohl's and wore fashionable clothes, but I feared that at the rate she was shrinking she might be microscopic by the decade's end.

"That's a gorgeous top, T," Trixie boomed.

"Thanks. It was on the sale rack. You can get some great stuff there, and so. Ya know." Theresa dragged out this last word. She tended to tag lots of unnecessaries to the end of her sentences. "What are you up to, Trix? And what brings you here, pretty Lilah?"

"She's getting the Crock-Pot for Pet!"

"Oh, okay."

There was a lull in the limited conversation, and I signed my name on the borrowed-item list and hoisted the box up. "Well, thanks, ladies. Pet will really appreciate this."

Theresa nodded. "Yeah, 'cause we've got the ladies' social coming up Friday, and I know they want Pet to make something. They all want her to go for the chili, to get right back on the horse, ya know. They're afraid she'll never make it again because of what happened, and the ladies don't want that. Pet is such a good cook, and so. Ya know."

"Yes," I said. "Well, that's nice of the ladies to show encouragement. Have they

116

told Pet they wanted her to make the chili for this Friday? Because I think she needs time to shop and prepare." And some of us have plans this weekend.

"Oh, I'm not sure. They'll probably call her today, ya know."

I paused for a moment, looking at the women who had spent so much time in this kitchen and who had been right in the thick of things on Saturday night. "What do you guys think happened?"

They exchanged what seemed, to my imagination, like a secretive glance. "Obviously someone got to the chili," Trixie said in a normal voice. She probably thought she was whispering. "But it's hard to track down. I mean, there were upward of twelve women in here, and a few men, and people were lifting pot lids all over the place, sniffing and admiring. We always do that. So . . ." Trixie leaned in, and I winced. "So it seems to T and me like whoever did it knew exactly what would happen. They would kill Alice Dixon, and in the process try to implicate Pet. That's what we think."

"But Pet hasn't been implicated. It seems like she's the one person people *don't* suspect, because it would be too obvious for her to do it to her own food. So could this person have had some other intention?"

Theresa sniffed, as though she were smelling the idea. Then she said, "Weeeeelllllll . . . I think that's a good point. Maybe someone just hated Alice Dixon, and they wanted her dead, and Pet's chili was just an easy way to make that happen." She lifted an arm full of jingly bracelets and scratched her cheek.

"Well, if they're looking for someone who hated Alice, they'll have to start making a list. God bless her soul," Trixie boomed.

I set the box down. "Who hated Alice Dixon?"

Trixie and Theresa exchanged another glance. "Well, start with her ex-husband. God knows he had good reason, but he was pretty fed up with that woman. Then his little girl toy, Pammy."

"Tammy."

"Right. You can probably put Pet on the list, because Alice was always kind of witchy to her. Heck, you can put me and Ang on the list, too. We got into it with her all the time."

"About what?"

"Oh, just her constant power plays. She was always making rules and saying it was church policy, except it wasn't. It was just Alice policy. She was a control-a-holic. We'd go to Father Schmidt and say we didn't know about such-and-such new rule, and he'd tell us there wasn't one, and then he'd go and have a word with Alice. But a week or two later she'd be doing it again, making that little tight-mouthed face of hers."

Trixie imitated her and did, to her credit, look remarkably like Alice Dixon when she was in judgmental mode.

Theresa laughed, then covered her mouth. "Sorry. That was just so funny, Trix. But you should also add Barb and Mel Hadley. They got into it with Alice all the time about the way she ran bingo night. They're kind of insane."

I couldn't disagree with that, either.

"And then there're those neighbors of hers. The Sullivans."

This surprised me. I pictured Alice's stern blue house. "Why didn't the Sullivans like her?"

"I guess she was always calling the cops on them. They would have Scout events sometimes in their yard — they have that nice big backyard, ya know — and Alice didn't like noise or kids. She said a neighborhood should be silent. That's what Maura Sullivan told me."

I remembered Maura's face when she asked me about Alice Dixon's death. She hadn't looked very sorry. In fact, she had almost looked cheerful.

I picked the pot back up. "I can't even believe that one of those people is responsible. I keep thinking it must have been an accident. I can't accommodate the idea that someone in our community intentionally committed murder."

Trixie shrugged. "I knew a murderer once. A lady in my knitting group. She killed her husband because he was cheating on her. She was just a kid at the time. She served twenty-five years, and then she came to live here in Pine Haven. I asked her once if she was sorry she did it, and she said no." Trixie plunged her cloth back into the soapy water and started scrubbing again.

Theresa, far from looking scandalized, chimed in. "I knew a murderer, too. Tony Portillo, from our neighborhood. He killed his dad, remember I told you, Trix? Shot him in the chest. He was such a nice boy," she finished on a disturbing non sequitur.

"Then why did he kill his dad?" I asked, shocked.

"Oh, they were fighting. You know how it is."

But I didn't. Was it true that murderers just walked among us, sitting in knitting groups and being nice boys? "What happened to him?" I asked.

"Tony? Oh, he went to jail. He's still there,

but he's getting out soon. He has a fiancée that he met while he was in jail. I guess she used to come and read to them or sing with them or something? I can't remember. Anyway, they're getting married when he gets out."

"And has his family — forgiven him?"

Theresa shrugged. "They never really held it against him. He's such a nice kid, and the dad had his issues."

I didn't know what this meant, but they were depressing me. "I'd better get this to Pet," I said. "Thanks for the chat."

"Bye, sweetheart," yelled Trixie.

"Bye, Lilah," said Theresa.

Mick had been wandering around, sniffing for mice, and he didn't seem eager to leave when I called him. Still, he padded at my side happily enough once we got outside. Mick loved running errands.

I drove home and stowed the gorgeous Crock-Pot in my house. If I liked it, I would put it on my Christmas list — my parents bought me one nice thing for my kitchen every Christmas and on every birthday. I was building up a fine pantry full of tools and dishes.

My phone rang while I was puttering around my tiny kitchen, humming a Harry Connick tune.

"Hello?"

"Hey, kid." It was my brother, sounding both lazy and busy at the same time. He was probably at the desk of his cool office at Loyola, which had one big window that looked right out onto Lake Michigan. "Are you going to this Halloween party of Terry's?"

"Yes! Are you actually coming out for it? I haven't seen you in ages."

"Yeah. I'm bringing someone, too."

"That's good. I'll be glad to meet your Italian love."

"You heard?"

"Yes — from Mom."

"You bringing anyone?"

"Nope."

"Good. Bringing no one is preferable to bringing Angelo."

"Geez! I wish everyone would stop mentioning him to me."

"No problem. Consider him wiped out of my memory banks. So how important is it that I wear a costume to this crazy thing?"

"Terry and Britt would love it. Just find something easy. Remember how much fun we had dressing up? Hey, do you want to do a buddy costume again?"

"I would, Lilo, but there's going to be this lady that I want to impress, and if you and I are dressed as Sonny and Cher or some other dorky thing —"

"Sonny and Cher would be awesome!"

"And yet, no."

"Fine. So you want to impress this woman, huh? Unlike the other poor things you drag around who beg for the crumbs of your affection?"

"This one's different," said my brother.

The hair stood up on my arms. "Oh my gosh, she's the one! Will I like her? She's not bitchy, is she? You tend to find bitchy women, Cam."

He laughed. "No, she's not bitchy. You'll love her."

"Great. I can't wait to meet her."

"So, what else is new?"

"I have sort of a crush on someone. But he really doesn't know I'm alive, so it's a pretty safe thing."

"Oh? Who is this?"

I sighed. "Did Mom tell you that a lady at our church got murdered at bingo on Saturday?"

"*What?!* No, Mom did not mention that!"

"Well, anyway, she dropped dead right in front of us — poisoned. And I think —"

"I'm still trying to absorb this. Someone died in front of you? At a church event?"

"Yes. I think it was cyanide, but they

123

haven't confirmed that."

"Oh, you do? And what makes you the great detective?"

"The cop who came out seemed to suspect that the chili had been poisoned, and I went up and smelled it, and it smelled like almonds. That's what cyanide smells like, according to my Web sources."

Silence for a while. Then Cam said, "And how does this woman's cyanide murder, which happened before your eyes, relate to the person you have a crush on?"

"In that he's the investigating detective."

"Holy cannoli! Your stories are always better than mine."

"There's actually a lot more to it, but I'm not going to get into it over the phone."

I could hear him crunching something into the receiver — probably chips. Cam tended to eat during phone calls, which annoyed everyone. "My God, I really do need to visit more often."

"Yes, you do. And sometimes you should just come to my humble home for dinner. I miss you, you jerk."

"I know. I'll be better about it now that summer's over and I'm not traveling as much."

"Great. And I don't recall getting a souvenir from your trip to Italy."

"I still have it, greedy. It's a necklace that I got at a museum gift shop. Beautiful."

"Then all is forgiven. I guess I'll see you Friday?"

"Yes, you will. Bye, Lilo."

"Bye."

I hung up, smiling, and in that instant the phone rang again.

"Hello?"

"Hi. Um — Lilah?"

I recognized the voice, and the *um,* instantly. It was Shelby Jansen, a girl from Pine Haven High who was also a sort of protégée of mine. She'd been there on bingo night, as well. Before I'd started my secret food business, I'd done all sorts of odd jobs for money, one of which had been tutoring Shelby in English. Even after that gig ended, Shelby and I had kept in touch, sporadically messaging each other on Facebook or occasionally calling each other to say hi.

"Hey, Shelby! Long time no see."

"You saw me on Saturday night."

"True — but I never even had a chance to say hello."

"I know." Her voice sounded a little bit quavery.

"Are you okay?"

"Yeah, I'm okay. I mean, I'm not freaked out about Saturday or anything, but there is something bugging me."

"Okay. What's that?"

"Do you have time for me to come over? I have fresh cookies. I was going to bring you some anyway. They're Halloween cookies that me and my mom made."

"My mom and I," I said, slipping back into tutor mode.

"Whatever," said Shelby.

"Sure, come on over. Mick misses you."

"Okay. And can I bring Jake?"

Jake was Shelby's boyfriend — he was big and sort of dumb, but nice enough. "Sure — the more, the merrier."

"Thanks, Lilah. We'll be right over," Shelby said.

I rooted around in my refrigerator to see if I had beverages to offer to the cookie-wielding teens. I spied a quart of skim milk and sniffed it: still okay. I always had some Diet Coke because it was something of an addiction for me. Even though various Internet sources assured me I would die very soon from its contents, I couldn't seem to give it up.

I looked at Mick, who sat resting by the stove (one of his favorite spots, especially when meat was cooking in it). "Crazy day, huh, buddy?"

Mick didn't nod because his chin was resting on his paws, but his eyes seemed to agree with me when they were open. He was indulging in some long blinks, which meant he would soon be asleep. Sometimes I envied Mick his gentle lifestyle. He was well fed and had two cozy beds, many fun walking routes, his own backyard for rooting out scents in any season, and a fairly attractive owner who loved him. He gave the phrase "a dog's life" a whole new meaning.

With a sigh I snapped open a Diet Coke, took a swig, and looked out at the gold leaves.

CHAPTER EIGHT

Shelby's cookies were wonderful: pumpkin-shaped and pumpkin-flavored, with cream cheese frosting. "I might gain five pounds eating these," I said, shoving a second one into my mouth.

"Aren't they great? It's a family recipe," Shelby said, and Jake nodded his appreciation. He was at least six feet tall and broad-shouldered, but his face was young and half-obscured by gold-brown hair that hung over one eye. The part of his countenance that was visible looked worried.

I decided not to rush whatever it was they wanted to tell me. Shelby carefully poured herself some milk and Jake concentrated on massaging Mick's back, much to Mick's pleasure.

"How's English going this year?" I asked Shelby, wiping frosting from the corner of my mouth.

"It's going good. I mean, it's going *well*,"

she corrected, rolling her eyes. Shelby didn't like the arbitrariness of grammar rules. "I'm getting a B right now. I promised my mom I'd keep it there or higher. Mr. Branson is pretty good about meeting with people if they have questions."

"Ah. Always a good thing in a teacher."

"Yeah." Shelby reached out to rearrange the cookies on the plate. Jake watched her do it as though the fate of Pine Haven hung on her actions. It was as tense as those "red wire or blue wire" scenes in suspense movies, where the hero has to snip one to defuse the bomb.

"Okay, what's going on?" I said, my voice snapping into the tense silence.

Shelby looked up with wide brown-eyed surprise. "What? How can you tell something's going on?"

"Well, for one thing, you're here. We haven't really talked since your last tutoring session. For another, you both look like you killed someone and are worried about where to bury the body."

This macabre joke did not have the desired effect; both of them looked downright guilty.

"What's going on, Shelby?" I said again.

She held up her little hand. "Nothing. Nothing like you're thinking. It's just — we were both there on bingo night. You saw us."

"Yes."

"And we saw that you're friends with that cop who was asking all the questions."

"Detective Parker? Actually we only met that day. We're not friends," I said.

"Well, anyway, you seem to know him, and he seems to like you. You're the only one he smiled at the whole night. He has sort of a scary face."

Jake nodded at this, one eye still obscured by his hair.

"He was just doing his job, Shelby. A woman had been murdered."

Shelby and Jake exchanged a glance. "Well — we were wondering if you could tell him — the cop — that we didn't have anything to do with it."

This silenced me for about a minute. Various thoughts darted through my head. Why were sixteen-year-old kids worried that they'd be suspected of murder? Was it because they were somehow guilty? Did they know something about Alice Dixon's death? But how would two teenagers have the wherewithal to poison someone?

"Now you look suspicious, too!" Shelby cried. "I told Jake that the cop looked suspicious of us."

I folded my hands. "Let's start at the

beginning. Are you telling me that you're innocent, or that you're guilty? Because you're both making really guilty faces."

"We're not guilty of *murder*!" Shelby said, her eyes so large they seemed to fill her face.

"We just *feel* guilty," Jake said, his expression helpful.

"Okay. And why do you feel guilty?"

They exchanged another glance.

I sighed. "Here's another question. Why were you even there?"

Jake decided to field that one. "We need service hours for school, and for college applications. Father Schmidt is pretty nice about signing our service hour sheets when we help with activities at the church. We've helped at the St. Bart's homeless sheltering events, and at the fall festival, and at bingo. Even though it's not strictly service, since the people at bingo aren't a community in need, Father Schmidt said it was okay, because we were working for our faith community."

That was a long speech for Jake, and I realized that he had more depth than I'd previously realized.

"So you were doing it as a service."

"Yes," Shelby said, nodding and smiling.

"Okay. I'm failing to see the reason you feel guilty. I assume this has something to do with Alice Dixon?"

Again they exchanged a glance. I was getting tired of this. It felt as obvious as a soap opera, although they seemed oblivious to the fact that I could see their dramatic reactions.

"Why do you think it's related to Alice Dixon?" asked Jake. He had been petting Mick, and now his hands froze, keeping Mick's floppy ears sticking up like strange antennae.

"Again, because you're *here* and she was just murdered, and you are concerned about the investigating detective."

"Right," Jake conceded, nodding. To my relief, he let go of Mick's ears and finally pushed the hair out of his eyes, giving me a view of his whole face. He was a handsome boy with a high, pale forehead and almond-shaped hazel eyes. "The thing is, we talked with Mrs. Dixon on that night. We sort of fought with her."

This was interesting. "I need a third cookie for this." I took one and bit into it, letting the cream cheese and butter disintegrate on my tongue. "You argued with Alice?"

Jake opened his mouth to explain, but Shelby cut in. "It's not like we were looking to fight with her. Jake and I were doing dishes in the kitchen, and she came in to put some sort of decoration on a cake she made. She was there with this bag of nuts and arranging the nuts on the frosting. And we were talking about animals, because Jake and I are both members of the Pine Haven High Animal Protection Club. Miss Grandy is our moderator."

I sighed. Of course she was. On the list of their many volunteer activities, the Grandy sisters worked in the local schools. Angelica coached soccer at St. Bart's, and Harmonia and Pet donated their time at the high school. I hadn't known about the animal club, though.

"So?"

"So Mrs. Dixon was talking about this dog she had. His name is Apollo."

This surprised me. I hadn't pegged Alice as a dog person, and I had never heard of Apollo.

"He was really Mr. Dixon's dog," Jake added.

"Okay." That made more sense.

"Mrs. Dixon said that she had the dog after their divorce, because Mr. Dixon's apartment building didn't allow them. But she didn't like how much Apollo barked; she said it was bothering their neighbors." Shelby's eyes looked indignant now. "She said she was going to have him debarked."

I laughed. Shelby had such hilarious terms sometimes.

"No, it's a real thing," Jake said. "It's a surgery vets perform on dogs when their owners don't want them to bark. They anesthetize them and go in through their throat and cut their vocal cords. After that, the dogs can never bark loudly again."

"What?"

Shelby nodded. "We learned about it in our animal defense club. Lots of people have it done to their dogs — people whose neighbors don't like barking, people who have their dogs in shows, or even drug dealers who don't want their attack dogs to make noise." She and Jake looked outraged, as they probably had that night. "And sometimes there are terrible complications to the surgery. Dogs can get excess scar tissue, which can interfere with their breathing. They can die."

I rubbed my arms where the hair stood up on my skin. "Well, that's not a very nice thing," I said inadequately.

"We didn't think so, either. And we had heard things about her and dogs before. She didn't like them. One time a little dog bit her on the ankle — it didn't even break the skin — and she demanded that the owners put it to sleep. They had to give the dog away to avoid it."

Shelby's eyes flashed with the special fervor of teen ire. "We started telling Mrs. Dixon all the reasons we thought it was inhumane and she shouldn't debark Apollo. She got all snooty and said we should stay out of it and shut up. That's when Jake got mad." Shelby turned to her boyfriend with a mixture of awe and pride. "He yelled at her."

Jake shook his head. "I didn't yell, exactly. I just said her dog couldn't speak up for himself, so we were speaking for him. I said that it was a cruel and unnecessary procedure that deprived her dog of his voice and identity, and it was selfish. Her face got all red, and she said I should mind my own business."

They were quiet for a minute, neither of them meeting my eyes.

"I'm guessing you didn't mind your own business."

Jake's brown eyes met mine. "I said that someone should hurt her the way that she was planning to hurt her dog, and then maybe she'd think twice about doing it."

"Oy."

"Yeah. And, like, an hour later she was dead."

I sighed. "So I'm guessing you didn't share this story with Detective Parker."

Shelby shook her head fiercely. "No! Because then he might think Jake was a violent person, or that he killed Mrs. Dixon!!"

I turned to Jake. "Did you kill Mrs. Dixon? Did you put poison in that chili?"

His face was white with shock. "No! I barely could believe I stood up to her. I would never hurt anyone, and I would never normally talk like that to an adult. I just — I was picturing her dog, and feeling so mad. . . ."

My glance moved to Mick, who was looking at me with his wise gold eyes and smiling while Jake massaged his neck. Mick loved barking, especially when he saw other dogs. I always thought of it as a kind of greeting, as though he were calling out to friends (or enemies). He had a few different vocalizations: a big, throaty bark for those who seemed threatening; a playful bark that he reserved for the dog park and various people he met on our walks; a little yip that sometimes escaped him if I took too long to feed him; and then his "eating sound," which was an appreciative little moan he sometimes made into his bowl. Cam called it his "nom-nom noise." Mick's voice was a key part of his personality, and I couldn't imagine taking it from him.

"It's good that you have things you believe in, Jake. You don't have to suppress those just because an older person tells you to do so. I think it's noble that you stood up for animals, and for Apollo."

They both smiled at me, their faces relieved.

"But," I continued, "I also think you should tell this to Detective Parker."

"Why?" Shelby moaned.

"Because. Think of it this way. He's trying to put together a big puzzle, which means he needs all the pieces. What if someone overheard your conversation and it made them angry, too? Whoever did this was, let's face it, not quite right. So what if you provided a motive and you didn't even know it?"

This shocked them; they hadn't considered it, but they did so now. Meanwhile I recognized my own hypocrisy. Wasn't I suppressing a very big puzzle piece by not coming forward as the chili maker?

"Lilah, you look nervous," Shelby said.

"Well, your story has me a little on edge. Did you tell this to your parents?"

They looked guilty again. "No," Jake admitted.

"Guys," I said. "No one is going to put you in jail, because you are clearly not guilty of anything beyond speaking your mind. But I think you will feel better, and it will be the right thing, if you and your parents go to the police and tell them what you told me."

"You don't think they'll be convinced we poisoned her?"

"Because you just happened to have the poison with you in your pocket, in case someone offended your animal-rights sensibilities?"

Shelby laughed, covering her mouth. Then she dropped her hand and turned to her boyfriend. "She's right, Jake. We don't have to be afraid of anything."

Now that they both felt relieved, their faces looked younger and more vulnerable, and I felt a moment of longing for my own teenage days, when things had seemed complicated but were really far less so. . . .

Shelby got up and hugged me. "Thank you, Lilah. I knew you would help us."

"Thank you for the cookies. But please take them away so that I do not eat them all. Call or text me after you talk to the police, okay?"

Jake shook my hand, seeming suddenly adult, and then the two of them wandered out, Shelby clutching her cookies (in an

138

enviable vintage Tupperware cake and cookie carrier with a removable transportation handle), and Jake with a casual arm dangled over Shelby's shoulders. They were well suited, I thought, watching them. Some people just met the right companions early.

Mick and I went for an afternoon walk and I inhaled deeply, appreciating once again the scent of someone's outdoor fireplace, making me long for days of yore, when my parents took Cam and me on camping trips and we roasted hot dogs over open fires.

We came across the remnants of a broken beer bottle, glowing green and dangerous in the middle of the sidewalk. I paused to push it all to the side, wondering why people persisted in breaking glass all over town. One always saw the evidence, but never the act. "So thoughtless," I murmured to Mick. Then we kept walking, past the Rite-Aid and the second-run movie theater, and then looping around the other side of Dickens Street. By the time we got home, Mick seemed to be flagging. This was odd, because he was only four years old and usually could outlast me on any walk.

"Feeling tired, bud?" I asked him as I unlocked the door and then unfastened his leash. He moved down the hall and headed toward his basket; that's when I saw the blood. Red, paw print–shaped bloodstains had appeared every time he set down his front right paw. I screamed at the sight, then ran to him. "Stop, Mick!" I said.

I lifted his paw, and sure enough, there was a shard of green glass sticking into one of his pale brown paw-pads. I pulled on it gently, and Mick yipped. "Sorry!" I said. The glass had come out and now he was bleeding even more. I ran to the bathroom and found a washrag, which I wrapped around his paw and then fastened with some masking tape I pulled out of a side-table drawer.

"Okay, that looks terrible. But you won't have to put up with it for long, okay? Come here, my sweetie." I slung my purse over one arm and then lifted Mick, who was a substantial canine, in both arms. I managed to lock the door after me and then stow Mick into the passenger seat of my car.

On the way to the vet I kept a watchful eye on Mick, who seemed happy enough to be in the car with me. He watched the scenery, as always, with his wise gold eyes.

I lucked into a close parking spot and wrestled my Labrador out of the car and into the Friends of Animals Veterinary Center. "Hello," I said to the silver-haired receptionist. "I don't have an appointment, but my dog stepped on glass and I need someone to look at him. Can anybody squeeze me in? I usually see Dr. Harkness."

The woman smiled and typed something into a computer. "Dr. Harkness is booked all day, but Dr. Trent can see you. You can go into exam room one."

I was still holding Mick, who had rested his big head on my shoulder and seemed ready to take a nap. I staggered toward the room and managed to set Mick down carefully on the examining table. "Geez, you're heavy," I told him. "Maybe you get too many table scraps."

Mick stretched out his legs so that his belly touched the table. Then he set his head on his good front paw. I patted his head and said, "Don't be nervous," even though he looked perfectly content. It was I who felt nervous, still rather traumatized by the sight of blood on my floor.

The door opened and Tammy walked in. Hank's girlfriend, Tammy. "Uh — hi, Tammy," I said.

She smiled, slipping her hands into the pockets of her white smock. "Hi, Lilah!"

"I had no idea you worked here. Or that you were a vet," I said. Or that she did anything at all. Why had I assumed that

Tammy was just some sort of professional husband-troller? Shame on me.

"Yes, I've been here at Friends for about eight months. Before that I was at the Chicago Animal Welfare League."

"Okay."

"What's your dog's name?"

"This is Mick. We were just walking, and I pulled this out of his paw." I showed her the shard of glass, which I had put into my pocket.

"Yuck. That's sharp. Let's check and see if you got it all. Okay with you, Mick?" She put her face in front of Mick's face while she gently massaged his big square head. Mick licked her nose. "Oh, you are a cute one," she said. Then she deftly took off my weird washrag bandage and studied Mick's paw while still talking to him in a soft voice. I massaged his back, hoping to keep him relaxed.

Tammy looked carefully in all the crevices between his footpads and then nodded. "Looks like you got it all. He's just bleeding a lot because that one piece happened to hit him at an angle and it went kind of deep. I'll put in a couple of stitches and he'll be good as new."

"Will it hurt him?" I asked.

"He'll be fine. I'll give him a little topical

anesthetic, so he won't feel much pain. Just some pressure, maybe. But I will need to clean the wound first. That's the only part that may hurt a little. I'm going to have Rich clean him up in the back, and then I'll do the stitches quick as a bunny and I'll hand him right back to you. Okay?"

"Thank you, Tammy." I was truly impressed with her bedside manner, and Mick seemed to like her, as well.

She surprised me again when she gave Mick a kiss on the nose and then lifted him up in one swooping motion. "Want to see the back, buddy? Let's go see the back room. Okay?"

Mick nodded. I felt a spurt of jealousy.

As promised, she brought him back about half an hour later, his paw bandaged in a clean and tight white gauze. "Hey, Mick!" I said as he loped over to me.

"He did great," Tammy said. "I didn't put on a cone, but I did put some nasty-tasting stuff on that bandage. Still, he'll probably work it off by morning, but that's no big deal. By then you can leave it off and just keep an eye on the stitches."

"Okay. Thank you. Thanks so much," I said. We were still in the little exam room; I was sitting in a chair and Mick was tucked between my knees, panting and drooling slightly. I decided to venture a personal question. "Is everything going okay — with you and Hank?"

She sighed and rolled her eyes. "The police questioned him and let him go, but of course he feels like they're watching his every move."

"Did he . . . get his dog back? After Alice —"

Her eyes widened. "You know about Apollo?"

"I didn't, but then I ran into a girl from the church who told me about him, and that Alice had wanted to — debark him? Is that really the term?"

Tammy sighed and nodded. "Debarkation. Or *devocalization,* it's sometimes called. I can't discuss — but then again, I guess I can. Hank doesn't care, and Alice . . ." She shook her head. "Do you know that's how Hank and I met?"

"What?"

She looked at her watch, then sat in the chair next to mine. "Alice came in here about eight months ago, asking about the operation. I said that we don't do it at our practice because we consider it unnecessary and unethical. I told her there were other ways to modify her dog's behavior. I could see it wasn't the response she was looking for. I knew that she was not the person whose name was on Apollo's contact card, so I called Hank. I asked if he knew about the procedure she was considering, and he was furious. He told me that they were divorcing and that she had Apollo for the time being."

She leaned back in her chair and looked at a framed picture of a Persian cat on the wall. "He came in the next day and said we were not to cooperate with anything his wife requested without contacting him. He was . . . really passionate about it. I told him I admired his attitude. Then he asked if it was appropriate to ask me out for dinner."

Her lovely eyes were dreamy as she smiled at me. "Probably not very romantic-sounding, but it really was. And we hit it off right away."

"So Alice — did she see it as a sort of betrayal that he ended up dating you after you refused to do her bidding?"

She shrugged. "Alice didn't like me for a lot of reasons. And the more I got to know her, the more that feeling was mutual."

"Did you know that she was still considering the debarking? Even on the night she died?"

Tammy's mouth turned into a thin line.

"How do you know that?"

"That girl I told you about — a teenager who was there doing service work. She and her boyfriend got into an argument with Alice about it."

"Is that so?" Tammy suddenly looked like a formidable opponent. In a battle between her and Alice, I would not have been able to predict the victor.

"Yes. They just told me that today."

"I guess Apollo had a narrow escape," she said. Her expression was reserved, but her voice had a victorious sound. Then she reached in her pocket, pulled out a cell phone, and started pressing buttons. Finally she held it up for me to see a picture of a truly beautiful German shepherd sitting in front of a rose trellis. "That's Apollo," she said.

"Gorgeous," I told her.

"He'll live with me soon. He and Hank both."

I nodded. It was good to know, somehow, that Apollo was with two people who loved him, and not with someone who resented him.

Mick leaned over to snuffle at a scent on the floor. Tammy — Dr. Trent — giggled and patted his head. "Mick's a great dog. Call if you have any problems with the stitches. You can make an appointment to have them removed in about a week."

I stood up and shook her hand. "Tammy, thank you so much. You're really good at this."

"Thanks. Sometime you and I should go out for coffee. Since our paths keep crossing," she said. For a minute I saw a look on her face that I sometimes recognized on my own in the mirror — a loneliness that had nothing to do with being alone.

"I'd like that. Give me a call," I said.

Mick and I left the room and I went to the counter to make a new appointment. So far Mick was not biting at his bandage, but he was sniffing it a great deal. "Leave that alone, Mick," I said.

I paid the receptionist and brought Mick back to the car. It was now late afternoon and I still had a list of things I wanted to accomplish. As I drove, I tried to work on that list, mentally ticking things off, but my mind strayed to Dr. Tammy Trent and her almost smug expression when she spoke of Apollo's "narrow escape." It seemed to me that she had more than one motive for wanting Alice Dixon dead, and that she, perhaps more than anyone, had benefitted from that death.

■ ■ ■ ■

When I got home, I tucked Mick into his basket as one might a sick baby, and Mick clearly enjoyed all the doting. Soon he was snoring, and I took my cleaning supplies to the hallway to clean up his bloody paw prints. I left the door open so that my bleach-smelling cleaner wouldn't dominate the house. "Out, damned spot," I quoted to the floor.

"Lady Macbeth," said a voice in my doorway.

I jumped and turned to see Britt Hansen, Terry's girlfriend, chic as always, even though she wore a casual rust-colored sweater and a pair of jeans. She waved and said, "Let's see, what else can I remember? 'All the perfumes of Arabia cannot sweeten this little hand.' "

"Very good! Did you major in English?"

She smiled. "I majored in art history, which in retrospect was almost a guarantee that I would find it difficult to be gainfully employed for the rest of my life. Thank goodness for the gallery and the Internet, which provides all sorts of opportunities for luring customers."

I stood up. "Come on in! I was just cleaning up after Mick. He cut his paw and got blood on the floor."

"Oh — poor baby! Is he okay?" Britt asked, looking around for Mick.

"If you listen closely, you can hear him snoring. He has been spoiled by both me and a very pretty veterinarian who smelled like a field of flowers, and now he's probably having happy dreams."

Britt laughed. "All's well that ends well. Oh — now I have Shakespeare on the brain."

"Come to the kitchen. I can make some coffee."

Britt followed me as I walked toward the back of the house, but said, "Oh, I can't stay. Terry and I are going to some fundraiser tonight. Mayor Emanuel will be there; I've never met him before."

I tried not to look as amazed as I felt. "Uh — me either, Britt! You guys are such jetsetters."

She waved the notion away. "Anyway, I wanted to borrow an idea from you. Normally I have things catered, but tomorrow Terry invited a couple of clients over in the morning, not exactly breakfast but before lunch, and I just wanted to put out a few things for them to eat, but I have no idea about what I would do with such short notice. And I know that you always bring such delicious things when you come over — maybe you have some ideas for me?"

She perched on one of my kitchen stools and crossed her slim legs.

"Well — let's see. When would you be going shopping?"

"Probably early tomorrow morning. Which is why I am warning Terry not to keep me out late tonight."

"Good luck with that." Terry loves going out, and he claims to need only about four hours of sleep.

"I know, right? Meanwhile he's saddled me with this meeting tomorrow. He just counts on me to provide sophistication at a moment's notice."

My mind was working; Britt had her own caterers, but she wasn't using them tomorrow. This was an in for me. "Listen, I think I can help you out. First of all, I have a couple of frozen zucchini breads. Everybody likes those. Take one now; it will be defrosted by morning, and you can just set it out along with your butter dish, if they want to add some calories. That's one thing. Then I have this really easy recipe for a brunch frittata — I made it up myself, actually — and it's very popular. I could whip up the batter tonight and all you would have to do is put it in the oven. Then put out some lovely coffee and tea, some jam and scones, and you're all set! I can bake up some scones for you in about twenty minutes."

"Lilah, I'm in love with you." Britt jumped up and gave me a hug. Her perfume was exotic and obviously expensive. With her 1920s hair and face, her scent always made me feel that I was getting a whiff of a bygone era. "And I am going to pay you handsomely."

"Well, just for ingredients," I said.

"Of course not. Your labor, which you are offering most kindly after a last-minute request, is also worth money." Britt had her wallet out; she dug inside and took out a satisfying stack of bills, which she left on my counter.

"When do you want to pick it up?" I asked.

Britt pouted briefly with her lovely red-painted lips. "That's the problem — I don't know when Terry is going to let me leave this thing tonight."

"How about if I just leave everything in the kitchen, and you can use your key — just grab it whenever you get home. I'm an early bedtime sort of gal."

Britt clapped. "That sounds great! Thank you so much, Lilah! You are a lifesaver, as I knew you would be. You're always so innovative." Then she studied my face. "But you can't always be an early bedtime girl. I'm going to drag you out soon for a girls' night on the town. In a week or two, maybe. Right now I have to get ready for the Halloween party."

I tried to keep the envy out of my voice when I said, "It must be weird to entertain constantly."

Britt smoothed her lovely silken hair. "It has its rewards and its drawbacks." She gave me another hug and ducked back out, telling me she had to change her clothes. I wondered what sparkly thing she would wear to her fund-raiser, where she would meet the mayor of Chicago.

With a sigh, I took out a dozen eggs and began cracking them into a bowl. I would be sure that everything I made for Britt was top-notch. Then sometime in the future I would ask her casually if she ever wanted me to be a backup to her current caterers. Yes, that was the plan.

I lost myself for the next hour, stirring and beating and blending and baking. I carefully labeled the frittata mixture and put it in my fridge. I let the scones cool, then wrapped them up with a note to Britt and Terry. I tucked Britt's generous payment into my client earnings drawer, let Mick out and in, and climbed wearily upstairs.

When I came down the next morning, the food was gone, but someone had left a smiley face on a Post-it note and stuck it to my refrigerator.

CHAPTER NINE

The next afternoon I worked my shift at the real estate office, answering phones and typing up files with only half of my mind on my tasks. I drove home at around five o'clock and passed The Pizza Palace, where a handmade sign in the window said, ASK US ABOUT OUR CATERING! It was written with a fading marker, and the words slanted upward; someone obviously couldn't be bothered to use a ruler. The sign made me angry. Who would want to hire a caterer who couldn't even make a legible advertisement? Who would want a businessperson who couldn't make a computerized ad, or at least locate an industrial marker?

I huffed and flipped on my radio, where a news announcer was saying, "The man was the second victim of poisoning in Pine Haven in the past week. Pine Haven police told reporters that they are investigating several people of interest but are not ready to make an arrest for either murder."

My hands went numb on the wheel. Someone else was dead. Someone had been murdered. Again. "Oh God," I said, and I sent up a little prayer for the anonymous victim.

When I reached my house I ran inside and let Mick into the backyard. He had indeed removed his bandage, but his paw looked good and he didn't seem to have bothered the stitches. I threw away the gauze he'd left on the floor and turned on my message machine. I heard my mother's voice say, "Lilah, call me when you get a chance. Bert Spielman has been murdered!"

"Oh no," I said, staring at the blue tile on my kitchen wall. Some sort of classical music was playing in my head; I didn't even recognize it, but my brain had probably heard it and stored it at some point in my life. Perhaps it was a funeral march.

Bert Spielman was the head librarian at the main library. This was bad, truly bad, for many reasons, but especially for Pet Grandy. Despite all of her volunteerism — at church, at the high school — Pet also had one part-time job, and it happened to be at the Pine Haven Library. This meant that the two people who had been poisoned were both connected significantly to Perpetua Grandy.

■ ■ ■ ■

I called my mother, who was, naturally, distressed. "Bert Spielman!" my mother said. "Who in the world would want to kill a librarian? He just dropped dead, they said."

"What do you mean 'dropped dead'? As in the way that Alice Dixon dropped dead?"

"Well — I got this from Annie Prince, who was there looking at cookbooks. You know how the cooking section is pretty close to the main desk?"

I did.

"She said Bert had gone to the back to get his little dinner, and he took a bite of his meatball sandwich, and then she asked him a question and his eyes got really big. At first she thought he found her question shocking, but then she realized he felt ill. And by the time she noticed how pale he had gotten and started running over there, he had already keeled over."

"That's terrible."

"I know. I mean, talk about a harmless person. Bert could not possibly have had an enemy in this town. If it turns out that he was poisoned, like Alice — well, I think the police will have to assume they've got some kind of madman or serial killer on their hands."

This was a terrifying thought. "Mom — was Pet there when it happened?"

"Pet? I don't know. Oh dear. Oh, poor Pet," my mother said. "You don't think they'll suspect her, do you?"

"Of course they will! What if it's the same kind of poison? What if she was working that night? They're going to think she's an insane murderer!"

My mother contemplated this in silence. "You don't think there's any chance that Pet *did* kill two people, do you?"

"Mom, really! This is Perpetua, the woman who got her arm stuck in a storm drain because she was trying to rescue a trapped kitten."

My mother giggled. "Remember when that was on the news?"

"She's also the woman who crocheted earmuffs for every child in the St. Bart's kindergarten class because it was an unusually cold winter."

"I know, I know. It's ridiculous. Poor Pet. What do you think we can do to help her?"

This was a good question. We certainly couldn't prevent the police from suspecting her, but surely there were other ways we could offer our support.

"I don't know," I said.

My mother sighed. "I have to go now, hon. Dad and I have some work to do tonight. Do me a favor and make sure all your doors are locked. I don't want some mad poisoner murdering you."

"That's a cheery thought," I joked before we said our good-byes. Still, my mother had me feeling just paranoid enough to open my refrigerator and check to see if anything looked tampered with. Then I checked the locks on my doors and windows. When the phone rang again, I jumped about a foot in the air.

"Hello?"

"Hi, Lilah. It's Angelica Grandy."

"Uh — hi, Angelica."

"Listen, I don't know if you've heard about Bert Spiel—"

"I have. How's Pet?"

"She's really upset. We're all sitting here, trying to distract her, but she's got something on her mind. She asked if we would call you. Would you be willing to come over?"

"Um . . . sure. Why does she —"

"Well, you two are friends, and she figured your sense of humor would cheer her up."

This was strange for two reasons. First, I did not think Pet Grandy viewed me as a friend — more like a co-conspirator in our covered-dish secret. Second, although I liked to think I was a humorous person, Pet Grandy had not, to date, found one of my jokes amusing. Pet didn't really have a sense of humor. For a chilling moment I wondered if I was being lured to the Grandy house so that they could poison me. Then I realized how crazy a thought that was and said, "Okay, I'll be over soon, Ang."

I decided to take Mick with me, just in case. The Grandys all knew and liked Mick, so I knew they wouldn't object to his presence. Mick followed me out to the car with no discernible limp. I let him in on the passenger side and he jumped up with his usual grace. Then we drove through a mostly quiet Pine Haven, where Dickens Street glowed with orange lights and lurid skeletons and mummies peered through store windows. I flipped on the radio and happened across the oldies station — *From the fifties to today!* — and caught the end of Sinatra singing "The Way You Look Tonight." For a moment I wished that a man were sitting in Mick's seat, and we were talking easily and throwing each other secret, desire-filled glances. Then I sighed and figured I was better off with Mick. Men ended up disappointing me, but Mick had never done so.

When Mick and I got to the white two-level house with the life-size scarecrow on the porch, we climbed the stairs, I knocked, and we were admitted into a room full of people. Harmonia and Angelica both had their "boyfriends" over — Ted Parsons and Carl Booth, respectively — and the four of them seemed to have been chatting near the fireplace when Angelica let me in. I stood in the doorway while Angelica returned to her chair. "You know everyone, right, Lilah?"

I nodded. Mick made his way into the room, drawn by the scent of some pizza on a table. Harmonia practically dove onto Mick and started petting him with her big hands.

"Uh, yes, I think so. Hello, Ted. Carl."

Ted, a fifty-ish man with the red nose of a drinker and the brown mustache of a lumberjack, worked at the Rite-Aid pharmacy and was an usher at church. Carl, who was bald and thin, owned Pine Haven's only car wash and was reputedly rich as a lord. They both waved to me, but none of them offered me a seat. Ted took pity on me, finally. "Pet's in the bathroom, washing her face. She had a little . . . weepy attack."

"Ah," I said, feeling awkward. I turned to study the picture gallery in the hallway, which seemed far preferable to making my way into the crowded living room. I turned to my left, contemplating a wall full of pictures of what seemed to be about a hundred years of Grandy history. One of the best shots was an eight-by-ten of three Grandys as little girls — and even though they were tiny, it was clear that it was Pet, Harmonia, and Angelica because they looked like shrunken versions of the women they were now — sledding in a snow-covered park. Perpetua, in a red coat, was trying to pull the sled. Angelica, smug as a little cat, sat on the sled, her face rosy inside her multicolored knit hat. Harmonia, the tiniest of them all, was crying and attempting to pull the sled the other way. It was obviously a family favorite, since it had been enlarged.

Farther down the hall and closer to the living room were some more recent pictures of the women; their hairstyles were slightly different, so the snaps were probably a year or two old. I wondered who had photographed them. These were great pictures, without the look of posed department-store portraits, and somehow capturing the personalities of all the women. Each of them had some sort of prop: Angelica, holding a bouquet of tiger lilies, looked dreamily into the distance; Harmonia, holding a little black dog, smiled down into his face; and Perpetua, holding a wooden spoon, wore the homey expression of someone who loved cooking. I was guessing that our chili arrangement had already been established when this shot was taken. I looked away from the wall of photos and tuned in to the voices in the room, which now included Perpetua's. She had emerged from the bathroom and sat down in a plush red chair to the left of the hearth.

"Pet, just let the police do their job," Carl said. "They'll sort things out and realize you had nothing to do with this, or with Alice."

Angelica agreed. "You weren't even at the library today! How could you possibly have poisoned Bert if you weren't there?"

Pet nodded. "Bert was my good friend. We were just talking about Edinburgh. I said I had never been there, and he had been twice, and he showed me some books with pictures of the city. He said if I ever went, he could give me an itinerary that was better than what tourists usually got." She wiped her eyes.

Mick, a therapy dog at heart, went to Pet

and put his chin in her lap. This earned a smile, and then Pet started rubbing his head in earnest. "You're a good dog. Thanks for bringing him, Lilah."

"Oh — sure. How are you doing, Pet?"

"I still can't believe it. I don't understand what's happening in this town. And why is it all happening right in the tiny little areas of my life? I'm a quiet person. I live a quiet life."

Harmonia sat on the arm of Pet's chair and stroked her short hair; then she reached down and started petting Mick. "Of course you do," she said. "Just stop worrying, Pet. The police can't touch you, because you're innocent. Innocence doesn't need a defense."

Everyone nodded, admiring this sentiment. I sat down on a chair near the door, wondering why I was there. Eventually Pet sent me a secret glance and said, "I think it would do me some good if I got some fresh air. Lilah, can I walk your dog with you?"

Curiouser and curiouser. "Sure. Mick loves walking in the evening." I stood up and called Mick; I snapped on the leash I had just removed and said, "Why don't we walk around the block? There are some great Halloween decorations out here."

Pet nodded; the other four people seemed

163

relieved to give up their roles as counselors. When we left, Ted was turning on the television and Carl was helping himself to some of the pizza that sat on a sideboard.

Now I paused at a tree so that Mick could sniff it with elaborate care. I looked at Pet, who again reminded me of a child, bundled as she was into her little jacket. Her short, graying hair stood up in an uncombed tuft on her head. "Pet, what's going on?"

"I don't know. I want you to know that I didn't do it. Whatever someone did, that someone wasn't me." Even in the limited glow of someone's landscaping lights, I could see the tears in her eyes.

"Well, of course you didn't! But why do you feel you need to say that to me?"

"Because you're involved, too! If they end up believing that I poisoned my own chili, and they interrogate me, then they might make me confess about who made it. I don't want to, but now I wonder what they'll do."

She sounded genuinely frightened. "Pet, they can't interrogate you without cause. As your sister said, you weren't there on the day Bert died. I would think they'll be looking at who was. Does the library have a security camera?"

Pet looked surprised. "Yes, I think so. By the front entrance."

"Let's be logical. If I were the police detective, I would study that tape and try to identify every person who had walked in that day. I would talk to witnesses and find out who had access to the back room where Bert kept his dinner. And then I would narrow it down, based on those two things, until I found my murderer. But before we get off this unpleasant topic . . . do you know of anyone who might have had a grudge against Bert? Any patron he'd disagreed with lately?"

Pet shook her head, frowning. "Everyone loved Bert. He was sort of a cumuldge — what's that word?"

"Curmudgeon?"

"Yes. He was a lovable curmudgeon."

"Okay. Maybe Bert wasn't the intended victim. Could anyone have mistaken his food for someone else's?"

Again Pet shook her head. "No. When Bert brings his own lunch, he has it in this distinctive Tupperware with red lids. Other times he goes out and picks up something to eat at a local place. I'm not sure which he had that night."

I sighed. "There are probably lots of other possibilities, but here's one more to consider, Pet. Maybe whoever poisoned him — if they did in fact poison him — didn't care whose food it was. Maybe they just wanted someone to die."

"Why?" Pet asked, scandalized.

"Either because they're crazy, or because they wanted to frame someone else — someone like you. In which case, the police will probably be considering those same scenarios."

Pet plunged her hands into her pockets and nodded. She seemed slightly cheered by this. "You're dating the cop in charge, aren't you?"

"What?" I was so shocked I dropped Mick's leash.

"Harmonia saw him in your driveway the other night when she drove down Dickens Street. He didn't look like he was on official business."

"I am not dating him!"

She grinned at me.

"I — we — I barely know him."

"Well, if he asks you, tell him I'm a good person."

"I've already told him that, Pet. Everyone knows you're a good person. Don't let this make you paranoid. Some evil person is doing bad things in this town, and for some reason both of those things have personally affected you. But it could be just a coincidence. I'm sure that the police know that coincidences happen all the time."

She nodded. "Thanks, Lilah." She scuffed her feet into the leaves for a while. Then she brightened. "Hey, you and I have another job to do!"

"Yes, I heard. I was wondering when you were going to mention it to me!"

"You *heard*?"

"From Trixie and Theresa. When I went to get the Crock-Pot. I told them it was for you, just like we agreed."

Clearly relieved, Pet cuddled into her fleecy coat. "I told them I could make something different — maybe a big platter of mac and cheese or baked enchiladas or something. But they said the ladies all want me to make my chili. Trixie said they trust me, and they don't want to change the tradition."

"That's probably a good idea. You know I will make it with care, Pet. And I will be sure it goes directly into your hands, and then *you* can keep it under close guard until people are ready to eat. Not to be paranoid, Pet, but I don't think you should take your eyes off of it until it's served. Have the ladies guard it in shifts."

Pet chuckled miserably.

"I'm not kidding, Perpetua."

She nodded. "All right. I'll arrange something with Trixie. You can bring it to the church like always, and then we'll watch it, I promise."

"And Pet — I know you have a lot going on right now, but don't forget that it helps if I have some notice before these events. Sometimes I'm working, and I don't always have time to run out at the last minute and get ingredients."

Pet looked stricken. "I know, I know! I'm sorry. It's just — there's been so much going on, and it cheered me up to have them ask me to cook for the next event. You know. It makes me feel proud and happy."

"I know."

"But now you look kind of mad, and that upsets me, because we've become such good friends over this last year!"

So her sisters hadn't been joking. Pet Grandy considered me a friend: not just a businesswoman from the parish, but a friend. I thought back. We'd certainly had many clandestine meetings, during which I passed a covered dish (with the solemnity of passing the Holy Grail) into Pet's impatient hands. I often teased her about this, and Pet had shown no humor at all. Perhaps she did in fact appreciate my little jokes, and just didn't show it that much. "Yes, of course, Pet."

"Remember when we sang karaoke for Father Schmidt?" she said, beaming at me. The event in question had actually involved Pet asking me to help her transfer a rented machine into the church hall and then me showing her how it worked (since I had sung karaoke at Terry's before, and got the basic idea). In the process I had sung "Proud Mary" for Pet and Father Schmidt, both of whom had clapped enthusiastically and told me that I should join the choir. After that Pet held the microphone while I showed her the various cords and attachments. Perhaps, in her memory, she had sung, too. I had never heard Pet's singing voice, and I had no idea whether or not she could keep a tune. Despite what I considered the boring nature of my own life, there was a chance that Pet had done a little vicarious living through me. This was oddly flattering but also sad, and on impulse I slung my arm around her and kept it there as we started walking back.

"You are a nice friend, Pet. And that's why you have nothing to worry about: because the police will hear that from everyone in this parish. That Pet Grandy is just a genuinely nice woman who wouldn't hurt a fly, and who gets kittens out of storm drains.

Whatever happened to that little cat, anyway?"

Pet looked up at me. "Didn't you know? We adopted him. His name is Stripey. You'll see him when we go back, I'm sure. He usually likes to talk to company; maybe he was afraid of the dog."

"Ah. Well, see, there's another sign of your niceness. You rescued a kitten from the drain, and then you took him in."

"We love him," Pet said simply.

I nodded, squeezing her shoulder and rounding the corner to find Jay Parker and the blue-suited woman from bingo night standing in Pet's driveway. Even in the dark I could see that Parker's eyebrows had hiked up at the sight of Pet and me together. "Hello," I said.

"Hello, Miss Grandy, Miss Drake." Jay gestured to his companion, who was pretty, in a dark and self-contained sort of way. My eyes darted to her ring finger and found it bare. "This is Detective Grimaldi."

"Hello," I said. "I was just cheering up Pet. She's suffered some terrible shocks over the last few days."

The detectives remained stone-faced. "It's a stressful time, we understand," said Grimaldi in a smooth, uninflected voice. "But if we could ask you some questions,

Miss Grandy? We could do it here, if you'd prefer, or at the station, if that's more convenient."

"Will her family be present?" I asked, feeling protective of Pet in her lamblike fleece.

"We'd like to talk to you alone, if that's all right," said Jay Parker.

I bristled at their attitude; I could feel Pet trembling under my arm. "I don't think Pet has to talk to you without someone present — either a family member or a lawyer — isn't that correct?"

Jay Parker shot me a surprised and slightly murderous glance. "Miss Grandy has every right to have counsel present during our interview. But since we merely want to establish a few facts about her job at the library, that hardly seems necessary."

I realized that when it came right down to it, I didn't totally trust the police. They had to do their job, which was difficult. Whoever committed murder was going to lie as a matter of self-preservation, and there was always the off chance that Pet was crazy and actually guilty of poisoning two people. My instinct, though, was that Pet was in a bad situation, sort of naïve, and genuinely frightened, and these two cops were scaring her even more.

I shrugged. "Then I'm sure you won't

mind asking those questions in front of her sisters and their friends."

"Thank you for your input, Miss Drake." Parker's voice was cold enough to freeze water. "If you'll excuse us?"

I gave Pet a hug in front of them. "Don't worry, Pet. I'll call you tomorrow to see how you're doing, okay? Keep a good thought."

"Thanks, Lilah. Thank you so much," Pet said.

I watched her walk in, followed by Parker and Grimaldi, who had a graceful walk, too, I noted with some resentment.

Then Mick and I went back to the car; he climbed in eagerly, and I realized he was probably a bit cold. "Sorry, buddy," I told him, flipping on the heater. He settled into the passenger seat and slitted his eyes, making me laugh despite my growing misery.

I had been harboring a fantasy that someday, after the murder was solved, Jay Parker might show up at my house for dinner again, his blue eyes glowing like moonstones in the dim light of my porch. Now I was pretty certain that I wouldn't have to worry about Jay Parker showing up at my house late at night, or at any time, ever again. I had questioned his authority and his integrity in front of two other people, and it seemed he had perceived it as a betrayal.

Picturing Pet's childlike face, though, I knew that I would do it again. The police had to suspect everyone, but I didn't have to suspect someone I knew. Pet Grandy was an innocent woman, and I would not look kindly on those who tried to suggest otherwise.

CHAPTER TEN

After work the next day I went to the grocery store to buy the ingredients for Pet's latest batch of chili. She had texted me that approximately fifty women would be attending the event, which gave me a clear sense of portions. The ingredients were expensive; I wondered how Pet was able to pay me on such a regular basis when she probably made little more than minimum wage at the library and certainly made nothing helping out at church. My mother had once heard a rumor that the Grandys had some sort of family nest egg, perhaps as the result of a lawsuit.

Curious about that, I called her when I got home, nestling the phone between my cheek and shoulder so that I could unpack my groceries. "Hey, Mom. Remember how you told me that the Grandys inherited money once? Money that made them sort of wealthy?"

My mother was humming some little song under her breath; she was probably doing a task, too — I pictured her arranging flowers. Now she stopped humming and thought about it. "Oh, as I recall, the grandfather was working on the railroad —"

"All the live-long day?"

My mother giggled. "Probably. Anyway, I can't remember who told me this, but he got hurt somehow. I want to say there was a lawsuit, and he got a big sum of money. He was a thrifty Irishman, that's what your father says, and so he saved it and made more money. And then he died and it got passed down. That's why all those daughters can sort of just pursue their hobbies and their little church duties, because there's some money there. I don't know how much."

"Huh."

"If you ask me, it's also why none of them was in a hurry to get married. Why get married, if you don't feel dependent on two incomes?"

That one silenced me for thirty seconds. "Mom! That is a far more cynical view than I would expect to come out of your mouth. Especially because your own marriage is happy."

She sniffed. "Yes, it's happy, but if I were

twenty-three again and had a bank full of money, I'm not convinced that I would have rushed into matrimony. It's just a reality. It's Marxism."

I stared at Mick, who nodded. "Who are you, and what have you done with Olivia Drake?"

She giggled again. "You'll understand someday, when you're ready to settle down." Then her voice changed. "What's bothering you, hon? Besides the murder, I mean."

"Nothing much. Mick got some glass in his paw and I had to get stitches for him."

"Oh, poor doggie!"

"He's okay now. The vet was Tammy. Hank Dixon's Tammy."

"She's a veterinarian?"

"That was my reaction — but she was good."

"Huh. Hey, guess who I ran into yesterday? That handsome policeman who talked to us at the church. The tall one with dark hair and blue eyes."

"Jay Parker?"

"Yes! Right."

"Where did you run into him?"

"Daddy and I went to the diner on Stark Street for lunch, and he was there, having lunch with his partner. They were wolfing down their food; I'm sure they're super busy. But he remembered me and he said hello, and he asked how you were doing."

"He probably suspects me of murder."

"He's very handsome," my mother said.

"You mentioned that."

"If you married someone like him, can you imagine what beautiful children you'd have? With your blonde hair and his blue eyes?"

"You just told me that women are better off having money and not marrying! And why, by the way, are you fantasizing about me marrying him?"

"Oh, no reason," my mother said meekly.

"Anyway. I'm pretty sure he hates me now."

"Why would he hate you?"

"Pet's sisters called me last night and said she was upset, and asked me to come over."

"Well, sure. You two have become good friends." Was I the only one who had missed this?

"Anyway, Pet and I went out to walk Mick, and when we came back, he and this woman detective were in the driveway."

"You said 'woman detective' in a weird voice. Was she pretty?"

"Annoyingly so."

"Oh, I'll bet it's the one I saw him eating lunch with. They didn't seem — you know.

Intimate. They seemed like colleagues eating lunch. Did you notice if she was married?"

"No ring."

"Ah," my mother said.

"And they said they wanted to question Pet. I had just gotten her sort of cheered up; she's genuinely scared about the whole thing. I had her laughing and cheerful, and we were walking back, and then those two were there, with these cemetery faces, and Pet literally started trembling."

"Oh, poor Pet!"

"So I basically told them to stop harassing her, and that she had a right to a lawyer."

"Well, that's true."

"I know, but he got really distant and cold then. He looked like he wanted to kill me, to be honest. And he basically told me to get lost."

"Ah."

"So. Not that I care either way — I'm just saying you can stop fantasizing about grandchildren."

"Oh, honey, don't sound like that. You want to come over for some ice cream?"

"I have to make Pet's chili. Maybe after that?"

"Sure! Come for dinner. Dad is making steaks on the grill. And Cam is coming with his new girlfriend, this Bellini woman. They're staying overnight, because they're going to Terry's party tomorrow."

"Oh, well then! I definitely want to be there! I need to meet this woman. Cam seems hung up on her."

"Something about the change of season, maybe."

"Yeah."

My mother started humming "I've Been Workin' on the Railroad." "Oh, Lilah, you put that song in my head!" she said, scolding.

"See you soon, Mom."

I hung up and looked at Mick. "You like steak, don't you?"

Mick nodded.

My parents' house — my old home — was a roomy Georgian on a one-acre lot, centered between two beautiful old elm trees, which now boasted an array of leaves in a whole spectrum of crayon-box autumn colors. When I pulled up I admired those leaves for a moment, on the trees, on the lawn, on the porch. Nature had blanketed the entire property with the shades of fall, and it was a refreshing sight.

Mick and I climbed the steps, and my brother Cameron, looking relaxed as always, came to the door with a glass of wine in one hand. His left hand was joined with the slender hand of one of the most beautiful women I had ever seen. Her tan skin and chocolate-colored eyes would have been her most arresting features, if it weren't for the gorgeous dark curls that tumbled down her back, almost to her waist, or for the ridiculously generous proportions of her figure, which made her look rather like a cartoon that had emerged from a twelve-year-old boy's fantasy. Leave it to Cameron to find these women.

"Hey, sis. This is Serafina Bellini. Serafina, Lilah Drake."

"Wow," I said.

Serafina let go of my brother and grabbed me in a surprising embrace. "Oh my God, you are lovely! Cameron told me, but is true! You look like my little baby sister, Abia! She is so blonde like you. Like a golden angel!"

I looked at Cameron over her shoulder. "Seriously?" I said.

Cam nodded. "She's always like this. She's super affectionate."

My mouth curled. I could only imagine how Serafina's *affection* paid off for him. Still, I enjoyed being hugged by her because she smelled amazing and everything about her was soft and comfortable. "It's nice to meet you," I finally said, when she let go of me. "How did you happen to meet my brother?"

Serafina laughed and clapped her hands. This woman *was* enthusiastic. "It's so funny. Cam is visiting Rome, and he meets my brother Carlo, who directs him to a museum that Cam is seeking. So Cam tells Carlo that he is from Chicago, and Carlo tells him that his sister is studying there for several years. He tells Cam to look her up when he gets back. And Cam keeps this promise — and that sister . . . is me!"

She clapped again, as though she really didn't think I'd guessed the ending of the story.

"Well, that is very cool."

My mother wandered in with a vase of roses. "Isn't Serafina beautiful?"

I could tell that she was doing that "future grandchildren" exercise, trying to morph together the best qualities of Cam and his girlfriend. I had to admit, they would be some amazingly cute kids.

"Yes, she is. Serafina, what are you studying here in the US?"

"I am working on my master's degree in chemistry," she said.

"Wow," I said again. Some women had it

all. I had a brief wrestling match with my own jealousy; finally my polite self won out and I told her how impressive she was.

She shrugged. "In my family, I am not the impressive one. My brothers and my sisters, they are all like young Da Vincis. That is why I wanted to study overseas. Easier to be impressive when they are not standing beside me!" She grinned at me with perfect teeth.

"I get that," I said, pointing at Cameron. "He graduated from high school at sixteen."

Serafina hugged him; it looked sort of like a gorgeous, sexy boa constrictor wrapping around his body, and Cam's face said that he would die happy. "Cameron is brilliant," she said.

"How long have you two known each other?" I asked, surprised at the level of their intimacy. In the past, Cam brought girls home to prove that they existed and then basically ignored them while he talked sports with my dad.

"Two months," Serafina said. "Two months yesterday. We celebrated in the city, at The Berghoff."

"Nice," said my mother and I together.

Cameron smiled; his face was half-hidden by Serafina's amazing hair. "It *was* nice. We had a terrific time." His expression was so happy it was almost stupid. I had never seen Cameron this way.

This pleased me and depressed me simultaneously: it pleased me because I was glad Cameron had finally found a love match; it depressed me because my own perfect Italian man, with similar dark curls and gorgeous features, had been roundly despised.

In my family's defense, Angelo had done a lot of despicable things. He tended to neglect me for days at a time and then make some grand gesture to make it all better. That worked at the beginning but got stale after a few months. And a couple of months after that, I realized he had cheated on me. If he hadn't already lost my family's allegiance, he did then.

"Hey, I'll have what they're having," I said, pointing to Cam's wine.

"Oh, sure, honey," my mother said. She poured a glass, put it into my hand, and whispered, "She's a bit much all at once, isn't she? Go say hi to your father."

I did, escaping into the cool, crisp air and the splendor of my father's deck. He had built it himself when I was about twelve, and since then it had weathered into a lovely, seasoned gray. The air smelled like charcoal and cooked meat; it cheered me considerably.

"Hey, Dad," I said, giving him a kiss on the cheek.

"Hey, doll. You look nice tonight."

"I'm feeling kind of like an ugly stepsister. I just saw the glory that is Serafina."

My father shrugged. "She's sexy," he said. "But you are the real deal."

I kissed him again. "You're my dad, so you might be biased. But I will take your compliment and enjoy it."

My father gave me an assessing look. "Anything on your mind?"

"No."

"Mom says some cop gave you a hard time."

"No, it's not like that. It's just — I thought we were friends, but then he got pretty angry with me. It's no big deal."

"It's never fun to play the dating game."

"Which I am not playing."

"I'm relieved I never have to do that again," my father said, with an innocence that I found charming.

I tried a new conversational tack. "Some men still play it after they get married."

"God knows why," he said, shuddering. "I hated dating. Even dating your mother I was a nervous wreck. I just remember sweating a lot."

"Oh, Dad." I sat down on the wooden

bench attached to the deck and watched my father as he expertly flipped meat and vegetables. "Have you sold that house? The one I was showing Sunday?"

My father squinted at me over his shoulder. "Oh — didn't we tell you? Yes. Hank Dixon and his fiancée made an offer and the seller accepted. He went well over asking price, so the other bidders didn't have much of a chance."

"Huh. Well, I'm glad for Tammy. She seemed smitten with the place."

"Yeah. She's kind of a strange woman, but she genuinely seems to love Hank. God knows why," my father said.

This was unlike him. My father tended to leave gossip and judgment to my mother and me, and to be honest, we had indulged in our fair share in our mother/daughter talk sessions.

"Why do you say that? Hank seems like a nice enough guy. Kind of stressed out."

"I don't know. Maybe he is. I just remember way back when, when you and Cam were little, he had a reputation as a womanizer."

"Even while he was married to Alice?"

"*Especially* while he was married to Alice." My father closed the barbecue lid and turned to look at me. "It was just talk, but enough people hinted at it that I always believed it was true."

"Strange, because he looks genuinely upset by her death. Grief-stricken, almost."

"You can love someone and still cheat on them," my father said. "Or at least you can tell yourself it's love." He didn't look at me when he said this, but I knew he was talking about Angelo.

On the night that I broke it off with him, Angelo came to my parents' house, demanding to see me, in his typical passionate way. My father, a decidedly unpassionate man, went out in the dark yard to speak with Angelo, and Angelo never contacted me again. I still didn't know what was said, nor did I want to.

I sighed and looked around the yard. "It's so beautiful here. Like a little sanctuary."

My father sat down next to me and patted my hand. "That's exactly what it is. Hey — your dog is sniffing around my grill."

"He won't steal anything. He's just waiting for you to offer something."

My father looked suspicious. "I'm not giving him a steak."

"Just some drippings, maybe, or some fat. Mick just loves the smell."

"Hey, boy," my father called. Mick loped over, smiling, and my father got to work rubbing his head. I wondered if my mother knew what a good man she had; I thought she probably did, even though she had speechified about money and independence.

My father's phone beeped in his pocket. He took it out, flipped it on, and said, "Hello."

He listened for a while, his face attentive, and then he said, "Okay, sure. Maybe in about half an hour? Come by the house, and I'll drive us out there."

I frowned at him. "Are you leaving?"

"Just for thirty minutes or so. That was Hank Dixon, speak of the devil. He and Tammy want to take a couple of quick measurements in the house. I'll just run them over and then come back. But we have half an hour to eat before they get here."

So we called out my mother and Cameron and Serafina, and the five of us shared a meal on the chilly deck, gazing at the glimmering leaves and talking about love and coincidence and Italy and wine.

I lost myself in those surprisingly happy moments, laughing when Serafina got down to Mick's level and kissed him right on his dog mouth. The woman was irrepressible. I looked at my brother and gave him a thumbs-up, and he looked so relieved and happy that I realized she really was the one, because Cameron had never cared what we thought of his girlfriends before.

Our autumn idyll was interrupted by the sight of Hank and Tammy, who had walked around the side of the house to find us on the deck. "Hey, I know you," Tammy said, pointing at me. She sported another pair of crazy-high heels, even though she wore jeans and a sweater, and I feared she would catch her foot in a gopher hole and break her leg.

"Hi, Tammy."

"Did you hear we got the house?"

"Yes! Congratulations."

Tammy walked closer and spied Mick. "Can I take a look at the paw?" she said.

"That would be great!"

She called my dog and he went over, head bowing and tail wagging. Tammy squatted down and picked up his paw, peering at his paw pad. "It looks terrific. Still nice and clean."

She stood up again and took Hank's hand.

Hank Dixon still looked sort of solemn, but Tammy's happiness had brought some life to his face, and I could see a trace of his normal good looks. "Thanks for doing this, Daniel," he said to my father. "I didn't realize we'd be interrupting a family event."

"It won't take long," my father said.

"Hopefully they'll all still be here when I return."

"Just a few quick measurements," Tammy said, winking at me. "We ladies like to start planning even before we move in, right, Lilah?"

Every woman seemed to think I was her pal. "We sure do," I said, smiling back.

My father grabbed his wallet and keys and walked around the corner with Hank and Tammy. My mother collected some dishes, and Serafina leaped up to help her, grabbing wineglasses and a Jell-O mold that undulated slightly less than Serafina did. My brother never took his eyes off of her.

"I'm afraid you might actually put her on a plate and eat her," I said.

He finally looked at me, laughing. "Can't help it. She's amazing."

"No arguments there. She's like Sophia Loren and Penélope Cruz got put into a blender."

"Right?"

"Are you going to marry her?"

"Yes, I am," said my brother. "If she says yes."

"Will my nieces and nephews have Italian accents and call me Zia Lilah?"

He laughed again. "You crack me up. And

no, because Serafina intends to live in America."

"Good. I was half fearing you'd relocate to Rome."

"If she asked me to, I would. But she knows we Drakes are a small family. She's got a big one, and they're spread all over. Three of her siblings are here in the US."

"Huh. Any brothers who look like her?"

"Some." Cam's look was assessing. "I thought maybe you'd had enough of Italian men."

"Maybe I have."

"What about this cop you said you had a crush on?"

"That's a no-go," I said.

My brother patted my head and gave me a sip of his wine.

When my father returned he started scrubbing his grill; he was meticulous about his barbecue routine. "How's the happy couple?" I asked.

"Fine," my dad said. He looked around to make sure no one else was with us. "But Hank grabbed me while Tammy was upstairs with her tape measure and said that he had been about to talk with Bert on the night he died."

I had been watching a moth that flew

persistently into my father's deck light and refused to learn from its mistakes. Now I spun on the deck bench so that I fully faced my father. "What? What do you mean, 'about to talk to him'?"

"Bert had called him and said he needed to tell him something. Hank said he'd stop by the library after work, but by then Bert was dead."

"So . . . ?"

"He thinks Bert knew something about why Alice died. And he thinks someone killed Bert to prevent him from talking."

There was silence, except for some tree frogs and cicadas, doing their surprisingly loud nighttime singing. "But — has he told this to the police?"

My father shook his head. "Apparently they put him through quite a grilling the other night. He's not eager to speak with them again. He only told me because it was obviously bugging him. It was on his mind, and I was there."

My father was easy to confide in, and many a person had spilled their sorrows to him over his lifetime, including his daughter. "Well, he needs to tell the cops."

"I assume he will eventually. Still, you might want to mention it to your friend, if you happen to see him again." He didn't look at me while he said that.

"It's not likely, Dad."

"No big deal, then."

At the end of the evening my mother came through with the promised ice cream, and we sat on the couches in the living room and watched *Houseboat* with Cary Grant and Sophia Loren, cuddled up in couples: Cam and Fina (as he called her), Mom and Dad, Mick and me. Because my mother knew I was depressed, she gave dispensation for Mick to sit on the couch and have his own ice cream.

Sophia Loren appeared on-screen; she yelled something with angry, beautiful fervor at Cary Grant, who looked handsomely confused. "There's Cam and Serafina in two years," I said, and everyone laughed. Then Cam and Serafina made out for a full minute while the rest of us watched without apology. They truly were attractive, just like Cary and Sophia. My mother murmured something against my father's ear; I could swear I heard the word *grandchildren*. My father was clearly excited to have my mother murmuring in his ear, so when the movie ended twenty minutes later, I looked at Mick and he nodded. It was time to go.

Everyone rushed to walk me to the door, and Serafina gave me a series of kisses all over my face as her good-bye. "Geez, Cam, if you break up with her, I'm asking her out," I said, and I left on the wave of their laughter.

"At least I amuse everyone," I said to Mick as we walked to the car. I had earned giggles from Pet, my mother, Tammy, and everyone in my parents' house. Only one person had been distinctly unamused by my behavior recently.

The memory of Jay Parker's cold eyes made the dark evening seem colder, and when Mick had finished his business, I locked us securely into the tiny house and found my fleeciest pajamas. We briefly watched a Western on my petite attic television, but I found that my eyes were drooping, so I flicked it off and pulled up my covers. "Tomorrow is another day, Mick," I said, although he was already snoring in his basket.

Then I thought of what my father had said about Hank. It seemed that Hank Dixon was the only one who cared about finding his wife's killer, and the killer of Bert Spielman. But then I remembered Hank Dixon's face in the window of his ex-wife's house. At the time it had looked sad, but in retrospect it seemed sinister. . . .

"I need sleep," I murmured and buried my face in my pillow. But even behind my closed lids I could see the faces of various people who had been there the night that Alice died: simple, friendly, innocuous people — one of whom had been a murderer.

CHAPTER ELEVEN

The next morning I was cheered by the thought of Terry's Halloween party. There were always plenty of cute guys at Terry's event, and I had decided to forgo the Elvira idea and to look amazing — Serafina-level amazing. There wasn't time to get a costume now, but I happened to have a little ace up my sleeve. Two Halloweens earlier the church had put on a variety show to raise money for a new playground. My parents had volunteered to do a skit and were given a script in which they played Batman and Robin (God knows why, or who wrote these things). My mother, a talented seamstress, made the costumes for herself and my father, as well as for me — whom my mother had persuaded to play a walk-on role as Catwoman at the end of the skit. "You don't have to say any words," my mother said. "Just look sexy."

Since my father was Batman, I had some

problems with this, but my mother had finally persuaded me by showing me the sad playground behind St. Bart's. So I walked onto the stage in three different shows, and the audience clapped appreciatively. It was a really dumb skit, which goes to show that people are desperate for a laugh.

I still had the Catwoman outfit, and now it seemed an appropriate thing to wear. My weight hadn't changed significantly, so I felt I could still stuff myself into the leatherlike costume.

I toyed with bringing Mick to the party, but I decided I'd leave him at home. I'd only be gone a few hours, and he could sit that long by himself without feeling left out. Our little house was so far down the driveway that we didn't tend to get trick-or-treaters, which was good, since that would send Mick into a frenzy. Terry got all the costumed children, and every year he and Britt managed to give out something memorable.

At noon I drove to St. Bart's and delivered Pet's chili. Pet came out looking sinister as ever with her envelope full of cash and her deliberate lack of eye contact. According to tradition, I offered to get out of the car, only to have Pet dance around like Rumpelstiltskin, assuring me that she was fine. This time she had brought the dolly with her, and she made quick work of the transfer.

"Thanks for bringing this from my house," she intoned loudly. I had grown fond of the whole process — it was Theatre of the Absurd that would have cost a lot more on a New York stage.

"See you, Pet. Happy Halloween," I said. "You are guarding that chili, right? All day long?"

"I am," she assured me. "No one will touch it."

God, I hoped not. I said good-bye again and drove off. When I looked in my rearview mirror, I saw that Father Schmidt had joined her and was holding the door open for her in a chivalrous way. I heard him saying, through my slightly open window, ". . . smells delicious, as usual!" So even Father Schmidt wanted Pet to know that there were no hard feelings about the poisoned chili — at least not toward her.

I had a message when I got home; it was from Toby Atwater, a guy with five kids, for whom I sometimes made a French toast casserole — a dish of my own invention. He saved his "special recipe" for kids' birthdays and his anniversary and such. He wanted one for Saturday morning. I stowed my money from Pet in my kitchen drawer where

I kept my covered-dish finances, and called him back, assuring him that I would have it ready Saturday morning, and that I would meet him in our usual place — the viaduct under Route 23, just outside town limits. Then I wrote the date on my calendar, in code, just in case I ever had a nosy visitor. It said "Breakfast with Toby." I wrote it in red pen, which meant a job. If I ever wrote a date in black pen, it was a real date.

On today's calendar square, there was a black notation that said "Terry's Halloween Party, 7:00."

That gave me about five hours. I did not want to spend it mooning around, so I got my cleaning equipment out and did a thorough washing, vacuuming, dusting, and decluttering of my little house. When I was finished, it was glowing, and the sun in the room seemed brighter because I had actually washed my windows. "Now, that's clean, Mick."

Mick agreed in his silent way, and it earned him some lunch. Then, feeling grubby, I retired to my bathroom and took a luxurious shower. It was fun, I decided, having hours and hours to get ready for a party. Who knew, on this day of devilish mischief, what treats awaited me?

By five o'clock I had squeezed my way

into the black costume. I left off the mask and ears so that I could really go to work on my hair. I never bothered with my locks. They were long and pretty straight, and I generally liked them that way. But sometimes, when I needed to feel gorgeous (after meeting someone like Serafina, for example), I got out the curling iron and gave myself what my mother and I used to call "Sleeping Beauty hair." This took me almost forty-five minutes, but at the end I had bouncy blonde waves that made me look a little bit like a pageant contestant, which suited my mood.

I still had about an hour. What to do? Read a book? I was too geared up. Watch television? Same thing. Mick wanted to go outside, so I decided to go into my teeny backyard and breathe in some fresh air. I flipped on the security light, which, thanks to my father, was laser-bright. I saw that I had left a rake leaning on my back shed. I headed toward it, inhaling deeply. It felt good. I loved cold weather, I loved October, and I loved a good dark Halloween night. I could hear the sound of children running up and down Dickens Street, enjoying their candy hunt. I laughed a little to myself, and Mick seemed to be smiling, too, as he sniffed along the line of trees at the end of our yard. I grabbed the rake; Mick lifted his head and barked, and I turned to see a dark figure coming toward me down the side path, like a man from a nightmare. My scream was so loud that even Mick stopped barking and turned to look at me. My eyes were blinded by the glare of my outdoor light, so I could only make out a silhouette of a bulky form and a head that seemed made of Medusa-like snakes and devil horns. I held up my rake as though it were a lance . . . then, in a sudden shift of perception, I saw that the visitor was Angelo, and he *was* wearing devil horns, along with a little red cape over his habitual black T-shirt and jeans. The latter outfit was one that Angelo wore particularly well.

"Lilah," he said in his sexy voice, putting out his hands in entreaty. "Put down the rake, eh? I come in peace."

I let out a shuddery sigh as I lowered my weapon. "What are you doing, sneaking up on me in the dark? I should go ahead and stab you."

He put on his patient look. "I was not sneaking up on you. You did not answer my knock on the front door, and I saw your back light was on. So. I came to speak with you."

"Dressed as the devil?"

"You are dressed as a cat. A very sexy cat," he added. "Consider what day it is, Lilah *mia.*"

Initially Angelo's sexy little Italian sayings had enthralled me — that was, until I'd realized he used them on everyone. Angelo knew how to work his foreignness to his advantage.

"Fine. I assume you're going to a Halloween party and you don't just intend to scare children who come to your house."

He laughed, but there was some misery in it. "Can we go inside? I need to ask you something."

"Angelo, if this is about us —"

He held up a hand. "There has been no *us* for some time, eh? I'm here about something else."

I put my rake inside the shed and snapped for Mick. We all trailed through my kitchen door. I went to the sink and leaned against it, steeling myself against any residual feelings that might pop up as Angelo bent his tall frame through my doorway and stood smiling at me, as he had once done almost every evening. "What's up?" I said.

He went to my island and sat on one of the stools. Mick moved forward, in the Mick tradition, and Angelo began to pet him automatically. "I have been approached by the police," he said. "Not once but twice."

"What do you mean, 'approached'?"

"Two people have been killed. . . ."

"What? You mean the poisonings? How does that lead them to you?"

He shrugged. "This is what I wonder, as well. In the first case, they said that they had analyzed the food that killed this woman who died in your parish. They came to me because the ingredients turned up peanut butter — not just any, but my special brand, with its distinctive ingredients."

Angelo, along with owning what was arguably the best restaurant in town, had started a lucrative sideline — marketing his own special recipes in a gourmet food line that was now carried by several Chicago-area stores. One of his bestselling items was Angelo's Gourmet peanut butter. It was delicious, and it was the secret ingredient of Pet's chili. My chili.

I stared at him, shocked. "But why would they analyze the ingredients if they knew that someone put cyanide in it? Why would it matter what ingredients were in the food?"

Angelo shrugged. "I don't know. But I know you use this particular ingredient in chili, don't you? So you made the food that killed this woman?"

"That's a pretty big leap," I said, keeping

my face expressionless. "And it wasn't the food that killed the woman, it was the poison someone put in the food. The cop in charge even told me. . . ." I paused. Why was Parker being so thorough? Did they do this sort of thing as a matter of course? "Did you tell them I made it, Angelo?"

He shrugged again, a casual lifting of his big shoulders that was, even now, inexplicably attractive. "I cannot tell them what I do not know. But I suspected, hmm? So I planned to come to you, and before I find a chance, here they are again at my door, because this man who has died —"

"Bert Spielman?"

Angelo nodded. "He was eating a sandwich from my restaurant! My eggplant parmigiana sandwich."

"I was told he ate a meatball sandwich."

Angelo looked annoyed. "No. It was eggplant. And now the police find this little oddity interesting, although I do not. I find it insulting. Anyone can buy that peanut butter. Anyone can buy a sandwich from me. This does not mean that I pre-poison things. If this gets out, it will affect my business. Both of my businesses." His handsome face was genuinely distressed. I felt myself softening.

"Of course it has nothing to do with you.

How ridiculous. I don't understand . . . but then again, he doesn't strike me as a man who would leave any stone unturned."

"He?"

"Parker. The detective in charge."

"And how is it that you know his name?" asked Angelo, with a little flare of his old jealousy. His eyes were narrowed and his hands went to his hips.

Now it was I who shrugged. "Because he told it to me, on the night that I myself was questioned. And I've run into him a couple more times." Then I paused — but, heck, why not lie to everyone in town, including my ex-boyfriend? It wouldn't be good, at this point, to start telling people my chili secret. "Anyway, here's what you need to know: the woman who made that chili is named Pet Grandy. She belongs to my parish, and she's famous for her recipe."

"And somehow she also uses your secret ingredient?" he said, his dark eyes suspicious.

"I, um — I told it to her once. In a moment of weakness."

"Ah. And so I am not to tell the police your name?"

"I would prefer not to be questioned again, since it has nothing to do with me."

Angelo stopped petting Mick and moved

toward me. I thought, for a weird moment, that he intended to kiss me, but he merely wanted to use my sink to wash his hands. I moved away, but not before I smelled his signature scent — some expensive Italian cologne that I had always found enticing.

Once his hands were clean, he ran them through his dark curls — another habit of his that I had at one time found alluring. Then he set his devil horns in place and said, "Where are you going tonight? Perhaps we are attending the same party." He flashed me his lovely smile.

"I don't think so. I'm walking down the driveway and spending time at Terry's."

"Ah. I am going to downtown Chicago, to the Four Seasons. A friend in the restaurant business who likes to throw costume parties."

"Someone famous, I'll bet. You always did have connections."

The shrug again. "He is quite successful. I like to have fun, but also to make some new business acquaintances. Perhaps find more places to market my Angelo's Gourmet line."

"It's very good, Angelo. I use it all the time — or at least when I can afford it."

He looked indignant. "You have a talent. You should be working in a restaurant. Running your own, really. Not toiling in some real estate office." He said the last words with a fair amount of scorn.

This had been the one thing in our relationship that I still looked back on with some gratitude: Angelo had been quite supportive of my foodie ambitions, and he had freely shared his European expertise.

"I'm working on it. Everyone has to start somewhere, Angelo."

"You can put my name as a reference on an application — it would get you an interview at any Chicago restaurant." This sounded egotistical, but I felt fairly certain it was true.

"But I don't want to be a chef, Angelo. I don't want those crazy hours, or to be cooped up in a kitchen all day. I want to run my own business, cater my own carefully chosen events. That way the job is always interesting, always new — and so is the menu."

He shook his head. "Hard work, very hard. And how would you get clients? In a restaurant they come to you."

"There are ways," I said. "It's called advertising."

"Ah — I've made the cat angry, and now I must fear her claws." He smiled at me, and I edged a little farther away. He murmured, "Your hair is lovely. Like a waterfall in the sunshine."

"You're very poetic. But I think you're going to be late for your party."

He shook his head, laughing. "Once my poetry inspired you."

"Once."

Then he sobered again. "You know this cop. This Parker."

"Not well."

"You should make clear to him that I have nothing to do with these deaths. It is a strange coincidence that my food has appeared in both cases. I cannot control who buys my products."

"If I see him, I'll tell him," I said.

He nodded. He leaned in and took a strand of my hair in his hand, sifting it through his fingers. "I miss you sometimes," he said softly.

Sometimes I missed him, too. "You should go, Angelo. Have a nice party."

"You, too, Lilah *mia*." He bent and gave me a quick kiss on the lips, before I could escape it.

Then he walked out, his devil's cape flying behind him. The scent of his cologne lingered like an erotic dream.

The door closed, leaving a deflating silence. I looked at Mick. "He's like high-calorie food — bad for you in the long run, but so appealing in the moment."

Mick nodded. I patted his head. "Keep an eye on the place for me, okay?"

Then I locked up the house, fluffed up my hair, and strolled down the driveway for Terry's party.

CHAPTER TWELVE

My mood lifted as I reached Terry's porch; my irrepressible love of Halloween had me feeling like a kid again. I climbed the curving stone stairs and reached the impressive wooden door, then rang the bell. The door opened to reveal Britt, dressed as a flapper. Her black hair hung in its usual silky bob, but on this she wore a rhinestone crown (which could well have been an antique from the 1920s) and a bead-encrusted dress that ended with a glittering silver fringe. She swung it back and forth while doing a contained Charleston, and I clapped. "It's beautiful!"

Britt leaned in and hugged me. "You look terrific! We're so glad you're here." She turned and yelled over her shoulder, "Terry, the party can start! Lilah's here."

I laughed at her flattery, but the reality was that, for whatever reason, Britt and Terry found me vastly entertaining.

She turned back to me and squeezed my arms. "You are a lifesaver! That food was a hit, and I think I ate more scones than our visitors! Delicious, Lilah. Thank you so much."

"I aim to please," I said lightly. She hugged me again and I got a pleasing whiff of her perfume, the stuff that smelled like the past. I'd asked her once what it was, and she'd said, "Place Vendôme." Based on the name and her French pronunciation, I had assumed it was out of my price range.

Britt pointed now, a diamond ring twinkling on her finger. "Lilah, pick a song and program it into the jukebox; if everyone picks a few we'll have music all night." I gazed at the gorgeous Wurlitzer tucked into one corner of their big foyer. It was currently playing a Phil Collins song.

"Oh, the jukebox! You know how I love it. I'll probably be spending half the party there."

Britt grinned. "Pick something good. Oops — there are some trick-or-treaters behind you. Let me just get them some candy." She whisked past me and gave out some giant Three Musketeers bars to a ghost, a mouse, and a Power Ranger respectively. I looked enviously at the little visitors.

"Unbelievable, Britt. I grew up in this town, and I never found a house like this. One lady on our block gave out sugar-free granola bars, and another gave out little laminated cards with the Ten Commandments on them."

Britt's laughter tinkled out of her like crystal jingling on a chandelier. "They did not, Lilah. You're making that up to be amusing."

"If only. Ask Cameron — he'll verify."

More guests appeared at the door, and Britt excused herself so that she could welcome them.

I sidled up to the jukebox, my beautiful neon-glowing friend. The selection of songs was immense, but I had a favorite music style, as everyone knew: show tunes. I selected "We Beseech Thee" from *Godspell*. Cameron liked that one. Then, just for me, I selected "Honey Bun," from *South Pacific*. Few people knew that I, as a high school thespian, had played the role of Nelly Forbush in that same musical. I had given my all to the role and forged a true love for Rodgers and Hammerstein. Mitzi Gaynor and Rossano Brazzi had played the lead roles in the movie version that I, in my self-schooling, had watched again and again. Rossano, in the songs that he sang to me of his lost love, continually broke my heart when I was an impressionable seventeen. I had written to my junior high Italian teacher, Miss Abbandonato, to tell her that I wanted to travel back in time to when Rossano Brazzi was young, find him, and marry him. Miss Abbandonato, always supportive, had written back that this was a good plan, and if I wanted her to come along in my time-travel spaceship, she could be the interpreter.

I took a photo of the jukebox on my cell phone and then wandered into the main room, where I greeted Terry, who was dressed, appropriately, as a circus ringmaster; my brother, Cameron; and Serafina. Cam had gone for minimal garb; he wore a tuxedo t-shirt and jeans. But Serafina, predictably, was breathtaking in a Cleopatra costume, which included intense, dark eye pencil, a black gown with a gold adder-shaped belt, and a gold headpiece on her amazing dark curls. Several men in the room were staring unabashedly at her.

Cameron pointed at my outfit and said, "You look cute."

I lifted my cat tail, which had been dragging behind me, and flourished it in a bow. "Thanks. Just something I found in the closet."

"Good thing Angelo isn't here," Cam joked. Then he said, "Why are you making that face? *Is* he here?" He looked around the room, seemingly as alarmed as if I'd said a wild panther was stalking the guests.

"No, he's not here, but he did show up at my place half an hour ago."

"What?" Cam's eyes bulged slightly.

"Never mind. Long story."

Terry, who had been whispering something to Serafina, now joined our conversation.

"She assured us that Angelo is out of the picture," he told Cam. "So don't worry about your little sister — she's going to meet someone amazing. Britt already has someone in mind whom she wants to introduce to you, Lilah. He couldn't make it tonight, but we know he would love you."

"Great. I can't wait," I said, my voice dry.

Terry laughed, then invited Cam to join him in the dining room, which had been transformed into a bar. "Let's get some drinks for our fair ladies," Terry said. Cam nodded, waved at us, and followed Terry, who was also leading a group of people who had just arrived. Serafina and I were left alone.

"You look great," I said.

"You as well," she responded in her pretty accent.

I felt like petting her silky hair; she was a life-size doll. "Do you love my brother?" I asked.

I had expected a spate of Italian and English, a stream of passionate words, and maybe even some tears. Instead she grew dignified. "I think I do," she said. "I wonder if he feels the same."

"I think you can count on that," I said.

"I do not mean just sex," she assured me. "That is very nice, but not forever. I think I have the love that will last when I am old."

Despite the rather garish paint and the red lipstick, this made Serafina look young and vulnerable. "Cameron has never looked at a woman the way he looks at you," I said. "And he's had plenty of pretty girlfriends."

She smiled. "I am hungry. Would you like food?"

"Always," I said, and I went to plunder Terry's amazing buffet with Cam's Italian girlfriend. We found that we liked some of the same foods, and that we had one other surprising thing in common: a fear of germs.

"This is a good table," Serafina said, nodding with approval. "Clean and careful, with heat under hot foods and cold foods kept cold. I do not like to think of what grows in food that is left out. I have studied so many compounds, you know. Many of them are created accidentally, when we fail to keep track of food. But of course people still eat it. Moldy bread is just one example."

"That's why when I cook for other people I'm super cautious about labels and expiration dates and refrigerating what needs refrigerating," I said. "You can't be too careful."

Serafina raised her kohl eyebrows. "You cook for others? As a business?"

"Uh — no. I just mean, you know — for gatherings and parties."

"Ah yes. I have become so meticulous, too, after my studies."

A new jukebox choice popped up: "Ruby Tuesday." Mick Jagger's weird and plaintive voice filled the room, as did about seven new party guests. Confident that the noise would drown me out, I leaned toward Serafina and asked, "Do you know anything about poisons?"

"Of course. You are curious about them?"

"Did my mother tell you about the murders?"

Serafina's eyes gleamed with interest. "No! Where did these happen?"

We took our plates to a long green divan in the corner of Terry's living room; it sat in front of some gorgeous maroon velvet curtains that looked like something stolen from the set of a British murder mystery. All we needed was a rope bell pull and we could summon a servant named Jeeves. As we ate, I told her the story of bingo night and Alice Dixon. Of Pet and her fears of being suspected. Of meeting Jay Parker and liking him. Of the death of Bert Spielman.

"This is unbelievable," she said. She had a little smudge of lipstick on her cheek, but I didn't tell her because it made her seem like a real person instead of a magazine ad. "And in both cases, the food was poisoned?"

"I don't know any details of the second case. At bingo night, the chili had a sweet smell — and Alice even commented on a sweet taste right before she died."

"Did she?" Serafina frowned. "And what does Jay tell you about the poison?"

"He didn't tell me anything. He's super professional, which I respect. But he did tell Pet and me to wash our faces and our hands, and all we did was smell the chili. I looked it up and thought it might be cyanide."

She nodded. "It probably is. It can have an almond-like aroma, more bitter than sweet. He feared that you could become ill from the vapor."

"I guess." I took a moment to eat a piece of coconut shrimp. "Oh my. Terry's caterer is so amazing."

"Yes. Delicious." Serafina had a good appetite — another humanizing detail.

"So why does cyanide kill so quickly?"

She ate a tiny meatball and said, "Mmm." Then she looked at the ceiling and squinted her eyes. "Cyanide poisoning causes what we call histotoxic hypoxia."

"Do we call it that?"

"It means that the cells of an organism are unable to, uh — claim oxygen. Use it, you say."

"So that kills you?"

"Yes, because the cyanide ion halts the cell respiration when it inhibits cytochrome c. oxidase."

I wrinkled my nose. "That sounds like the name of a scientist on a kids' cartoon."

Serafina giggled. "You are so funny, Lilah."

I stabbed at some salad drizzled with a fragrant raspberry dressing. "But what does that look like? When it kills you?"

"Well" — she pursed her lips — "weakness, confusion, dizziness, headache. Sometimes seizures. Or perhaps, if it is ingested in a large dose, just a collapse, from an immediate effect on the heart."

"That's what it looked like, Serafina! She

looked confused, and dizzy, and then she touched her head, like maybe it was hurting her. Then — she just keeled over." Sympathy for Alice Dixon rushed through me once more.

Terry and Cam appeared in the doorway, looking for us. We waved, and they strolled over. "Extreme Ways" started playing on the jukebox. "I want that machine," Cameron said. He was holding a beer and looking much more cheerful than he had when I'd mentioned Angelo.

"Fill your plates and join us," I said. "Before the line gets long."

Cam did what I suggested, but Terry flitted off, saying he had to mingle with his guests. Cam found a chair and set it across from Serafina and me. "You ladies are easily the loveliest in the room," he said in a fawning way. "What were you two talking about, with your heads bent together?"

I shrugged. "This and that."

"We spoke of poison," said Serafina. "Lilah told me of these murders, these crimes. I imagine it will be quick work to find the perpetrator."

"Why is that?" asked Cam, eating a tiny meatball.

Serafina shrugged. "Because few people have access to cyanide. So either it is someone who already had it, who has it through their profession, perhaps, or who specially ordered it. The first one is not as easy to trace, but the second one is easy."

Cam leaned forward, almost spilling the contents of his plate. "Lilah said this before, but how can you be sure it's cyanide? You can't just Google something like that and assume you know."

I pointed at Serafina. "She's the chemist. I told her the symptoms and such, and she told me the type of poison."

"Ah." Cam nodded, sending an appreciative smile to his girlfriend. "She is smart."

Serafina shrugged her well-shaped shoulders. "Our laboratories are often consulted by the police."

We all sat quietly for a moment and ate our food. "Some Nights" started playing. A weird time to hear a song by Fun, I thought as I studied my plate. I wondered how it must feel to eat a favorite dish in all innocence, not realizing that something evil and deadly is hidden within. And by the time you realized that you had been poisoned, it was far, far too late. . . .

"Oh, look at the dessert table!" Serafina cried.

Cam laughed. "Fina's got a terrible sweet tooth."

"It's true," she said, shaking her head. "Someday I will be very fat."

"If there is justice in the world," I said, and Serafina laughed and patted my head.

"Your sister is so funny, Cam. Let's go find some cheesecake," she said. My brother followed her away like a puppy.

I was tempted to wander back toward the jukebox, but Terry ran into the room. He looked around, spied me, and ran over.

"Lilah! I've been looking for you, babe. I've got the karaoke set up, and Britt's going to turn off the jukebox in a minute. We're going downstairs for a show, and you're up first!" He pulled me up from my chair. "Come on. Time to be a star!"

And so we relocated to Terry's basement, which was a grand, carpeted, cedar-beamed space that Terry had turned into a party area. He had DJ equipment and a dance floor, but right now there were a bunch of folding chairs set up in front of a stage where karaoke hopefuls could jump up and choose their favorite song.

Terry went to the mike and spoke to the crowd of about forty people. "Hey, everyone! We're ready for some Halloween karaoke! I'm going to start us off with my favorite duet partner, Lilah Drake. Lilah, come on up here — I've picked out something I think will be perfect for you and me."

I looked apologetically at the audience and ran up onto the steps. I lived a solitary existence, but when Terry got out the song machine, I became a ham. I was wearing a mask, anyway, so it was even easier to lose myself in a stage persona. *Catwoman sings.*

Terry handed me a mike and pointed at the song he'd selected: "Stop Draggin' My Heart Around," the great Stevie Nicks and Tom Petty duet. "Perfect!" I said.

The song began, and Terry strutted around, doing his best Tom Petty swagger and getting a big laugh from the crowd. The vocals started with me, and I tried to put a lot of Stevie Nicks's grit into my voice as I sang. Then Terry joined me on the refrain and we harmonized, our heads together. By the end of the song the audience was singing with us, and we got a big burst of applause. I hugged Terry and ran down the stairs. Terry called for the next volunteer and an older man, someone Terry worked for, climbed on the stage and requested the Sinatra songbook.

"You wear that outfit well," said a man's voice at my shoulder.

I turned. A man I did not recognize stood there; he was perhaps thirty years old, and he sported a Luke Skywalker outfit, complete with a lightsaber holstered on one side. I would have labeled him as the world's biggest nerd if I hadn't coveted his outfit so much. Didn't everyone want to be Luke Skywalker?

"Thanks," I said. "It's not super comfortable, and yet Halloween comes but once a year."

He laughed. His face was nice enough — sort of round and earnest — but I wasn't in the mood to encourage any suitors, if that's what he was trying to be. "Are you a friend of Terry or Britt?" he asked.

"Both. I've known them for a couple of years."

"That's cool." He watched the older guy onstage as he launched into "Strangers in the Night." "So what's your name?"

"Catwoman."

He laughed, sort of uncomfortably. "I mean your real name."

Terry had just said it, but apparently this guy hadn't been paying attention. "Lilah."

"I'm Steve. Steve Ralston."

"Nice to meet you."

Now Terry spoke into his mike. "Who's next?" he called.

Serafina climbed up, looking like any man's fantasy come true. She glanced over the song selections and finally settled on some Adele song that I only vaguely recognized, especially once Serafina started singing. In an instant I liked her even more because she had proven to be human after all. She was almost entirely tone-deaf, but she didn't seem to realize it. I found Cam's eyes in the crowd, and he sent me a wry look. Even love-blind Cam recognized that his girlfriend couldn't carry a tune in a trick-or-treat bag. We all suffered through the song and Serafina stepped back down to some polite applause. I gave her a big hug; it was so nice, really, to know that she hadn't made some kind of deal with the devil.

Steve Ralston was edging closer to me; I just wanted to hang out with my brother. I waved at Steve in a friendly fashion but quickly followed Cam and Fina upstairs when I noticed that they were leaving the karaoke scene. "Sorry to be a third wheel," I said to them on Terry's stairway, "but that guy was about to hit on me, and I'm not in the mood."

"How will you meet someone, then?" Serafina chided.

"I'll stick with my dog," I told her, and she laughed, because she thought I was kidding.

Some people had started a trivia game in

Terry and Britt's parlor, so we formed a team of three and joined up. This whiled away a pleasant hour, and I learned that my brother's girlfriend was truly a whiz when it came to math and science questions. Cam and I did fairly well on the humanities questions, but none of us fared well in the sports categories. Still, we came in second, and Britt suddenly appeared to award prizes to the winning teams: tasteful black cat statuettes with orange rhinestone collars. They had sort of an art deco look and cried Britt in every detail. "Thank you!" I told her. "This is lovely. It's going on my mantel. I always wanted a cat, but I don't think Mick would share the house, so this is as close as I'm going to get."

Britt laughed and darted out again. Our trivia team of three wandered back to Terry's beautiful dessert table, where Serafina began filling her plate with chocolate strawberries and a white-coated server appeared again to put out a new cheesecake and some sort of chocolate fondue. In addition to that were an almond torte, frosted hazelnut cookies, a blueberry cobbler, a pan full of bread pudding with caramel sauce, and amazingly moist-looking brownies with Dracula heads painted on them.

The server left again and Britt appeared

to survey the table. "Who does your catering?" I asked Britt, trying to hide my drool.

"Haven of Pine Haven."

They were the biggest name in catering in town, even in Chicagoland. They were classy, sophisticated, and, from what I'd heard, fairly affordable.

"Do you know they're closing down, though?" Britt asked.

"No!"

Britt pursed her pink lips. "The owner is retiring. I don't know what I'll do without them. I throw a lot of parties."

"I have an idea for you," I said, before I could think about it further. "Can we talk sometime this week? Maybe have lunch?"

Britt tucked a silky wave of hair behind her diamond-studded ear and sent me a bright, inquisitive look. "Sure! This sounds fun and mysterious! I'll call you tomorrow."

"Okay, great." The doorbell rang, and Britt looked distressed. This was not surprising, since she had been doing about five tasks simultaneously.

Britt said, "Oh, shoot. More trick-or-treaters. Darn Pine Haven and their generosity. Lilah, could you get that one for me? The candy's in a bucket by the door." Pine Haven, unlike most local towns, had no set trick-or-treating hours, except that everyone had to be off the street by midnight, and children under thirteen had to be with parents. Lots of people, even the parents of grade-school children, made it a tradition to not even start until about ten o'clock.

"Sure," I said, and I went to the door to find Mike and Maura Sullivan, with their two boys, looking surprised to see me in a catsuit, answering the door of a large and stately house.

"Oh — hi!" said Maura. "Lilah — do you live here?"

"No, no," I said. "This is a costume party, and I was invited." I found Britt's bowl of giant candy bars and gave one to each of the Sullivan boys. Their eyes goggled appropriately.

"I know, right?" I said to them. "The hosts here are very generous with the candy. I think I'm going to slip one of these in my purse before I leave," I said. The boys both laughed, because they thought I was kidding.

The boys started down the steps, followed by their father. Maura leaned toward me. "The police were at Alice's house today. Well, Hank's house now, I guess."

"Really? Why?"

She shrugged. "God knows. I feel bad for Hank. He's a friend of ours, you know?

More than Alice ever was. And we know he didn't do it, because the guy is broken up. He feels bad about his wife's death, especially now that he got the news about his inheritance."

"Oh?" I asked.

Maura looked behind her, then edged even closer to me. "He inherited her house and a bit of money. But he was also still the designated beneficiary on her life insurance policy, to the tune of five hundred thousand dollars. He's going to be very wealthy, assuming he can get the cops to leave him alone. I guess it looks like a good motive for murder — unless you know Hank."

"Sure," I said. But I was thinking that, when murders happen and reporters interview the neighbors of the people who get arrested, they always say that same thing: *We never would have thought Bob was capable of this. Carol was not that kind of person. Trevor wouldn't kill his wife — he loved her and was devoted to her.*

That was the common denominator — no one ever saw it coming — because no one ever bothered to look for murder under a seemingly placid domestic exterior. And yet, based on the people Parker was haunting like a determined ghost, the domestic spaces were the likeliest ones to hide a killer in plain sight. I thought of Hank's dog again, potentially deprived of his voice. Tammy had said that Hank had been angry. . . .

"I'll see you around, Lilah," said Maura, following her sons. "Probably next Thursday!" she called over her shoulder.

"See you, Maura." I was about to go in when I saw a little figure marching down the sidewalk in a knight costume — sword and all. He held his sword in one hand and his treat bag in the other, and his mother's hand, resting on his faux-metal shoulder, guided him up Britt's walkway. Once they came into the light I recognized Mariette, Jenny Braidwell's sister, who happened to be Henry's mother.

"Henry!" I cried. "You're a knight!"

Henry lifted his little visor and looked at me. "Hi, Lilah."

"Are you Sir Henry of Weston?"

"Yes. My mom made the costume. I'm a real knight, actually."

I gave Marietta a quick hug and she said, "What are you doing here?"

"I live back there," I said, pointing at my house. "And Terry is my landlord. He's having a party."

She smiled. "Henry told me he wanted to go to the really big houses. He thinks that they give proportionally larger candy, about which, so far, he has been wrong."

I bent down and peered at Henry's cute little face. "This house is your jackpot, Sir Knight. Britt and Terry have got your back."

"Good! This other candy is *hideous.*"

"I don't know, Hen. You've got an iron grip on that bag — I'm guessing something in there is valuable."

Henry glanced to his left and right, where other trick-or-treaters scuttled in the night. Someone in monk's robes moved past in the shadows. "That guy smells like markers," he said.

This non sequitur had us all laughing, and I gave Henry a giant hug before treating him to two of Britt's giant candy bars. I figured she wouldn't mind.

I went inside and returned to the buffet table, where there was quite a line now as people discovered the desserts — people dressed in a variety of bizarre costumes. A very tall Frankenstein was dipping pound cake into the chocolate fountain; a Sponge-Bob SquarePants was taking a generous helping of bread pudding; and a brown M&M was dipping into a bowl of M&M's. She smiled at me through the face-hole. "Life imitates art," she said.

I moved back toward the red sofa where Cam and Fina had once again taken up residence. Suddenly the room was plunged into utter darkness, except for the glow of carefully placed orange lights. Terry's voice spoke into a microphone somewhere, or perhaps a PA system? He did his best spooky laugh, and then said, "If you want light, you must dance in the dark!"

Suddenly a throbbing bass was playing loudly, and Eurythmics were singing "Sweet Dreams." Everyone was up and dancing, so I joined, too, enjoying the anonymity of darkness, which allowed me to do whatever dorky dance I wanted to do. It's much more fun to dance, I realized, when you can be totally free with your movement.

Terry's disembodied voice forced us to dance in the dark for four more songs, and by the time the lights went back on, people were breathing hard and sweating but in a great mood. Serafina and Cam had apparently spent the time kissing, and now they looked eager to leave.

Cam left the room and came back with a pretty little wrap for his Cleopatra, and then he told me, "Fina and I have to get going."

"Right," I said. "Let me guess why."

"Don't smirk at me. She has to get up early to write a paper."

"Fine. Do me a favor and walk me to my house on your way out. It's dark out, and

I'm just a wee fair maiden."

Cam laughed. The three of us thanked Terry and Britt and made our way out their mighty oaken door and into the cold darkness.

"It smells great out here," Cam said. "Like someone's fireplace. Nice and woodsy."

He had an arm around me and one around Serafina, and he looked quite content with his life.

"It does. I love fall," I said. We started down Terry's long driveway, and I laughed. "I can hear Mick barking from here. Do you think he heard your booming voice, Cameron?"

My brother tried to strangle me with one hand, then gave up. "He's probably just lonely. Does he usually bark while you're gone?"

"No." I stepped on a crackly leaf and enjoyed the satisfying *crunch.* "He's normally a perfect gentleman." I looked at Cam and Serafina, wondering if I should invite them in. Clearly they wanted to be alone, but it was still polite to ask. . . .

"Lilah, stop," my brother said.

"What?"

"Stop. Don't go any farther." He tightened his arm around my shoulder and Serafina gasped.

"What the hell . . ." I started to say, but then I followed his gaze and saw the message scrawled across the white siding on the front of my pretty house:

You're Next.

"Oh my God," I said.

Cameron's face was grim. "Don't go any closer. I'm calling the police. In fact — Serafina, you call them. I'm going to check on something." He darted away into the dark, producing a tiny LED flashlight from his key chain and heading for my backyard.

Serafina was dialing 911 on her cell phone. "They'll be busy tonight," I said. "It's Halloween. Ask them to tell Jay Parker. Tell them it's related to the poisoning case."

But was it? Is that what the message meant — that two people had died of poisoning, and I would be the next to die? Or was it just some crazy Halloween prank, some kids doing graffiti on a dare?

Serafina spoke into the phone in her lilting accent, her voice solemn. I liked the way she said, "Jay Parker." Coming from her, they sounded like beautiful words.

Minutes later Cam was back, and he and Serafina stood with me, contemplating my house. Cam said, "I didn't see anyone, but I think they must have just been here, right? Otherwise why would Mick be barking?"

I shook my head. I hated to contemplate someone wishing me ill, especially to the extent that they were willing to vandalize my home, my sweet and private space. Why me? What had I done? What had Bert or Alice done? Why was this happening?

"That is scary stuff," Cam said, echoing my thoughts. "Lilah, I know there's a murderer in this town, but I didn't think it had anything to do with you!"

"Neither did I!" I said. "I don't know what it's about." I could hear Mick whining at the hallway door; he had heard our voices and he wanted to join us.

"Not yet," Cam said, restraining me.

We waited for a few minutes. The first car on the scene was Parker's. He jumped out and strode toward us; even in my shaken state I found myself glad to see him.

Before he said a word to us he went close to my house, looked at the graffiti, and then spoke into his phone. Then he came back and looked at me. "Are you all right?" he asked.

"Yes. I wasn't home — I was at Terry's Halloween party until about fifteen minutes ago." I pointed at Terry's house. Parker nodded. His eyes flicked up and down, taking in my outfit.

Cam said, "I think the person was just here. I can smell that spray paint strongly, as if particles of it were still floating on the air. And we heard Mick barking when we came down the driveway."

"Don't touch anything," Parker said. Then he turned and walked swiftly into my backyard, as Cam had just done. When he returned he said, "No one there. This seems recent, though, as you said." He sniffed the air.

"Henry!" I yelled.

They all looked at me.

"I'm sorry?" said Parker.

"Henry — he's a little boy that I know — he said earlier that one of the trick-or-treaters smelled like markers. He probably meant those industrial-strength markers that smell like paint. We all laughed at him."

"Did you get a look at the person he meant?"

"Just someone going past in the darkness. Dressed as a monk."

Parker said something into a voice recorder, then looked back at us. "We can look for security-camera footage of this person. Lilah, you'll need to find somewhere else to stay tonight. I need my team to examine this, and I don't want you — I mean, you shouldn't be alone."

"She won't be," said Cameron. "She'll be with us."

"No," I said. "I'll go to Mom and Dad's. They're closer. You can drop me off there, right, Cam?"

He hugged me against him. "Of course we can. And you'll stay there until this is resolved." He turned to Parker; even in the dark, I could see it dawning on my brother that this was the man I had mentioned to him. He did a good job of hiding his reaction. "Do you think you're on the verge of getting this person? Will this little incident help in apprehending him?"

Parker shoved his hands in his jacket pockets. "I can't really comment on that, Mr. . . . ?

Cam stuck out his hand. "I'm Cameron Drake. Lilah's brother."

It was probably just my imagination, since it was dark out, and we had illumination only from Terry's landscaping lamps and my little pumpkin window lights, but I thought Parker looked relieved. "All I can tell you," he said to my brother in his official voice, "is that we'll be asking neighbors what they saw and combing this scene for evidence."

"But there have been people running all

over the place. It's Halloween, for goodness' sake!" I said.

Suddenly Cam was pulling Serafina away. "Lilah, we'll be right back. We're just going to tell Terry what happened."

They disappeared rapidly up the driveway.

Parker looked ominous. "Tell me what you think. Who might have a grudge against you?"

"I can't think of one soul. Seriously. I mean —"

"Yes?"

"It's nothing."

"Then say it."

"I have an ex. But we're fine with each other. He was just here earlier tonight."

"Why was that?"

"Well — because he thought I knew you well, and he asked me to vouch for him to you."

Parker scratched his head. "Why?"

"Because you've questioned him. Uh — something about his peanut butter and the sandwich Bert Spielman ate."

Parker started. "The Italian?"

"Angelo, yes."

"You dated *him*?"

"Why is that hard to believe?"

"I don't know. So you think he might have done this?"

"No! I'm telling you he wouldn't have. He's at a party downtown, in any case, so I'm sure he has a nice alibi."

Parker's face was unreadable. "Fine. Who else?"

"I don't know! Up until now I didn't think I had an enemy in the world!"

"Any real estate deals gone bad?"

I snorted. "I'm just a receptionist. This is something else — I just don't know what that something is."

Parker was feeling for his phantom cigarettes again and, as he had done on the day that I met him, he settled for a piece of gum. Then he said, "Lilah, you're shaking." He took off his jacket and put it around my shoulders. "Listen, I'm on this," he said in a low voice, his hands still resting on my shoulders. "Tell me your parents' address and I'll have a guard put on the house."

"I need my dog," I said, as Mick's plaintive barking grew louder. My throat felt tight as I spoke. "He can't stay in there alone!"

"I'll get him for you. I don't really want anyone on the porch right now, okay? Give me your key."

"His leash is on a nail just inside the door, on the left," I said, touching his arm.

He sent me a quick look in the dark; I

didn't know what it meant. Then he went carefully up the porch steps, used his shirt to cover his hand so that he could turn the doorknob without leaving prints, and retrieved Mick, who came bounding over to meet me.

"Thank you," I said. Parker handed me Mick's leash, and I clipped it on. Mick leaped all over Parker as though he was a long-lost friend, which in a way he was. Finally Mick settled down and wandered over to sniff Terry's linden tree.

"I wish I could go into my house," I said. "I wish this person had never done this and ruined my evening, and that I could just invite you in for dinner again, like the last time. That was nice," I said.

Parker looked surprised. "It was. And this will be over soon, and you can invite me again. Lilah —"

We heard Cam and Serafina's voices in the distance, and I remembered something. "Listen — you should know that Hank Dixon thinks Bert Spielman was murdered because of him."

"What?" Parker stiffened.

"He told my dad, when they were looking at a house Hank bought. Hank said that Bert told him he had figured something out about Alice's death, and he wanted to talk it over with him. Hank said he'd come by that night, and then Bert was dead."

Parker's mouth was a straight, unsmiling line. "Was he planning to share this information with the police?"

"I don't know; my dad said he felt like if he sought you out it might turn into another big interrogation."

"That's a risk you run in a murder investigation," Parker said, his voice cold.

"Hey, don't blame the messenger. I just thought you should know."

My brother called from mid-driveway. "Lilo, Fina and I are going to get the car and drive it back. See you in a couple of minutes."

They disappeared again, and I was left with Parker in the cold, cold dark. I looked up at him and got a whiff of his minty gum. He said, "Listen, Lilah —" just as I said, "Do you have any idea who killed Alice?"

He looked at me; even in the dark, his eyes were blue as moonstones. "No. We don't. But I'm going to find out, very soon. Do you still need this on?" he said, touching my mask. I had forgotten it was there.

"No. Geez, I probably look ridiculous." I yanked the mask and the cat ears off my head and shoved them into the pocket of Parker's jacket.

"You don't look ridiculous," Parker said. Again, his eyes did a quick assessment of me, from top to toe. "Your hair —"

Mick started barking and Parker grew tense. "My team will be here any moment. You should go, Lilah. Go to your parents' house, and I'll be in touch."

"I can't," I said, miserable.

"Why not?"

"Because you're standing on my tail."

For a moment he looked at me, his expression blank. Then he stepped back, almost embarrassed. "Sorry," he said.

Headlights illuminated us briefly, and I saw the tired lines around his eyes.

Serafina jumped out of Cam's car and walked to us, tucking her arm into mine. She still smelled lovely. "We will take her now, Detective." Then, looking closely at Parker, she said, "I'm sure you know this — but if this person left prints, you should study them for traces of the poison. They would have been wise to administer the cyanide with gloves, but this" — she pointed at the weirdly scrawled letters — "this is reckless. And cyanide can linger on the skin."

Parker turned toward her, stiff and surprised. "What makes you think it was cyanide?"

Serafina shrugged. "It seems likely."

Parker glared, looking from Serafina in her Cleopatra getup to me in my cat attire. I was sure he was sick of civilians telling him how to do his job, especially knowledge-able people like Serafina. I called Mick and grabbed his leash, and we started walking toward Cam's car. I heard Parker's voice calling after me. "I'll be in touch, Lilah."

By the time our car pulled onto Dickens Street, the first police cars had already arrived.

In my old bedroom, which my mother used now as a guest room and a storage area for her scrapbooks, I sat on the bed, my Cat-woman outfit gone and replaced by a pair of my mother's pajamas. They smelled like lavender and were as comforting as a hug. My glittering cat trophy sat on the bedside table, its little orange collar glinting.

I lifted Parker's jacket and retrieved my mask and ears, putting them with the outfit on a chair beside the bed. Mick, already asleep on the plush carpet, made a snuffling sound in his dreams. Then, curious, I went through Parker's pockets. It was a nice jacket, a brown leather thing with a mascu-line scent. In the left-hand pocket were a roll of breath mints and two quarters, along with a receipt from the gas station on Dickens. Parker had bought forty-two dollars' worth. It probably hadn't even filled his tank. I also found one solitary Milk Dud. I disposed of this for him; if it melted it would damage the pocket lining.

In the right-hand pocket was a small appointment book with a leather-look cover, a single dollar bill, a pen, and a business card from Cardelini's. Angelo's restaurant. Of course — Angelo said Parker had been there recently. I knew that I shouldn't look through the appointment book, but my hands were already doing it. I certainly wasn't in danger of learning any police secrets. Parker had terrible handwriting, and most of the things he had scrawled were illegible, although I could pick out the occasional word or phrase, like "St. Bartholomew's," or "P. H. Library."

I turned to the last page, which had nothing on it except one name: Lilah Drake. Beside it was my phone number. I dropped the book back into Parker's pocket. Had I given him my phone number? Had he asked for it? Or had he looked it up on his own? I did not recall giving him the information. And Parker had never called me on the phone. Perhaps he had written the number in recently? Perhaps he had been planning to call me? If so, was it for the case, or for personal reasons?

I didn't know. I set Parker's jacket on the chair and climbed under the covers. I didn't want to think about the way my house had been vandalized, or whose hand might have been wielding the can of paint.

My name in Parker's appointment book provided a nice distraction. What had he said, when we were standing there in the dark and I'd felt his blue eyes looking at me with that careful, Parker-like scrutiny? He'd said I could invite him for dinner again soon.

I turned out the light and lay back against the pillows, planning an elaborate menu for a fantasy evening with Parker. We would eat fondue with long, slender forks, feeding each other instead of ourselves, and moonlight would pour in the window to illuminate his eyes.

Parker was not like Angelo; he was stiff and stern and sometimes awkward. He wasn't a smooth talker, and he had none of Angelo's easy charm.

And that was precisely why I liked him.

CHAPTER THIRTEEN

I was up early the next morning, preparing Toby Atwater's French toast casserole in my pajamas. In my head the Plain White T's were singing a love song to Delilah.

My father appeared, looking slightly disheveled and searching for coffee. "You're up early," he croaked.

"I'm working. Doesn't this smell good?"

He agreed that it did. "Where are you headed with that?"

I hesitated. "Well, this will sound weird, but Toby and I always meet under the viaduct by the expressway. He's a little paranoid."

My father scratched at his mussy hair. "Well, I'm a little paranoid, too. Especially because someone recently threatened my daughter. So give me a minute to take a shower, and then I'll go with you."

"Dad, it's not necessary. Toby's a regular customer, and . . ." It was too late; he was already jogging out of the room.

"Give me five minutes. I'll even ride shotgun," he called, suddenly much more alert, even without his coffee.

He needn't have rushed, since the casserole took another fifteen minutes to prepare, after which I had to attend to my own morning routine, taking what my parents had always called "an army shower" (due to its brevity), and then rushing out to pack the car, my hair still damp and my shoes untied. Mick hopped into the backseat, determined not to be left behind.

Finally we drove to our clandestine viaduct location, where Toby lurked in the shadows like a parking-garage mole. He eased into the sun to claim the large pan, and he thanked me profusely. "It smells like heaven," he said. "It's one of the few things my kids appreciate me for, which is sad, since I don't make it."

"You arrange it," I said. "Which still makes you a great dad."

He grinned and handed me the money, and I climbed back into my father's car. "Kind of weird, meeting people in these out-of-the-way locations," my dad said, gazing out his window at the bright sun, which had been steadily ascending as we drove.

"Keeps things top secret," I said.

"But it could be dangerous. Don't arrange any more of these meetings until things settle down, okay?"

I sighed. "I make good money, Dad. I'll just be sure to have a bodyguard with me."

"Hmm," he said. Mick leaned up from the backseat and licked his ear.

We returned to their house and I went back to the stove. My parents knew that I cooked when I was upset; I liked to lose myself in the process, and eventually it calmed me and helped me think clearly. They turned their kitchen over to me, then sat in the living room and read their Sunday papers, watching me with anxious eyes. My mother hated to contemplate the thought that I had an enemy, and she was actually relieved when the PHPD car pulled up outside and settled in for the long haul. I peered out the window, wondering if this was Parker, but of course it wasn't. It was a lowly beat officer — a young woman, it looked like — and she was just following orders.

I sniffed and returned to my canvas — a counter spread with all sorts of delectable things. At the center, a fancy rice made by Angelo's Gourmet, flavored with herbs. Two fat, firm peppers, one green and one red. A big white onion with a luminescent peel.

Some fresh chicken breasts, still tucked into their packaging. Some Angelo's Gourmet tomato sauce (my mother had his food in her cupboards, too, but she tended to hide it from my father, who did not want to support Angelo's business) and a bottle of red wine for a finishing touch.

I got to work with my mother's sharpest knife, slicing the onion, then the peppers, into thin strips. I flicked a pat of butter into a large pan, scraped the vegetables off of my cutting board and into the heat, and enjoyed the aroma that almost instantly permeated the air. I was working on a new covered-dish recipe that I thought would have appeal for many of my clients. Often people asked me for something original, and I liked to continually expand my repertoire.

I went through my mother's spice cabinet, pulling out likely bottles and sprinkling them on my sautéeing vegetables. I poured in a dollop of wine and Angelo's fragrant sauce.

"Smells great in there!" my dad called.

"Good! This is your lunch."

I found a glass casserole dish and started layering rice, vegetables, chicken, and some shredded Swiss cheese. Then I slid it all into my parents' oven and set the timer for thirty minutes. Casseroles were so easy to make; it was the inspiration that was sometimes difficult. I had once read about a great author — Flaubert, maybe — who agonized for hours over the selection of one word. I sometimes felt that way about spices; it was always about finding the perfect blend, and that took time and imagination.

I sat in the kitchen and watched some yellow leaves blow across the lawn. I'd started the day just like this when I made the chili that killed Alice Dixon. I had set out my ingredients with love and care; then I had sliced and diced and scooped it all together in one cooking pot, creating a delicious smell that had caused Mick to whine with appreciation. Mick had loved the chili I'd saved for him; in fact, I realized with a start, I had taken a picture of him eating it. If Parker ever ended up suspecting me of colluding with a murderer, I could show him the photo. But, of course, that wouldn't really be evidence, since Mick could have been eating any chili.

I sighed. Someone had added a toxic ingredient to what should have been wholesome, delicious food. How strange it was that in this world there were plants that could heal us and plants that could kill us. Even cyanide originated in a plant. And what sort of person could actually bring him- or herself to put poison in food, knowing someone would eat it? Knowing someone might die? Did that feed some terrible hunger in them, some longing for destruction? Or was it an act of desperation by someone who really needed to silence Alice Dixon and Bert Spielman? If so, why? What had Alice or Bert ever done?

My father appeared and put his hand on my shoulder. "You know, I realized something," he said, patting me and then sitting down across from me at the table. "Whoever vandalized your house could have been some little kid doing a trick-or-treat dare. It doesn't necessarily relate to the poisonings at all."

I had thought of this the night before, but then rejected it. I brightened slightly.

"Still, Mom and I don't want you eating anything unless it's prepared by you or us. Nothing from a restaurant or anything — until the police get to the bottom of it."

My spirits plunged again. "Yeah, I guess you're right."

"On the other hand, we don't want you to feel trapped in here. So just tell me where you want to go today, and I'll go with. Your personal bodyguard. Just like this morning."

I reached across and took his hand. "You're so sweet. But how long can we possibly do that? You guys have to work."

"Luckily, you work with us, so we can all go in together."

"But —"

"We'll take it one day at a time, Lilah. They might solve this thing today."

"And they might not."

"Your brother tells me this guy seems sharp."

"Parker? Yeah, he is."

"What does that little smile mean?" my father asked, looking suspicious.

"Nothing. Just that I realized I have his jacket, and I should probably give it back to him today."

"Great. When we go out, we'll stop at the police station and drop it off. I'll check this guy out for myself."

"Dad."

"Hmm?"

"I'm a big girl now."

"Still my only daughter," he said, brushing some imaginary crumbs off his shirt. "When is this food going to be ready, anyway?"

I laughed and checked on the casserole, which had baked to a lovely gold. I served it to my appreciative parents, and we carefully talked around the subject of murder while we shared our noon meal.

My mother volunteered to wash up, so my father went with me when I walked Mick around the block, golden with leaves and full of attractive scents for Mick's questing nose.

We came home, dropped off my Labrador, and climbed back into my dad's car. Suddenly I felt eighteen again, a passenger with my father at the wheel, as I'd been every day of high school when my father drove me to Pine Haven HS on his way to work. He still had all the same habits that had driven me crazy then: the constant fiddling with his dashboard — the radio, the heater, the change compartment — which he probably did without realizing it; the aggressive driving, which had him pulling far too close for comfort to the car in front of him; and the penchant for talk radio, something I despised because I felt there was not one likeable radio personality. My father claimed he learned a lot from the various shows he favored.

Our first stop was the library. My father liked books about travel (he and my mother were contemplating a trip) and wanted to find some picture books for them to peruse together. I told him that I wanted to speak to Pet, who worked the afternoon shift.

The library wasn't crowded, and I saw Pet

leaning moodily on the front desk, her elbows on the wood as she stared down at a book. As I got closer I could see, even upside down, that it was a picture-heavy biography of Princess Diana.

"Hey, Pet," I said.

She looked up, surprised, and then beamed at me. "Hey, Lilah! What brings you here?"

"I want to look for a couple of books. But I also wanted to talk to you — about Bert."

Her face fell again and she looked near tears. "The police asked me about him. I know it looks bad, how I made the chili that killed Alice, and I just happened to work with the other person who died."

"But maybe the police will realize that almost seems too obvious — something a murderer would never do for fear of detection."

"I don't know. It's just terrible — about Bert, and Alice, and being questioned all the time. It's really upsetting my whole family."

"Of course. That's understandable. And I know you're sick of being questioned, but I wanted to ask you a couple of things, too. Just so I can work it out in my own head. You're not the only one who has a connection here," I said.

Pet nodded gravely. She closed the Princess Diana book and said, "What do you want to know?"

"Well — why would anyone want to kill Bert? Was there any link between him and Alice?"

Pet shook her head. "I don't think they really knew each other. But you know Bert — he was sort of a gossip, and he loved mystery novels. So he was asking me all sorts of things about the night Alice died. He joked that he was going to solve it just like Sherlock Holmes, using deductive reasoning."

This was chilling. What if Bert had solved the mystery? What if someone found that out, and killed him before he could talk to Hank Dixon? Or what if Hank Dixon was the one who silenced Bert, but then told my father a different story to take suspicion off himself?

I pointed at some red leather chairs in the cooking section. "Since no one's around, can we go over there? If we talk quietly?"

Pet thought about it. "I guess so. I can keep an eye on the checkout desk from there."

We went to the chairs and sat down; my father wandered past on a quest for books.

Pet sighed. "It's so funny. I still expect

Bert to walk out of the back room, kind of hunched over like he always was, with his face all squinched up because he was thinking hard. We were all used to that sight. I wasn't here on the day he died, and I'm glad I wasn't."

"Have the police examined all the check-outs, and the camera and everything?"

"Oh yeah. They went over this place with a pine-tooth comb."

"Fine-tooth," I corrected automatically.

"What?"

"Never mind. Go ahead."

"They shut us down for two days. I don't know what all they did. And they took the little refrigerator that we had in the back room — the one where Bert had put his sandwich. Once a week he got an Angelo's lunch, and he always looked forward to it."

Two giant tears gushed out of Pet's eyes, surprising both of us. I touched her small, plump hand. "I'm sorry, Pet."

"Who would do this? To Bert — or anyone?"

I nodded. We had all been asking the same questions, it seemed. Murder, I was finding, held a whole town hostage to uncertainty and fear.

"Pet — tell me what sorts of things Bert wanted to know. What was he asking that potentially got him so close to the truth?"

Pet sighed, then stiffened, about to run to the desk, but the person who had approached it walked right past into the children's section. She relaxed again. "Well, of course he asked me who all had been there. He said it was like a locked-room mystery. And that once you knew all the suspects, you just had to find out the things no one knew about them — and their links to the dead person. He said that was the plot of every Agatha Christie novel."

It was true. I'd already learned more than I'd expected — about Alice and Hank's marriage, about everyone's resentment of Alice, about Tammy's profession, about Alice's dog and her plans for a cruel operation, about Hank's inheritance, about Alice's resentment of the Grandys and their relationship with Father Schmidt, about Alice's bad relationship with many of the bingo patrons. Even Theresa and Trixie, according to their accounts, had viable motives for wanting Alice dead. If I knew that much through casual conversations, how much more must the police know? Shouldn't they have been close to solving it by now?

"So who was a likely suspect, according to Bert?"

Pet shrugged. "He never told me that. But he loved talking about it. It was a game to him — the strategy of it, comparing potential motives. I didn't understand half the words he used, to be honest. Bert was really smart."

He had been smart. Pine Haven had been lucky to get Bertrand Spielman as their librarian; he had multiple degrees and was a true connoisseur of literature, history, and Chicago lore. "So what was the last day you saw him?"

Pet sighed. "It was the day before he died. I worked that morning, and Bert kept coming up to me while I was shelving books, asking this or that. He asked me whether or not Hank was going to inherit money from Alice. I said I didn't know. He asked if Alice had ever sued Father Schmidt or the church. I said I didn't know, but I didn't think so, since Father Schmidt probably would have told us that. He asked if we resented Alice for all the things she said to us."

"What do you mean?"

Pet blushed. "Sometimes I would let off steam to Bert about Alice — when we had to work together at the church. He liked hearing the stories, because he thought Alice sounded kind of crazy, but he also sort of admired her. I think Bert liked eccentric women."

I sniffed.

"Anyway, I had told him that Alice had said some mean things to us the week before she died. She was frustrated with us — she just seemed to hate it that we always had Father over for dinner. I don't think he ever once went to her house." Pet looked weirdly proud of that.

"What mean things?"

"Oh, just typical Alice stuff. We've learned to take it in stride. She told me I was too old to be chasing after a priest."

"What!"

Pet shrugged. "Father Schmidt told me that Alice was like a child, and that when she was hurt, she lashed out. After he said that, it helped me never get too upset by what she said. She seemed so fashionable and mature, but she really was like a spiteful little girl."

This was pretty sophisticated psychology; I wondered how Father Schmidt had determined that. Perhaps I would visit him next.

"What else did she say?"

"She told Angelica that she intended to sue her. Alice knew that we had some family money that we inherited, and she told Ang, just a week before she died, that she would sue her for all of it. It was kind of

257

crazy, how extreme she got."

"Uh — sue her over what, Pet?"

Pet jumped up and darted to the circulation desk, where two teens waited to take out books. She checked them out, chatting in a friendly way and handing them library bookmarks before they left. Then she jogged back over to me. She was wearing a sweat suit again, but this was a sort of classy black velour with a white appliqué of the New York Public Library logo on the front of the jacket. I wondered where she shopped.

She sat down, slightly out of breath, and I said, "Sue her over what, Pet?"

She laughed, but rather miserably. "One time Angelica saw Alice out to dinner with a man. Angel and Alice both saw each other, because this was back when Alice and Hank were still married. Angel never said anything about it, but once recently when Alice was complaining about Hank and his new girlfriend . . ." She leaned in and whispered, "Alice called Hank's girlfriend a slut."

I sighed. This did not surprise me.

"Anyway, Ang finally had enough and said, 'What do you care? You were seeing some other guy when you were married!' "

This had me leaning forward. "Get out! What did Alice do?"

"She got crazy. She said that was none of

Angelica's business and she had no idea what was going on, and then she said she knew a lawyer who could take us for all the money we had."

"Oh my God! Do the police know this?"

"Yeah, we told them. But you'd have to know Alice. By the end of the day she was acting all friendly again."

"Was she insane?"

Pet looked at her hands. "No. I think she was really lonely."

"Did you like her, Pet?"

Perpetua nodded. "Sometimes. She wasn't always crazy. Sometimes she was nice. And she was always sort of chic and worldly. She gave us beautiful gifts at Christmas — all the members of Altar and Rosary. And my sisters and me, because she said we were so important to the church. Alice was like two different people."

She pointed at the sweat suit she was wearing. "She knew I liked velour lounge suits, because of how comfortable they are. I'm too old not to dress for comfort, I told her once. And she found this when she was on a trip to New York, and she bought it for me. I think it cost more than a hundred dollars."

I thought about this. *Alice was like two different people.* So which of Alice's personalities had an enemy — the good one or the bad one?

"Who was the man?" I said.

"What?"

"The man Angelica saw her with. Who was it?"

Pet looked surprised. "I don't know. I assumed he was just some stranger. I'll ask Angelica."

I would ask her, too. "Did she say anything else? While she was on this mean streak?"

Pet shrugged, her eyes darting to the checkout desk. "She told Harmonia that she was too old for a boyfriend. That she should either marry Ted or move on. She said it was ridiculous that the three of us lived together when we were old enough to be grandmothers."

I stared, my mouth gaping. "I can't believe — the gall!"

Pet shrugged again, looking not at all embarrassed. "We are old, but so what? I'm the oldest, and I'm fifty. But we're not just sisters, we're friends. We get along, and we love the house we grew up in, so why not live in it? We're a unit. We always have been."

"Of course."

"The thing is, my mom had eight kids, but the first five were much older. Then she and my father — I don't know — they had

260

a second wind." Pet smiled at me with a rather innocent expression. "So then came me, and Angel, and little Harmonia. They always called us "the little ones," and we did everything together. That's just how it is. Some people don't understand that, but that's our family. Angel and Harm, they like living at home. And the guys are happy with that, too. They just like to come and hang out and watch television. We're all comfortable. So I couldn't imagine why it made Alice so uncomfortable."

"Good question." What had gone through the mind of Alice Dixon in the weeks before her death? I could see how this sort of work would drive Parker crazy. How was one supposed to determine the secrets of a dead person?

I thanked Pet for talking with me and watched while my father checked out his travel books. Two of them were about Italy. "Serafina has been telling us such wonderful stories — about the little towns, and the warm people, and the food that your taste buds can't forget," he told me.

"I'll bet. She probably wants you to meet her whole giant family."

My father grinned at me. Pet handed him his books in a little Pine Haven Library bag. My father said, "Thank you, ma'am," in his charming voice, and Pet blushed. Then my dad slid an arm around my shoulders and we made our way back to the car, where Parker's jacket sat on the passenger seat.

"To the police station?" my father asked.

"I guess. I hope he won't think I'm interrupting him."

"He'll think you're being thoughtful."

My father fiddled with his CD player until Paul McCartney's voice filled the car; he was singing "Hey, Jude," with beautiful sincerity and perfect pitch.

"That man could sing. Still can," my father said. He had said this a million times in my lifetime — almost as many times as he had assured me that butter pecan was the best ice cream flavor and that my mother was a beautiful woman.

He pulled into the police station parking lot and I got a case of the butterflies. I saw my father looking at me out of the corner of his eye, so I feigned nonchalance. "Come on, then," I said. "Since you want to meet him so badly."

We walked into the drab lobby and a receptionist asked our names. I told her and said that I needed to speak with Detective Parker.

"Just a moment," she said. She lifted a phone and spoke into it; then she said,

"Detective Grimaldi will be with you in a moment."

Sure enough, Parker's partner emerged in a blue suit and some attractive low-heeled shoes and smiled at us. "How may I help you? You're Miss Drake, are you not?"

I found my voice. "This is my father, Daniel Drake. Dad, this is Detective Grimaldi. Mom and I met her on bingo night."

"And I saw you with Miss Grandy the other night," said Detective Grimaldi with a wide smile.

"Yes. Pet is my friend."

My father nodded. "We were here to see Detective Parker?"

She was still smiling. "I'm afraid he is not here at the moment. Did you have a question or comment regarding the case?"

My hands tightened on the jacket. I didn't want to give it to her, and I tried to imply as much in an urgent look that I sent to my father, who immediately misinterpreted it. "My daughter wanted to leave his jacket here. He left it at the investigation scene last night."

Detective Grimaldi tucked a strand of her glossy black hair behind her ear. "Thank you very much for bringing it by. I'll see that he gets it." She held out one well-manicured hand, and I relinquished Parker's jacket, trying to surreptitiously sniff it once more before I gave it away.

"Is he pursuing a lead?" my father asked.

Detective Grimaldi gave him her expressionless cop face. "I'm afraid I can't comment on that. I can assure you that we're doing all we can to find this person."

"Who?" I asked. "The poisoner, or the graffiti artist who painted my house? Do you really think they are one and the same?"

"We don't know. But finding that out is our primary goal. Our only focus, right now. Please believe that, Lilah." She touched my arm. Her gesture said *I am a trustworthy public servant who cares about you.*

I nodded, wondering if she ever touched Parker's arm when they rode around together, fighting crime. "Thanks. Meanwhile my parents are worried about every bite that I eat."

Grimaldi looked a little miserable then. "We are advising the entire community to take precautions, of course. Just eat homemade food for the time being, and always lock your doors. Since you in particular seem to have been targeted, we have an officer assigned to your house and you'll be protected. Believe me — no one's getting near you."

I saw then that even though Grimaldi was

rather pretty, her eyes looked like Parker's — weary and dejected.

Bereft of Parker's jacket, I pouted in the car while my father drove me home; an old Eurythmics song called "Who's That Girl?" was floating around in my head, until my companion turned on the car radio and Train drowned it out with their insistent positivity. My father sent me a couple of sidelong glances, seemingly ready to have a chat, as though I were sixteen and wanting to confide. To head him off, I started talking about Mick and something funny he'd done the week before. My dad took the hint and didn't say a word about our short trip to the police station.

He pulled into our driveway five minutes later. The house smelled like pumpkin bread, and we were confronted with even more music: my mother was strumming her guitar while looking at tabs online. I marveled anew at her easy talent; she played the guitar quite well but had never taken a single lesson. She taught herself, she told me once, so that she could sing to Cameron and me when we were little. It had paid off. Back then, a few refrains strummed softly, and Cam and I conked out like we were under sedation.

"I made a snack," she told us, and then went back to humming "Here, There and Everywhere" while she played along. I was on the verge of musical overload.

My father made an approving sound. "One of the best songs ever written." He took my jacket and removed his own, then went to hang them up in the hall closet.

Since my mother was busy, I went into the kitchen, jammed a piece of warm pumpkin bread in my mouth, and then climbed upstairs to my father's office, where I sat in his black faux-leather chair and dialed Trixie Frith. Then I held the phone about a foot away from my ear.

"Hello?" Trixie boomed.

"Trixie, it's Lilah."

"Hey, sweetheart! What can I do for you?"

"I wanted to ask you a question —"

"Lilah! Are you by a computer?"

"Yeah, but why —"

"Lilah! Go on Skype."

"What?"

"Theresa and I are trying to learn how to Skype. Our kids are always bugging us about it. So we're practicing."

"Go on Skype!" I heard Theresa yell in the background.

With a sigh, I logged on to the computer and signed in to my father's Skype account.

"I have to hang up this line, Trixie, so I can call you on the other one. Okay?"

"Okay!" Trixie boomed. Theresa, apparently still in persuasion mode, yelled, "Go on Skype, Lilah!"

I hung up the phone and then dialed Trixie's number online. Soon enough we were connected, and there was Trixie with a different neon lipstick, her blonde hair slightly mussed. She was, predictably, looking away from the camera, as was tiny little Theresa, who peered over Trixie's shoulder at something unknown.

"You guys. Look into the camera. Look at me, in other words."

They shifted their gaze and then both burst into appreciative speech, drowning each other out. Trixie stopped first, so I caught the end of Theresa's sentence, which was "always telling us to Skype, so . . ."

"Hi, ladies."

"Hi, Lilah. You look pretty today," Trixie said. "I wonder if your mom's hair was that blonde when she was young."

"I think it was. She still has some blonde, mixed in with the silver."

"It's a beautiful color," said Theresa brightly. She was wearing some sort of little blue-jean overall outfit that looked as if it had come from the Kohl's girls' department, but it looked good on her.

"Listen," I said. "Did you guys ever hear that Alice Dixon might have been seeing another man? Like when she was still married to Hank?"

Trixie and Theresa, forgetting that they were on camera, exchanged a significant glance but said nothing.

"I can see you," I reminded them.

Theresa jumped and Trixie smiled guiltily. "That's right. Well, we did hear rumors. But it wasn't a man from the parish. That's all we knew — that she had been seen out and about with some guy. I'm not sure if Hank found out about it or not, but that's why a lot of people sided with Hank when they announced they were divorcing. We all remembered that little rumor, especially when Alice tried to suggest that it was Hank's girlfriend who broke things up. Hank didn't meet her until later."

"Yeah — I just heard the story of how they met. Sort of romantic."

"She's a lady doctor," said Theresa, sounding like Mrs. Andrews, my file nemesis at the real estate office.

"Or you could just say a doctor. A veterinarian, actually."

"Yeah. Very impressive," Trixie said, nodding. "Young people are so accomplished these days. All Alice did was sit around and think of ways to be miserable. Hank is better off, I have to say."

She didn't have to say, but since I had encouraged the gossip I couldn't really complain about it.

"I should get going," I said. "But let me ask you this. Do you know of anyone who might have a grudge — against me?"

Both women's eyes opened wide. "Against you?" cried Trixie, her loud voice causing static on the microphone. "Why, hon? Did something happen?"

"Not much. It might not be related. Maybe just a little Halloween mischief, my dad thinks. But who knows? People have been dying." My throat suddenly hurt. If I wasn't careful I would burst out crying in front of Trixie and Theresa.

"I can't think of anyone who would hold a grudge against you," said Theresa in a comforting grandma sort of voice. "Your family is kind and generous in the parish, and always willing to lend a hand."

"Pet and Father Schmidt just love you," Trixie added. "They're always saying what a fun young person you are."

"That's nice," I said. "Hey, I've got to go. I'm having an early dinner with the parents. Have a good day, both of you."

"See you later, Lilah."

Just before the screen went dark, I saw the smiles vanish from their faces, as though they thought they were already off camera. I wondered what had suddenly sobered them — the questions I had asked? The reality that I had been victimized? Or was it, perhaps, that they'd been forced to lie to me?

Thanks to the murderer running loose around the city, I was becoming utterly paranoid, and even church ladies had started to seem sinister.

That evening after dinner I sat watching *Charade* with my mother. We were both partial to Cary Grant; my father said he couldn't see the appeal. Men, my mother assured me, were envious of Grant's effortless masculinity. This offended my father, who huffed into the kitchen to do the dinner dishes. When the phone rang, I heard his muffled hello and then a brief silence. Then he appeared in the doorway, a dish towel over his shoulder and one hand over the phone. "Lilah. It's your boyfriend from the police station."

"He's not my boyfriend, Dad," I said, sounding and feeling about fifteen years old. Then, continuing the theme of immaturity,

I ran to my father, yanked the phone out of his hand, and went running up the stairs with it so that my parents couldn't eavesdrop. In a rather traitorous choice, Mick stayed curled up at my mother's feet, snoring slightly even though his eyes were open.

"Hello?" I said, safely in my room and breathing hard.

"What did I interrupt? Were you doing jumping jacks?" Parker joked.

"No. I had to run down from upstairs. What's up? Did you find him?"

"No. Sorry to get your hopes up. I just . . . wanted to thank you for dropping off my jacket."

"Oh, no problem. Thank you for letting me wear it. It's nice and warm."

I caught a glimpse of my own dismay in the mirror above my old dresser. What a lame response! For some reason I thought of Mrs. Andrews and her dome of white hair; back in her day they probably taught people how to have proper telephone conversations.

Parker's voice sounded the same, but somehow it seemed sexier to me than before. "I'm sorry I missed you. I mean, I *was* sorry, when I came in and Maria told me you'd been there."

"Maria?" Jealousy stabbed me in the gut

and had me scowling at my reflection. I turned away from the mirror and faced the window across the room.

"Detective Grimaldi, my partner."

"Oh yes. She's pretty, isn't she?"

"Hmm? Sure. Anyway, I was upset that I missed you. So I thought I'd call."

"I appreciate it. It's nice to hear from you — although it would be better if you said you'd caught someone."

"We will catch him, Lilah, and soon."

"Is that so?" My voice sounded bleak.

"Of course. Try not to worry." Now Parker's voice was no-nonsense; I pictured that stern teacher face he was making on the day I met him.

"Easier said than done, I'm afraid."

"This case is our top priority — Maria and I are working twelve-hour days. Few criminals escape a truly disciplined and relentless investigative team."

"I know you're a hard worker, Jay. And I trust you to get this guy soon."

"I will." His voice held a certain intensity — but of course he was just feeling passionate about his job.

"Anyway, thank you for calling, Detective Parker."

"Lilah, I promise to keep updating you, all right? I'll call again soon," he said.

I said good-bye and clicked off. Then I turned off the light and went back down the stairs to replace the phone in its charger.

"What's wrong?" asked my eagle-eyed mother from the living room. She had, ever thoughtful, paused the movie for me so that I didn't miss anything.

I returned to my spot on the couch and hugged a pillow against me. "You can both stop staring at me."

"Why so glum, chum?" asked my father, borrowing a phrase that I was guessing could be traced back to the Great Depression.

I shrugged. "He just called to talk about police stuff. And to thank me for handing in his jacket."

My father made a wry face and exchanged a look with my mother. "Lilah, normally I would not get involved in my daughter's love life. But since you really seem to like this guy I have to tell you something from a man's point of view: he didn't need to call you about the jacket. And he could have some clerk call with updates about the case. And he wouldn't have given his jacket to any other person in the first place. Do you see what I'm saying?"

"No."

"Lilah, he called you at home in the

evening, probably from his house."

"He works long hours."

"He doesn't need to keep contacting you, Lilah — he just wants to."

"What?"

"It's obvious," my father said, rolling his eyes.

"It *is* obvious," agreed my mother.

"What's so great about this guy, anyway?" my father asked.

"He's very handsome," my mother told my father, as though I weren't sitting right there. "And so polite. He questioned me on the night Alice died, and I was struck by his polite manner."

I hugged my pillow. "Let's just watch the movie. But turn it up a little; Mick's snoring is getting kind of loud."

"Sure, honey," my mother said.

My father wasn't finished. "And here's another thing," he added. "He clearly can't resist getting in touch with you. He probably told you he called for official reasons, but that's a classic gambit. I'll bet he told you that he's going to call back."

Parker had said that; he'd said he would call back soon.

"*There's* that pretty smile!" my mother said.

I ignored them both. "Let's just watch the movie," I said.

CHAPTER FOURTEEN

For the next week things fell into a daily rhythm: in the morning I drove with my parents to the realty offices; in the evening I would use their kitchen to keep up with my covered-dish business. With Parker's advance permission, my father accompanied me to my much-missed little house so that I could retrieve my calendar and a variety of kitchen tools and dishes that I needed. Terry had seen to it that the offending writing had been removed and the wall repainted. The front of the cottage looked as good as new.

My life got back to as normal a pattern as it could with me living away from my home. The new sound track of my life included the recurring plaintive songs of Emmylou Harris. I didn't know the words to any of them, but they played some folksy Muzak at the real estate office, and I had absorbed a lot of her haunting melodies. One of them had the words "icy blue heart," in it, and that one in particular was rattling around in my head.

On the Thursday after Halloween I delivered another casserole to Danielle Prentiss, my smoky client, who had indeed loved the addition of cumin and had requested that I make "the exact same thing" for her next poker party.

We met at our usual spot and she bounced toward me like a spring to claim the dish. "Lilah, I have to tell you — your food is an addiction! And not just for me. Everyone in my poker party thinks I'm a culinary genius. It's a shame you can't get the credit." She gave me a sly smile and I laughed.

"I'm getting paid," I said.

"Still." She shook her head as though my anonymity were a real shame. After thanking me again, she drove off, and I went back to Mick, my delivery companion.

We drove to our place, which I looked at with wistful longing. Mick, too, seemed ready to walk down the driveway and settle into his regular basket. "Not today, buddy. We're just here to talk with Britt."

I had made an appointment to speak with Britt about catering. Despite the fact that she was my friend, my hand was clammy on Mick's leash, and my heart was racing as I rapped on the door.

Terry answered, looking calm and rested, as usual. I felt a sudden longing for Terry's lifestyle. I was willing to wager it was full of things like naps and capricious journeys to beautiful places. "Hey, Lilah," he said. "Great to see you. Did you have fun at the party? I mean, before the whole thing afterward?"

"It was the greatest party ever, and you guys are the best hosts."

His look held affection and a bit of concern. He waved me after him and we walked toward his big kitchen, where we sat on two copper-legged stools under about five thousand dollars' worth of gleaming pots and pans, hanging from the ceiling on metal hooks. Terry offered me some of his expensive coffee, which I declined; I was wired enough without caffeine. He poured some for himself and took a sip, then patted my hand. "I got your place all cleaned up. Looks good as new."

"Yeah, Dad and I were in there the other day. Thanks so much, Terry."

"You're okay, right? I mean, you're not — scared?"

"No, not exactly. I mean, I'm not ready to live in there alone, but I'm not trembling in fear all over town. Mick and I are running errands tonight just like we always have."

"Good." He gave my hand another pat. "I don't want anyone taking your independence from you. That's important." His sincerity left me momentarily speechless. I nodded at him, and he pulled me into a hug.

Britt walked in and sighed theatrically. "I turn around for one moment, and you start an affair with Lilah."

"She's a temptress," Terry said, letting me go and winking at me.

I wiped my eyes and Terry hopped off his stool. "You sit, Britt. I have to go pay some bills." He waved to me and kissed Britt on the lips, then strolled off with the ease of a man on his way to some sort of leisure — perhaps to smell the flowers in his garden or to take a bicycle ride.

Britt stared after him. "He's priceless, isn't he? But he's so sweet."

"He really is. I've never met anyone like Terry."

"And you never will again," Britt joked. We laughed, then she grew serious. "I know Terry probably already said this, but . . . we're here if you need anything. You know that, right?"

"Yes. Thank you." I took a calming breath and said, "But that's not why I'm here. I want to tell you about a little business I've had for the last year or so."

Britt raised her eyebrows, and I told her about my covered-dish company — what sorts of foods I'd made, how many clients I had, the various happy responses I'd received. "It's like a catering company, but on a rather limited scale. Still, I have a book full of clients who call me on a regular basis, and I might be able to convince a few of them to provide references, despite the clandestine nature of the thing. And of course you're kind of a reference, too, since I made you some food the other day."

"Absolutely," she said.

"And I was wondering if you'd be willing to give me a try for one of your future parties," I said. "Something small, so that you can get a sense of my cooking without having to risk ruining a giant dinner party."

Britt laughed. "Lilah, I would never believe you could ruin anything. I think you have a magic touch."

"Hardly," I said.

"I would love to hire you. With Haven going out of business, this is a great new option. In fact . . ." Britt's eyes widened.

"What?"

"Well, I know Esther Reynolds pretty well. She's the genius behind Haven of Pine Haven. She hearkens from New England, but she long ago decided that Chicago was her sweet home, like the song on Terry's jukebox says. Maybe I could introduce you to her."

I tried not to lunge at Britt, but I didn't quite succeed. I grabbed her wrist and said, "If you could arrange a meeting I would be forever indebted to you. Maybe she wouldn't go out of business if she could find an energetic young worker who knows her way around the kitchen."

Britt sent me a sparkly smile. "Maybe you're just what she's looking for!"

Britt and I were both busy in the next week, but she promised to speak with Esther Reynolds and to get back to me in the near future. In return, I promised her eternal devotion.

Feeling like a true professional, I began to suggest to my parents that it was probably time for me to go home. I mentioned it again on Thursday evening while we ate spaghetti together in their kitchen.

"I don't like the idea," my mother said. "This person is unpredictable and probably insane, and he knows where you live!"

I nodded. "But what if they never catch him? What if I'm forty years old and still living here?"

My father cleared his throat. "Why don't

you put a little faith in that cop you like so much? He said he's on it twelve hours a day, right? So give him some time. It's only been a week."

This was true, and I had no real argument except that I missed my home. "That's a good point, Dad, and I do trust that Parker is working his hardest. But maybe this person is a genius. Maybe he or she is so clever that they'll continue to elude everyone. Meanwhile, my little house sits empty. Don't you think the cop they assigned me would watch me out there?"

They frowned at me. "Let's think it over and talk again later," my mother said, her favorite stalling tactic. "You know, your brother thinks you should stay here, too."

You win this round, family. "Well, I'll need to kick you out of your kitchen again tonight, because I have a business to run, and I have a delivery tomorrow."

"No problem," my dad said. "I have some accounts to look over, and Mom has a sewing project, don't you?"

"Yes, indeed," my mother agreed. "I'm making a quilt for Serafina. It will have the Italian flag in the center. It's going to be beautiful."

"I'm sure it will, Mom." She was clever at the sewing machine, too. She had endless creative outlets. "And I think I'm next in line for a quilt. Cam got one for his last birthday, remember?"

"Sure, honey. How about if I make one with little Labradors on it?"

"Awesome." I slipped Mick a piece of meatball where he sat under the table. He took it softly, without baring any teeth, and ate silently. Mick could be stealthy when needed.

We soon left the table and my mother gave Mick some leftovers in his bowl. The secret to getting lots of food, Mick had learned, was to be patient and adorable.

My mother and I cleaned up the kitchen, and I prepared another quiche Lorraine casserole for the Sullivans, who had become renowned in their Scouting circle for their baked contributions. While I worked, I thought of Cam and Fina. I wondered what it had been like when he first looked her up — just the sister of a friend that he met in Rome. Had it been love at first sight? Had Cam felt some sort of lightning flashing inside him? And if so, how lucky that the feeling had been mutual. Aye, there was the rub. The feeling had to be mutual. I stirred my batter with extra vigor and then spooned it into the dish.

By the time I was finished with everything,

it was quite dark outside. I started packing up the food, and my father loomed up behind me. "Hey, Li."

"Hey, Dad."

"Not to get all protective on you, but how about if you deliver that one in the morning? You can come in late to the office. I'll cover for you with the boss," he joked.

I hadn't been looking forward to making the delivery, even with a companion. My paranoia worsened in the darkness. "Okay," I said. "Provided this fits in your fridge."

It did.

Once again we gathered in their cozy living room to watch a movie. This time it was *Zorro.* I knew that my parents enjoyed having me back home again, and a part of me enjoyed it, too. I decided to count on Parker to solve things soon, so that my visit ended while we all still enjoyed one another's company and before I became a rather burdensome guest. I sat with Mick's head in my lap and admired Catherine Zeta-Jones's perfect beauty.

"That Antonio Banderas reminds me of Angelo," my mother said. "So handsome."

"Not a name to be discussed in this house," my father said with a rare burst of emotion.

I sighed, finding a certain irony in the fact

that my brother and I, who had grown up with a mutual fascination for Italian culture, had both found Italian loves. His was so popular that my mother was making her a quilt. Mine was so disliked that my father couldn't even bear to hear him mentioned.

The next morning I drove the casserole out to the Sullivans' house. Mike was in the front yard raking leaves, and he waved at me when I drove up. His dark hair had grown a bit long, and it blew into his face in a strong gust of autumn air. He wore only blue jeans and a Notre Dame sweatshirt, and he looked a bit chilled.

I walked toward him, leaving Mick in the car. He seemed happy to stay there; Mick didn't always like cold air.

"Hey, Lilah," Mike called to me, leaning on his rake. "Looks like you're going to enhance our reputation once again."

"I'd like to think so," I said, smiling.

He tossed the rake aside and took the pan from me. "Let me put this inside and get your envelope," he said. He darted up his stairs and disappeared into his house; a large Dracula still graced the front door, despite the November date.

I glanced down the sidewalk and saw someone walking a dog. I looked away, then looked back. The dog looked familiar, as did the walker. . . . I realized with a start that it was Shelby Jansen, my little teenage friend. I waved at her, surprised, and she jogged toward me with her canine companion.

It was a beautiful dog, a long-haired German shepherd with a remarkably handsome face; his snout was mostly black, but his fur was a mixture of black, buff, and cream. He was panting; he seemed to be smiling at me. I knelt to pet him, and I heard Mick whining his disapproval in the car. Mick was a gentleman, though — he didn't cause a barking scene the way some dogs might have done.

"Who's this guy, Shelby?" I asked.

"Isn't this funny that I saw you?" she gushed at me. "This is Apollo, Mr. Dixon's dog."

"Oh? And how do you happen to be walking him?"

"Oh — it's something we do through our animal club at school. The one I told you about? We volunteer as dog walkers for people who work. We take turns — us kids and Miss Grandy."

"So how did you end up walking here?"

She shrugged. "This is where Mr. Dixon lives." She pointed at the blue house where

Alice Dixon had lived — the house Hank had inherited.

I looked at the house through narrowed eyes. "Hank lives here? I mean, he moved back in? I thought he was going to sell the place."

She shrugged again. "This is where he told me to come, and he left the key and money and stuff. But, I mean . . . the house looks lived-in. By a guy. It has guy stuff around. I mean, it's his house now, right? So why wouldn't he live in it?"

Sure, why not? Maybe he was just going to live here temporarily until he and Tammy moved into the big, gorgeous place they'd purchased. But then why wasn't he staying at Tammy's?

"Lilah?"

"Hmm?"

"I said Apollo really likes you!"

I smiled, massaging Apollo's beautiful neck scruff. "I like him, too. But my dog is getting jealous, so I'd better stop."

I stood up, still admiring Apollo's beauty. Mike Sullivan came back out of his house and walked toward us. "Hey, Apollo," he said. "And who are you?" he added brightly, looking at Shelby.

"I'm from the Animal Protection Club at Pine Haven High School," Shelby said. "We walk animals as a service to the community. If you have a pet you want walked, you can contact Miss Grandy through the high school number."

"No, thanks," Mike said with a smile. "We just have a hamster. But it's nice to see Apollo back in town." He squatted down and did what I had just done; Apollo looked regal and took it as his due.

"I should get going," Shelby said. "I have a mile-long circuit I like to make with him, and I'm seeing a movie later with Jake."

"Have a nice time," I said. Mike and I watched her walk down the sidewalk, and then Mike produced an envelope for me.

"Here you go," he said. "Thanks, as usual."

"Sure." I tucked it into the travel purse that I had slung crosswise over my shoulder. My mother had made it on her sewing machine — a brown-and-orange autumnal bag with a little zip top. "Hey, Mike — can I ask you a question?"

"Sure. What's up?"

"I was talking to some ladies at the church — and to Pet Grandy — and they both suggested that Alice Dixon had been seen with some other man while she was married to Hank. Did you ever see her with someone?"

Mike had three reactions to this, all of

them surprising. He turned quite red in the face, and his perpetual smile disappeared. Then he turned abruptly and went to retrieve his rake. When he came back, his face had returned to its normal joviality, but by then I had figured it out.

"It was you?"

"No. Why would you think that?"

"Because you basically just said as much with your body language."

We stared at each other for a moment; a big burst of wind came along and sent my braid flying into my face. I pushed it back and looked into Mike's eyes, which were guilty.

He sighed. "We weren't having an affair, so don't jump to that conclusion."

"Okay."

"The fact is — sometimes we just wanted to gripe about our spouses. So we had dinner a couple of times. It was no big deal — just neighbors having dinner." His face turned red again. Mike was a terrible liar.

I shoved my hands in my pockets; it seemed to have grown a couple of degrees colder outside. "I get why you were attracted to her. She was pretty and stylish."

"Like I said, it didn't go further than dinner."

But that didn't mean that Mike hadn't

wanted it to. "I understand."

"And I would appreciate if you didn't say anything to my wife."

"Of course not. Why would I do that?"

"Well, why did you want to know at all?" Mike asked, his smile disappearing again.

I pulled some more hair out of my eyes; the wind was persistent. "I've recently been threatened — possibly by the person who did these poisonings."

"Oh God. I didn't know. I'm sorry, Lilah."

"It's okay — it's just that I thought there might be some connection between this mystery man and whoever killed Alice."

Mike held up a hand. "Whoa. First of all, I don't know if I'm even the guy your friends are talking about. I admit I had dinner with her, but only a couple of times."

"I get that."

"But Alice was just kind of a sounding board. Someone to talk to. To be honest with you, it was nice to get out and just be away from home — and yes, with someone other than my wife. No, don't look at me that way — I mean that Maura is the only person I ever get to socialize with. I don't really have guy friends I'm still in touch with, or women friends, either. And neither did Alice. We talked about that when we were out. How we were both essentially in these little islands of our marriages, and we had no other connection to the outside world. It's like we had lost touch with a part of ourselves."

"Huh." Mike, too, had to brush some hair out of his eyes. I realized then that Mike was a good-looking man. Acorn-brown hair, ruddy, slightly freckled skin, straight white teeth, and a perpetually smiling face — a lot of women would find that charming.

"But I had nothing to do with Alice's death. I was shocked and saddened, just like everyone else." He met my gaze with an earnest expression.

I thanked him for the money and the information and went back to my car, where Mick seemed to be pouting on the passenger seat. He might just have been cold; he was scrunching up into the upholstery.

"Sorry, bud — that took longer than I thought. Let me get the heat on for you." I turned on the motor and the heat, and Mick seemed to thaw by degrees.

I petted his head. "I'm guessing you were a little jealous about the Apollo thing."

Mick nodded.

"He's a handsome dog, but he's no Mick Drake. That's you, by the way. I don't think I've ever given you a last name. It sounds kind of weird: Mick Drake." I smiled at him and he seemed to smile back. I even got a glimpse of some doggie teeth.

I pulled back into traffic and realized that I'd reached another dead end. Mike Sullivan did not have the look of a murderer, despite his guilt at having been caught out. Then again, he had been very serious about the fact that he didn't want me to tell his wife. What if Alice Dixon had decided she wanted to tell Maura about the dates she'd had with Mike? How far might Mike Sullivan have gone to protect the little "island" that was his marriage?

When I got home I ran up to my room and dialed Jenny's house. "Hello?" she said brightly.

"Jen," I said.

"Well, hello, stranger! I feel like we haven't talked in ages!"

"I know. Let's go out next week. This week I'm booked."

"Me, too," she admitted. "How boring our lives are now."

"Hey, listen. I wonder if I could have your sister Mariette's number. I have a question for Henry."

"For Henry?"

"Yeah. I saw him on Halloween, and he gave us some information about the person who might have vandalized my house. I have some . . . follow-up questions, I guess."

She laughed. "You sound like a cop. Maybe that's your real calling."

"Hardly. I'm far too cowardly."

"No, you're not. Why are you so down on yourself lately?" I said nothing, so she sighed and said, "Okay, here's Mariette and Jim's number."

I wrote it down, then said, "Thanks, Jenny. We'll go out next week, for sure. Let's not let our workaholism talk us out of it."

"No way. See you, Li."

I hung up, then dialed Henry's parents' number. "Hello?" It was Jim, Henry's dad.

"Hi, Jim. It's Lilah Drake, Jenny's friend?"

"Oh yes — Lilah. You came to our Christmas party last year with that amazing Crock-Pot dish. Did you ever give Mariette that recipe?"

"I did. Hasn't she made it?"

"I don't think so," he said, sounding indignant. I laughed.

"Hey, this sounds weird, but I have a question for your son."

"For Henry-bear?"

I heard some giggling in the background, so I guessed that this name pleased Henry for some reason.

"Yeah — I saw him at Halloween and he told me something that might actually help the police with something they're investigating. I just wanted to ask him a couple more questions."

"This sounds intriguing!" Jim boomed in my ear. "Let me lift up this little bear so he can sit on the counter and talk to you." More giggling. "Henry, do you know someone named Zila?"

Henry laughed harder. "It's Lilah!" he yelled.

Male bonding sure was loud. I waited while they goofed around some more, and finally Henry was on the line.

"Hey, Hen. It's Lilah."

"I know," Henry said, impatient.

"Remember on Halloween, when you said that one person smelled like markers?"

"Yeah. He was dressed up as a holy person that lives alone in a castle."

"And why do you say 'he'? Are you sure it was a man?"

"Yeah. He was big and tall. At least the parts that I could see. And he walked like a man. And it's men who commit crimes, not ladies."

"No? What about Poison Ivy and Catwoman and Harley Quinn?"

Henry groaned. "Those are just Batman enemies. It's not like in real life."

"No, huh? Anything else you can think of

about that monk guy?"

"Nope. Just that he was walking fast."

Yes, of course he was. And he managed to get away right under our noses.

"Thanks for your help, Henry. Are you and your dad making lunch?"

"Yeah. We're making sandwiches. My mom is doing her homework, which is boring."

"But it will make her smarter. She wants to keep up with you, because you're so smart now, at six years old — imagine how smart you'll be when you're twenty!"

"Yeah," Henry agreed.

"Well, go make your sandwiches, and I'll talk to you soon, Sir Henry."

"Say hi to your dog," Henry piped, and then his father swooped him away and called a good-bye to me before hanging up the phone.

A man, Henry had said. So could it have been Mike Sullivan, who might have been on the verge of an affair with Alice? Or perhaps Hank Dixon, her estranged husband, who might have had more of a motive than anyone knew?

Or perhaps it wasn't linked to Alice's marriage at all. As ever, Alice's murder was a true mystery, and any clear reason why someone would be so cruel, and take such a risk, was beyond me.

Chapter Fifteen

I had gained a little confidence from my solo delivery (even though I knew my police officer had followed me from a distance), and I was starting to feel that my father had been right, and that the graffiti on my house had been a weird Halloween prank, probably perpetrated by a stranger. My late grandmother had always said that one could adapt to anything if given enough time. At the time she had been talking about old age, to which she felt she had adapted well (although she'd advised me not to get old myself). Now, though, I applied her idea to my night of fear, and the fact that the more time and distance I put between me and the event in question, the less real it seemed. The offending message had long since been cleaned away, and my pretty house awaited Mick's and my return.

I talked about this with my parents that evening, and my mother agreed — in a way.

"Why don't we say that we'll move you back in one week? That way Dad and I get to spend some more time with you, but you'll have a set date to go back to your cozy home."

We both knew that this was just my mom putting off the inevitable, which was her specialty. She had talked me into a year of commuting to college so that she didn't have to watch me go off to school. She had convinced Cam that he would save money *after* college if he lived at home for a year. In both cases she had been attempting to stave off our unavoidable departures — but in her defense, when the time came, she didn't go back on her word. She'd cheerfully accompanied us both to our new residences, providing plentiful linens and extra furniture.

So I went along with my mother's plan: one more week, and then I would return home.

I had no deliveries the next day, so my evening was free. My mother asked if I'd go with her to the church, which hosted a homeless shelter evening once a month (taking turns with other churches in the area). My mother, while not a constant volunteer, did commit to the hosting-the-homeless setup evenings because she believed in the goodness of it, and she was a firm proponent of the "there but for the Grace of God" mentality.

My father felt the same, and sometimes accompanied her, but this evening he had committed to going out for coffee with his friend Sam, a long-lost college buddy who had recently moved to Pine Haven. Since his arrival, my father suddenly had a new best friend. As I watched my dad dig out his old Indiana sweatshirt and pull it over his head, I remembered Mike Sullivan's longing for someone to talk to outside of his marriage.

"Dad," I said, as he ran a brush through his thinning hair. "Do you ever feel that your marriage is a little island, and you've lost all connection to the outside world?"

My father cocked his head slightly. "Why do you ask that?"

"Just something someone said the other day."

He shook his head and brushed some Mick hair off of his jeans. "I married your mother so that I *would* be on a little island with her. That's what you want when you love someone. It's a happy island, and I have no need for the mainland. And that's all the

metaphor I choose to indulge in this evening."

I laughed and hugged him. He kissed my
mother, grabbed his keys, and went out for
his evening of nostalgia.

"He's a good guy," I said to my mom.

"He's okay," she joked.

Then she and I bundled into her car and
traveled to the church. "That police car is
following us again," she said. "I wonder how
long they're going to do that. It's got to be
costing a lot of overtime money. I can't
imagine the Pine Haven PD will want to
fund it much longer, can you?"

I hadn't really thought much of the sala-
ries of the people involved, but this made
sense. Like all of America, Pine Haven had
been forced to tighten its municipal budget
belt, which had been discussed ad nauseam
in the local papers. I felt a burst of gratitude
to Parker. He was making this happen, and
there were probably people who opposed
him. "I wonder if I should tell Parker to let
it go," I said. "This can't be making him
any friends over there."

"Maybe just a few more days," my mother
said, and I laughed.

My mother got busy in the kitchen when
we got there; Pet Grandy and Father

Schmidt were handing bedrolls to volunteers and asking them to set up sleep stations. I stood in a line of about ten people who had showed up to help and waited for my pile of freshly laundered linens. I realized, as I watched Pet rush back and forth between a big wheeled laundry hamper and the counter where Father Schmidt was holding court, that I was among the people who took it for granted that things just got done: clothing got laundered, food got made, people who needed feeding were fed. But all of that only happened because of people like Pet, and Father Schmidt, and my mother.

"Hello, Lilah," Father Schmidt said. "You look nice this evening."

I was wearing jeans and a purple sweater with some rather grungy gym shoes, but I took the compliment. "Thanks, Father. What do you need me to do?"

He picked up a bundle and studied it. Then he made a wry face at Pet, who had just bustled up to us. "Perpetua, we have a problem," he said. "That sounded like I'm from NASA. Houston, we have a problem!" They both laughed at his lame joke. Father Schmidt loved to laugh, but none of his jokes were ever funny, including the ones he insisted on telling in his sermons. I had often wondered if the parishioners who forced out laughter at those times weren't, in fact, sinning.

"What's wrong with it?" Pet asked. She took the bundle, studied it, and then laughed again. "Okay — you got me!" Then she turned to me, taking pity on my blank expression and my inability to get the joke. "All of these should have a sleeping bag, a washrag and towel, a Baggie full of necessities like toothbrush, toothpaste, soap, all that."

"Okay."

"Look at this one!" Pet said. "It's just a sleeping bag and an empty Baggie!" She and Father Schmidt laughed again. This moment was apparently priceless for them.

I was struck, as I looked at their laughing faces, by how comfortable they were together. Even though Alice had been cruel to suggest that Pet had romantic designs on Father Schmidt, it was clear that their friendship was almost like a happy, platonic marriage. Even the way Father Schmidt had said her name sounded like a doting husband speaking to his wife. It was sweet, the way they interacted with each other.

Pet went to fix the faulty bundle, and Father Schmidt found me a new one that was not quite so hilarious in its oddity. I took it from him. "Now just find a cot and set up the station. When you come back you can grab another," he said.

I paused. "Pet sure does a lot around here," I said.

Father Schmidt beamed at me. "St. Bartholomew Parish would crumble to the ground if it ever lost Perpetua Grandy," he said proudly. "And I probably would, as well. I'm another old ruin that she somehow keeps in shape." He grinned at me, and I grinned back.

I took my bundle to the line of cots in the north side of the hall. The room looked different from the way it had looked on bingo night. The chairs and tables were gone; now the space would function, in essence, as a hotel, and the parishioners who bustled around were attempting to make it comfortable and pleasing for those who would come here, trying to make the best of a difficult situation. I found the first free cot and spread out the sleeping bag, unzipping it and folding back the top coverlet. At the foot of the bag I laid out the towel, washrag, and Baggie full of necessities. Angelica Grandy came past and handed me a pillow, which I centered neatly at the top of the sleeping bag. Harmonia followed her with a bag of cards and chocolate kisses; I took one of each and read the card. "God Loves You. From St. Bartholomew Parish Members."

I centered this on the pillow, along with the kiss. This was a class-A shelter — it provided chocolate on pillows. I liked that.

I set up two more beds, and by then the rest of them were completed. I felt that I hadn't done much at all, so I found my mother in the kitchen, where they were making sloppy joes for the evening meal. "Need help?" I asked.

"You can start pouring drinks and setting them on the counter there," she said. "Fill half the cups with milk and half with the Coke. If they want coffee, that's self-serve." I found the little disposable cups and started filling them with the required beverages. If I were tired and hungry, I decided, I would find this place most hospitable.

While I was filling the cups, Father Schmidt began admitting people for the evening. What surprised me most about the people who needed shelter was how little any of them looked like stereotypical homeless people. They looked, for the most part, like people you would see every day at shopping malls or restaurants. They were men and women, and they were all particularly polite as they filed in to the tables that the volunteers had set for dinner. Some of them came over to claim a beverage; they knew the drill from previous stays at St. Bart's. "Thank you very much, young lady," said an elderly gentleman who wore a white dress shirt with a bow tie.

"You're quite welcome. I hope you enjoy your dinner."

He winked at me and made his way back to a table, where he seemed to know a couple of other people. They talked quietly while they ate the fruit cups that had been set on their plates.

Perpetua appeared in the corner with a little trolley full of cleaning supplies. So she'd been here for setup, and she was on cleanup detail, too. I wondered what Pet got out of all this volunteering. Did it bring her joy? Did she feel it was necessary to ensure her a place in heaven? Did she just enjoy being around her friend Father Schmidt?

Harmonia approached me with her bag of chocolate kisses. It looked small in her big Grandy hands. "I have some extra, Lilah. Would you like one?"

"Sure." I took a kiss and unwrapped it. "It's nice of you guys to do this. I feel guilty, looking at the Grandy family."

Harmonia shrugged. "It's what we do. We

just grew up doing all these things, and we kept doing them. We like it." She smiled at her sister Angelica, who was blushing while one of the diners flirted with her. "It's nice to have everything back the way it was."

I nodded. "It's been pretty crazy around here, hasn't it?"

My mother approached. "Okay — the dishwashing crew is here, so I guess I'm off duty."

"Thanks for coming out to help," Harmonia said. Angelica, having extricated herself from the amorous diner, came to join her. Both women wore cross medallions on delicate silver chains.

"Those are pretty," I said.

Harmonia lifted her necklace. "Pet gave them to us last Christmas."

Perpetua Grandy, I marveled as we walked out. Seemingly, she was everything to everyone, and this church hall was her kingdom.

I wondered, as I followed my mother into the cold, dark parking lot, if a proverbial queen like Pet could really kill to protect her throne.

But where had that thought come from? This was Pet, of the velour sweat suits and the secret chili. She was a lot of things, but a murderer wasn't one of them.

Chapter Sixteen

Britt called me at work on Monday. "Hey, Lilah. Can I pick you up from work today? I've set up a little meeting with Esther Reynolds."

"What? Oh my gosh. I don't know if I'm wearing something nice enough —"

Britt laughed. "We're not meeting the queen. Esther is down-to-earth. But you have to see her kitchen."

"I do, I really do. Oh, Britt, you are my best friend."

Britt giggled. "I'll be there at — what time — four?"

"Yeah, that's great. Thanks so much."

I was so thrilled at the thought of meeting the Haven creator that I didn't get angry when Mrs. Andrews cornered me and started telling a boring story about her dot matrix printer and how it used to be the norm in offices. I eyed her giant white hairdo and wondered if I could hide a pencil in there.

My father appeared with some file folders. "Celia, could you file these with the recent closings?"

Mrs. Andrews took them with a flourish, leaving a trace of lilac perfume in her wake.

"Lilah, I need you to make some calls, see if these people are still interested. If anyone sounds ready to make an offer, transfer them to me."

"You got it, Donald Trump."

My father scowled. "Never compare me to him again."

"Just kidding, Dad. Why are you so grumpy?"

He yawned. "I didn't sleep well last night. Your mother wanted the window slightly open, and it was freezing! Sharing a bed with that woman is a constant challenge."

"*That woman* got up early to make you coffee. And fresh air is good for you."

"That's what she said. It was forty-eight degrees last night, Lilah."

I laughed and ruffled his hair, which also made him scowl. Then I got to work on the phone calls, which were mostly failures, but my last try generated enough interest that I patched the guy through to my father. Maybe he'd get a sale out of it — that would cheer him up.

■ ■ ■ ■

Britt picked me up in her sea glass–blue Passat, which had been a gift from Terry. Yeah, that was how people like Britt and Terry rolled — giving each other cars and throwing lavish parties. Since they were both particularly kind and down-to-earth, I couldn't even resent them for their luxuries; I simply admired them as one would admire royalty from another world.

"Hey, Lilah! Oh, don't you look cute, with that pretty knitted sweater!"

My mother had made it. I tended to wear it when I felt nostalgic for my childhood, when much of my clothing (and Cam's) had been mother-made. Today's sweater had been knitted with a multihued yarn in autumn tones. It was lovely, and people always commented on it. I wore it with brown corduroys and flat brown Aerosoles. I had thought it was an attractive outfit, although it didn't hold a candle to Britt's elegant brushed-suede jacket in an unusual shade of purple, worn over an understated blue pantsuit. Her dark hair hung in a glossy, fragrant sheet on either side of her pretty face.

"Thanks. You look amazing."

"You're too kind." She fiddled with the windshield wiper switch; a cold drizzle was falling.

"I'm actually having second thoughts about meeting her today," I said.

Britt laughed. "That's called cold feet, and I will not allow it. Esther is expecting us, and she said she was making gingerbread cake."

"Oh," I said. One couldn't argue with Britt, no matter how nervous one might feel.

Moments later we pulled up in front of Haven, a darling little storefront right next to the Village Hall, with a hand-painted sign of white letters on a green background, and a simple graphic of a fork and knife with smiling faces. The sign read HAVEN OF PINE HAVEN: CATERING FOR EVERY OCCASION.

The moment we crossed the threshold I knew that we were in the presence of greatness; the aroma alone told me that. This wasn't just the smell of gingerbread — buttery tones over cinnamon, ginger, and nutmeg with a slight vanilla base — but some extra, indefinable ingredient that made me feel nostalgic, happy, and sad all at once. Nothing can elicit emotion — and memory — like the scent of food, and this came home to me in an instant in Esther Reynolds's kitchen.

We were in a little green-tiled lobby, and before us was a long white counter that held a cash register and a big sample book full of photographs of food. I opened this and began to page through it, but my eyes kept straying past the counter to the giant kitchen beyond. Everything was stainless steel and spotless. I felt a burst of envy for the giant island in the center of the room — how easy it would be to prepare multiple dishes on that work space! Pots, pans, and bowls were tucked under the island on a variety of wooden shelves; it was clear that the furniture had been designed with their profession in mind.

I returned to the book in front of me and flipped to a page with the heading "High Tea." Beneath a picture of a long wooden table filled with food were various menu options, including things like sun-dried tomato–asparagus muffins, spiced blueberry scones, olive and cream cheese sandwiches on pretzel bread, caramelized puff pastry with hazelnut praline mousseline cream . . .

"Oh my! You're here. I thought I heard the bell. Hello, Britt." Esther Reynolds appeared before us, placid and bespectacled, white-haired but not old. She embraced my companion with a warm smile. Then she turned to me. "And you must be Lilah. Britt told me you're quite a cook."

"Oh — well — I like to think so. I've enjoyed your food at many events, and it's all been fantastic. I'm a bit in awe — you've always been the go-to catering company of this town."

She smiled at me. "That's nice of you, dear. We have held our own, I'll say that, and we have a loyal client base. But my husband and I are the main chefs these days. My daughter Marian and her husband used to work with us, but they had a great opportunity to relocate to Philadelphia. And our sons have no interest in cooking — Mark's a computer whiz and Luke's a teacher. So here we are. We're considering retirement; maybe finding out what it's like to live in Florida or California."

"Or maybe you can just find someone who's experienced and a great helper, like Lilah," Britt said. She really was selling me, which I appreciated.

"Why don't we all sit down," Esther said.

We moved past her front counter and into a side room where she'd set a table with a white linen cloth and delicate china teacups. The teapot looked at least fifty years old, and it bore a pattern of pale pink tea roses. "That's lovely," I said.

"Thanks. Sit down, sit down. Help yourself to some gingerbread cake and tea. I always like to talk over a meal, don't you?"

"Yes," Britt and I said in unison. We did as Esther urged and helped ourselves; soon I was tasting the wonder that the lovely aroma had promised.

"This is amazing," I said. "I think I can pinpoint all the ingredients except one. I can taste the ginger, the nutmeg — vanilla, butter, cinnamon —"

"Cloves," said Esther with a smile. "And molasses. And some of my husband Rick's homemade applesauce. And some almond paste."

"Almonds! That's it. I never would have paired almonds with those other things, but somehow — God, this is good."

We ate for a moment in silence, Britt groaning her agreement as she sampled her own cake from the tiny rose-patterned plate.

"Thank you so much, Esther," Britt said. "The tea and cake — such a soul-warming treat after that cold rain outside."

"Food warms the soul, indeed," Esther said, smiling. Then she turned to me. "What sort of things do you like to make, Lilah?"

I stared at her, awestruck, and then, as I had done with Britt days before, I told her about my undercover business. How I had expanded from my first few clients; how I had to keep people's secrets as a part of my service; how I had invented various new covered dishes to meet the demand of school events, bingo suppers, Scout meetings.

Esther stirred some sugar into her tea and nodded. "That is clever," she said. "Very innovative. You found your niche clientele. But obviously you'd like to be able to come out of the cooking closet, as it were. Establish a name for yourself."

"Yes, that's the goal," I said. "Although whatever I did, I'd keep a lot of my clients, since I generally make their food on my own time — evenings and weekends."

"Hmm." She cut some more pieces of cake and offered one to both Britt and me; we accepted. "I wonder if you might like to try working at Haven. We could call it a trial period for you and for us. Jim and I still aren't sure that we don't want to retire. On the other hand, if we had some capable help around here, we might not have to think about closing our doors quite so soon."

"I would love it!" I said, my mouth full of the cake I couldn't resist. "Esther, I would love that! Just tell me when to start. And give me some time to break it gently to my parents, who like having me work with them at their real estate office. But they'll be happy for me, believe me, once they get used to the idea."

Esther nodded. "We have a lot of requests at the holidays. It's going to get busy soon. What if you started in two weeks?"

"I'll be here. Just tell me the day. I have my own car, so I can help with deliveries. Oh, and I have a dog, Mick, who is usually my security when I deliver things, if that's okay —"

She giggled. "We love dogs," she said. "Cats, too. If you went through that door" — she pointed at a cheerful, red-painted door behind our table — "and went into our living quarters back there, you'd find a whole menagerie. I'm surprised the canines aren't barking away right now. They must be napping."

I stared. "You live on the premises?"

"Oh yes. This building was quite a find. Roomy living quarters with a view of Crandall Creek out back. And the seller happened to be very motivated, so it was affordable. He had gotten a job in Sacramento."

"Wow," I said.

"This building has great bones," said Britt, looking around with a sculptor's eye. "And that brick wall at the back — gorgeous!"

Esther nodded. "I admit it, we've been lucky. We've got a good place here. We wouldn't mind staying."

We continued our little tea party, but more than once I caught Esther looking at me with what seemed a measuring expression; I probably looked at her, and my surroundings, in the same way. Haven, for me, might live up to its name.

Britt dropped me off at my parents' house, her face smug. Mick was waiting for me at the door, even though my mother assured me he had been walked and watered. "Hey, boy," I said, sitting next to him in the foyer. A fragrant bowl of potpourri beside us scented the air with pumpkin and spice.

Mick allowed me to pet him for a while, until his seemingly hurt feelings mellowed.

"Is that better?" I asked, admiring the sincerity of his chocolate eyes.

Mick waited a minute, but he couldn't resist. He nodded.

"That's my boy," I said, hugging him.

Mick sat under my chair when we ate dinner, and I slipped him the occasional piece of my hamburger. Eventually, after we watched some television together and my parents both dozed off in front of the books they were reading, I called my dog and made my way up to bed. Somehow, despite the comfort of a loyal canine friend, a mother-made sweater, and the promise of a bright new career, I was haunted by the memory of words scrawled across my house, and of Alice Dixon saying there was something wrong with the chili.

I lay in the dark, my eyes on the blue-white crescent moon, which sat on a pile of gray clouds. How could I pursue my future when something dark obscured my present? When in the world would this murderer be exposed?

CHAPTER SEVENTEEN

On our way home from work the next day, we stopped at St. Bart's. My mother had agreed to be one of the planners of the Christmas boutique, and she had to drop some things off with the parish secretary, whose name was Erin Hartley. "Let me just run this envelope to Erin," my mother said and bolted out of the car in her brisk way. My father and I both knew that she was going to talk with Erin, as well, and that we might be looking at a ten-minute wait. His hand went to the radio dial and started roaming stations. I spied Father Schmidt on the side lawn of the church, kneeling in front of a flower bed.

"Hey, since Mom's going to be gone for a few minutes, I'm going to talk to Father Schmidt," I said. My father grunted, and I left the car and made my way toward our parish priest. He was wearing jeans, a Notre Dame sweatshirt, and gardening gloves, and he was busy pulling weeds that poked out between some purple mums. Even in early November, the hardy mums were still alive, as were some of the determined plant intruders that insinuated their way into his garden.

"Hello, Lilah," he said.

"Hello, Father. A priest's job is never done, huh?"

"Oh, I suppose not. Although this is less of a chore and more like therapy. I've always needed to get my hands in the earth now and then. It's like a prayer, don't you think?"

I had never considered this before. "That's a lovely way of putting it." I squatted down and said, "Father, I've been thinking about Alice Dixon."

He nodded sadly. "I'm sure we all have. She's been in my daily prayers. Alice was devoted to God, and I trust that she is with him."

"Yes." I paused. "I've been thinking more of her life on Earth, and who might have wanted to poison her."

He looked up at me. "Could you push my glasses up on my nose, Lilah? My hands are covered with dirt."

I did so, and he smiled. "There. Now I can see you properly. I need to get those fitted better. They're always sliding off." He sat back on his heels and wiped his dirty hands on the grass. "Pet told me that you are friendly with the police officer who is investigating Alice's murder."

I sighed, not bothering to deny it. This was the power of the St. Bart's rumor mill. "Do you have any ideas, Father? Can you think of anyone who wished Alice harm?"

He shook his head. "No. Alice was not an easy person, we all know that. She was rather like a rose — elegant and lovely, but quite prickly when handled. So yes, she created some conflicts in the church community. But I wouldn't go so far as to say she made enemies. You knew Alice. She was . . . complicated. In many ways she was like the girl I remember — she and I both grew up in Chicago, did you know? On the same street, right near Cumberland and Foster. I was just starting seminary school when Alice was still a little girl, perhaps a first grader, and I remember visiting home and seeing her on the block, running and playing. Even then she was quite particular. She didn't like to get dirty when she played. She would take her little dolls out in a wagon, but she would put a blanket between the metal of the wagon and her dolls' dresses because she didn't want to soil them."

He wiped his hands some more on the grass, then took off his glasses and wiped at his eyes with his forearm. Only then did I realize he was brushing away tears. I felt in my pockets for a tissue; I usually carried one in case I had a sneeze attack. I found one and handed it to him.

He thanked me and wiped his eyes. "It's hard not to feel sad, even though I know Alice is with God. But to die that way, without last rites, without a chance to say good-bye or perhaps to say sorry . . ." He shook his head.

"And to whom do you think she might want to apologize?"

He nodded. "You want to know this for your friend. He wants answers, right?"

"I think I just want to know for myself. I don't know if you're aware, Father, but someone threatened me recently. After Bert died. They painted the words 'You're Next' on my house."

Father Schmidt's eyes grew wide, and he grasped my hands with his dirty ones. Then he remembered the dirt and dropped my hands. "Oh — I got dirt on you."

"It will wash off."

"Lilah, this is terrible! I had no idea. You must be frightened and angry."

"Both of those."

He nodded. "So you want to know who I think resented Alice Dixon. The answer is, everyone. There were some women who resented her for having a higher rank than they in the women's club. Yes, some resentments are just that basic. Then there were those who were angry at her for perceived slights, real or imagined. As I said, Alice was not a cuddly person. I wouldn't even say she was a *nice* person. But she was a woman with feelings, and those feelings could be hurt. She knew that people didn't always like her, but she couldn't understand why. She was one of those people who didn't see herself the way others saw her; she didn't understand that she seemed cold. More than once she came to me crying, saying, "Father, why don't they like me?""

"Oh my."

"Yes. And I would sit down with her and counsel her, and ask her to make more of an effort to empathize with others. She tried, I know she did. But her nature worked against her; she was not an empathetic person. Poor Alice. I so often saw the child in her."

I nodded. "Who else resented her, Father?"

"Well, her husband, of course. Their marriage was tempestuous and largely unhappy.

In their case, I think separation was the healthiest thing."

"I didn't know priests could say that."

He shrugged. "I'm speaking more as a psychologist. That was my minor in school. Hank had many resentments, some of which were quite justified. But he wasn't perfect, either. Marriage is such a difficult challenge, really. I think of it as two boats, sailing side by side. But how difficult is it to remain side by side when the storms come? Boats can become separated."

This was like trying to get answers out of Confucius, although I did admire this philosophical side of Father Kurt Schmidt. "What about the church ladies? The Grandy sisters, or Trixie or Theresa, or Mrs. Breen, your housekeeper?"

Father Schmidt grinned. "Mrs. Breen disliked her intensely. They are both strong women who like to take charge. You can imagine how those interactions went, especially if Alice tried to take control over something in the rectory."

I giggled. Then I said, "Why would anyone do that? I mean, don't these people have lives of their own?"

His eyes were wise. "No, not always."

"Huh. And what about the other women?"

He sighed and stretched his long arms.

"Alice had a strange relationship to the Grandys. I think, in an odd way, she envied their sisterhood, their connection to one another. Alice was an only child."

"Ah."

"But she considered them her friends, as well, and often they would work side by side without conflict, mostly peacefully. They would joke with one another, and Alice would lavish them with presents. That was one thing about Alice: she was a woman of some means, and she was always generous. To the church, to the poor, to her friends. No one could call her stingy. Once she gave Perpetua a lovely ring that she said had been a family heirloom. But you know Pet — she's not the ring type. I think it hurt Alice's feelings that Pet never wore it."

"Did they fight about it?"

"Not exactly. Alice was more of a cold freeze kind of person. You had to wait out her anger the way you would wait for a glacier to melt."

"Did she ever give you the cold freeze?"

"Oh my, yes. All the time. But I wouldn't play her game. I would say, 'Alice, I will be happy to speak with you after you've gotten over your feelings.' It was best on those occasions just to leave her alone and let her stew."

I stared at him. "Don't you ever just get totally sick of people? Don't you just get tired of their weird personalities and their nonsense and their shallowness?"

His expression was cheerful. "Of course. All the time. And then I get out here and dig my hands in the earth and recite Psalms, and I am nourished anew."

"You're kind of saintly," I said accusingly.

He laughed. "No, I'm not. But it's my job to be good, so I try to be good. At least in public. Ask Mrs. Breen — I have my moods and my tantrums."

I tried to picture calm Father Schmidt throwing a tantrum. I failed.

"So if you had to investigate Alice's death, who is the one person that you would talk to first? The one person you felt might have had something to do with it?"

He sighed. "To be quite honest with you, Lilah, I have given some thought to the idea that Alice did this to herself. That it was one last act of spite against Perpetua for some perceived slight that Alice couldn't forgive. I mean, her last words were to suggest that Pet's chili wasn't right. She knew how proud Pet was of her chili."

"Oh my gosh." My legs were starting to cramp in their squatted position. I stood up and jogged in place for a moment, trying to come to terms with the bombshell Father Schmidt had just dropped on me. What if Alice was depressed, suicidal? What if Alice had poisoned herself? She had access to the chili, certainly, and she would have been able to engineer the whole situation. And yet — I had seen her face when the poison began to affect her. Either Alice had been the best actress in the world, or that had been genuine panic.

I looked down on Father Schmidt, who contemplated the dirt on his hands. "But, Father," I said, "if that's true, then who killed Bert Spielman?"

"I have no idea, unless it was an unrelated thing. A copycat crime, perhaps."

"Did you share this idea with the police?"

"No. Not in so many words. I hinted that Alice had been unhappy."

"Do you mind if I mention it?"

"Of course not. We all want to get to the truth. This is something that I've only been considering lately."

I saw my mother come darting out of the parish office; my father pulled the car into a recently vacated spot so that she wouldn't have to walk as far. "Looks like my ride is ready," I said. "Thanks for talking with me, Father."

Father Schmidt bowed his head in acknowledgment. "You're welcome, Lilah. Be safe. I'll keep you in my prayers."

I got back in the car and we pulled away from the curb. I watched Father Schmidt as he knelt there in the flower bed; his eyes seemed to be closed. I wondered how many people he prayed for each day, and whether his frail petitions had any impact on the juggernaut of fate.

Despite my mother's worried noises, I moved back into my little house one week later. Mid-November had brought ice-cold air and a few windstorms, which batted the last of the leaves off of the trees. My block was bereft of color when we drove down the street, and the skeletal trees offered stark welcome.

Cam and Serafina had insisted upon moving me back, and they'd also insisted (probably after being strong-armed by my parents) upon staying the first night, on the pull-out couch in my living room. It was always rather close when I had a visitor staying in my "spare room," almost as if we were sailors in our respective ship's cabins, but I was glad they were there.

Mick seemed the happiest to be back. He marched straight to his basket by the fireplace and made some smacking noises with his mouth — the kind that signal contentment — and went to sleep. I was tempted to do the same thing, but Cam and Serafina were there, nosing around my house and commenting on various things — the art on my walls, the rag rug in my hallway, the well-stocked pantry in the corner of my kitchen. "This is a great place, Lilo," Cam said, his arm around Serafina. "You've made it really homey."

"I love it," I said. "You two sit down and I'll make some dinner. What sounds good?"

"How about that thing you make with the veal?" Cam asked. "It's got that sort of tomato sauce and the crusty topping. . . ."

"Veal pie?" I asked. "I don't have the right ingredients. Let me go see —"

"No, no," said Serafina. "We will order Italian — Cam will pay. You sit and relax, Lilah."

Serafina was growing on me; sitting and relaxing made sense. I was happy to let her take charge, and, forty minutes later, it was as she had willed it. We sat down with pasta and wine and I told them about my new job opportunity.

"You like to cook this much?" Serafina asked. "To make food constantly for others?"

"Yes. It's an art. Food is my medium."

Cam stroked Serafina's hair. "Lilah does have a flair for cooking. She always did. She used to make my birthday dinners, and Mom made the cakes."

Serafina nodded. "Maybe you will make a birthday dinner for me someday. I am a terrible cook. Everyone thinks I should not be, because I am Italian, but I only like to mix ingredients in the test tubes."

We laughed, and Cam poured some more wine for everyone. "Good thing we're not driving," I said.

Cam looked out my living room window, though only darkness was visible. "Li, aren't you supposed to tell that guard cop about your new location?"

I choked on my wine. "Oh God, I forgot! I was supposed to call Parker." I looked at my watch. "Seven o'clock. I don't know if he'll even be there. . . ." I ran into my kitchen and dialed the number for the police. A bored operator told me that Parker was there, and that she would "connect me through."

"Parker," said Parker. His voice was clipped, distracted.

"Uh — hi, Jay. It's Lilah."

"Lilah." His voice was significantly warmer. "Is everything all right?"

"Well — yes. In fact, things seem back to

normal, so I've moved back home. To my little house."

Parker sighed. "Lilah, I wish you had consulted me. Us. I would have advised against it."

"Well, no offense, but this could be unsolved forever, and I have a life to live and a business to run."

"You mean the real estate business?" he asked, sounding confused.

"Yes, okay. I mean, I have to go to my job every day, and it got a little crowded at my parents' house. My brother and his girlfriend are here, and they'll be spending the night. So I should be fine. But I don't know if your police person is still doing night duty —"

His voice was clipped again. "I'll inform them. But I'm not sure how much longer you'll have that protection, Lilah. I have to get clearance from the chief of police, and he is not fond of overtime hours."

"It's okay. I'll lock up tight, and I have Terry and Britt in the house next door. If anything scares me, I can call them."

There was a brief silence; I tried in vain to imagine what Parker was thinking. When he spoke, he sounded tired. "Lilah, there's not just a danger of someone *scaring* you."

"I know, I know. But I have to live. Seriously. This has gone on long enough. I'm reclaiming my territory and my life, and the mad poisoner can just deal with it. I also have a big, brave dog." I looked at Mick, who was drooling in his sleep. "Big, anyway."

I heard some voices in the background on Parker's side. He spoke to them, his voice muffled. Then he said, "I have to go, Lilah. Some things are . . . happening here. I'll be in touch." He hung up without saying goodbye.

"Geez," I said. I looked at the phone for a while, just sitting and holding it in my hand. In the other room Cam and Serafina were talking to each other in Italian, something that should have annoyed me but that I found strangely beautiful.

I stared at the cool blue tile on my kitchen wall and realized something. It was never going to happen with Parker; he was too straightlaced, too uptight, too professional. I was always going to be a case to him. At this moment I couldn't even imagine Parker as anything but a cop, with that ramrod posture and those narrowed eyes. I wondered if he had ever loved a woman, or if that was something he simply made no time for. I was almost tempted to call Ellie, to ask her discreetly about her son, but I had my pride. I was also halfway tempted to call Angelo, to let him flirt with me in his predictable way so that I'd feel pretty and feminine and desired.

"Lilah?" It was Cam, peeking around the corner, finished with his own Italian flirtation. "Are you okay?"

I wiped at my eyes. "Ugh. Yeah. Just a long day, I guess. I called Parker, and he said he doesn't know how much longer I'll have the police protection. I don't care, though — I'm staying."

Cam's face transformed into a look I'd seen before: I called it "protective older brother face." He had worn it when we went trick-or-treating as kids and someone's mean dog barked at me; he had worn it when I fell down the stairs at the age of eleven and broke my arm (we were home alone at the time, and Cam had called an ambulance with remarkable calm, then sat at my side and stroked the arm that wasn't throbbing in pain); and he had worn it when my first boyfriend, circa freshman year of high school, had broken up with me because he said I was boring (Cam had also punched that person the next day, although I didn't learn that until four years later).

Now my brother, protective face established, came forward and gave me a hug.

"You know what? It's a really beautiful night. No more rain, and a bright half-moon. Let's go for a walk."

I let him coax me into a jacket and lead me outside. He and Serafina each took one of my arms and walked me down the driveway, where we saw the police car sitting on the street under an elm tree. Cam went to the window and spoke to the officer briefly. Then he returned, his expression cheerful. "I told him we'd be right back," he said.

We walked down Dickens and toward Main — the same route Mick and I always took when we went on nocturnal jaunts. The trees were silhouettes against the blue-black sky, and the leaves that fell were dark shapes floating downward, elemental and poetic.

Serafina told me about her sister Abia, the one who supposedly looked like me. Abia was twenty-four and studying to be a lawyer. She had a fiancé named Paulo who had proposed to her most romantically. After they finished university, they took a trip to Sorrento and the Amalfi Coast. "So lovely," Serafina said. "The town is so colorful, like multicolored stones beneath the sun, with the sea right there, breathing and sighing."

"You're very poetic, Fina," I said, trying out the shortened version of her name.

She kissed my cheek. "You must go there,

Lilah. You look like a girl who thrives in the sunshine."

"So how did he propose?"

"Oh yes. The best part is yet to come. They go from Sorrento to Capri, where they take a trip to the Blue Grotto. You have heard of this?"

"No. But it sounds gorgeous."

"Oh, my. Pictures cannot describe. It is a sea cave, you see. You enter in a boat — with your lover, is best — and you are illuminated by light that shines up through the water — light tinted like gemstones, either sapphires or emeralds, you would think. And you are immersed in this beautiful light, like another world. If you put your hand in the water, it glows."

We crossed Main Street and started heading home on the opposite sidewalk.

"Serafina, you should be a travel agent. I'm almost crying from that description," I said.

My brother squeezed my arm. "You were kind of sad anyway. But yes, Serafina is a poet. That's how she won me over."

"Oh yeah — *that's* how," I said drily. Serafina's laugh tinkled in the darkness.

"Anyway, my sister is in the boat with her Paulo, and they are immersed in the blue light, and he tells her that she has never been more beautiful — like a statue of a goddess — and that he cannot be silent anymore with his passion. He displays a ring, which glows blue but is a diamond. They don't dare take it out, for fear it will fall into the blue water and be gone forever."

"So she said yes?"

"Oh yes. They are so happy, and she has that story to tell always. That was a gift from Paulo. We all approve of him."

"Is he a lawyer, too?"

"No — Paulo is a builder, very talented. He is a true craftsman. They will have most talented children."

"That is so . . ." I stopped, distracted by the sight of a figure walking away from Terry and Britt's house, still in the distance. The street was illuminated by only streetlights, but there was just enough light to make the figure look recognizable — both in form and movement. It looked like Pet Grandy.

Had Pet gone to my house and found me gone? Had she been, for some reason, at Terry's house? Or perhaps it was not Pet at all?

Then another thought struck me — literally struck me, so that I almost fell down on the sidewalk. "Whoa, Lilah. Did you trip?" Cam asked, steadying me.

"Just — saw someone I thought I knew."

My mind was racing. What if Pet Grandy had been waiting for me to leave so that she could vandalize my house once again? What if Pet was actually guilty? What if Pet was crazy? Had I been wrong about her all along? If not, what was she doing by my house — which was nowhere near hers — in the middle of the night?

By the time we reached Terry and Britt's place the sidewalk was deserted and the police officer sat still in his spot. I studied my house carefully as we approached — no telltale paint marks or offensive scrawled words. Perhaps I was imagining things.

We went inside. I let Mick into the backyard, and Cam and Fina, with much hilarity, set up their bed in the living room. It looked very cozy. They found a channel on which *The Bourne Identity* had just started. It happened to be my favorite movie.

"Watch this with us, Lilah," my brother said as he snuggled under the covers with his luscious girlfriend.

"Are you going to be making out all through it? Because if so, I think I'll just head up to my room and call it a night," I said.

Cam shook his head. "We're not teenagers," he said with his professorial expression.

"Fine. I'll make some popcorn."

The Bourne Identity was a pleasure to watch, as always, but it did nothing to reduce my paranoia. Everyone was after Jason Bourne, and now, lying in my bed and jumping at every shadow that painted itself on my wall in the bright moonlight, I thought again about Pet Grandy. What if she was guilty? What if she had poisoned Alice Dixon and perhaps had considered implicating me? What if my making of the chili was all part of her elaborate murder plan? But then, of course, the police had said they didn't suspect her, so Pet kept quiet.

That didn't quite work as a theory — why would Pet bother to involve me at all? I'd been making that chili for her for more than a year. Then again, Pet had worked with Bert Spielman, and he was poisoned. Was Pet the type to poison people? Did Pet have what it took to end a person's life? Did she have a valid motive for killing Bert?

It still didn't feel right. Pet's grief over the deaths was too authentic, assuming she wasn't some sort of sociopath who could wear any sort of mask.

I sighed in the darkness. There was something there, right in front of me — some answer that would solve this puzzle once and for all. I couldn't imagine why Parker wanted to do this for a living. I hated having to wonder who had poisoned people, who had stood on my porch and painted a threat on the pretty white wood siding. I would make a terrible cop.

Mick snuffled on his pillow, and that was the last thing I heard until morning.

CHAPTER EIGHTEEN

At Pine Haven Realty, Mrs. Andrews was picked up for lunch by her husband, Alf, who was a true gentleman. He always wore a three-piece suit and a silk tie. He used words like *glorious* and *splendid* and spoke politely to everyone. I loved Alf and often fantasized that I could travel back in time to about 1950, which was probably the last time Alf was young, and meet him and fall in love. I had once seen Mrs. Andrews's wedding picture, and Alf had been a handsome young man.

I watched Alf park his 1998 Oldsmobile next to the office by putting it in drive and reversing about a hundred times, until he was satisfied that it was truly parallel to the building. A minute later he appeared and walked down the main aisle, greeting my parents and then me. Mrs. Andrews was off powdering her nose. She always acted nervous when he came for her, as though they were on their first date.

"Hello, young lady," Alf said. "Are you working hard, or hardly working?" I made a little Roman numeral on a sticky note I had on the bulletin board at the back of my desk. I was at forty-eight, which was how many times Alf had made that joke to me. I needed a new job. Still, Alf was sweet, so I said, "Oh, hardly working, as always."

Alf laughed. He was one of the few people I'd ever met who said, *Ho, ho,* when he laughed. "Ho, ho! Such a funny lady, and a pretty one."

"Will you marry me?" I asked, batting my eyes at him.

"Well, hot dog! A proposal! I'm flattered as can be, but I guess I'd better stick with my bride."

Mrs. Andrews came floating toward us on a cloud of lilac scent, her hair shellacked into its usual Dairy Queen cone style. "Alf, you could have waited in the car," she said, although she loved it when he came in to get her.

"Nonsense, sweetie." He took her arm and tucked it under his. "Where shall we go for lunch?"

"How about Mary's Diner?" she asked.

They always went to Mary's Diner, but they always pretended it was a new idea. I wondered if everyone descended into a sort of oblivion when they married, choosing to share the same illusions and to ignore the same realities.

"You're dark as a storm cloud today," said my mother, perching on the edge of my desk. "Are you coveting Alf again?"

"Yes. But also I'm just sort of depressed. I don't know why. I got enough sleep and all that."

My mother brushed hair off of my forehead and felt it with her palm, as she had done when I was six. "You seem a little flushed."

"I'm physically fine," I said. "Just a little moody."

"My baby Lilah. Things will look up, I know. You're just still sad about all these terrible things that have happened in town."

"Yeah."

"What song is in your head right now?"

I was reluctant to tell her. " 'All By Myself.' "

"Oh my. Do you want to come over for dinner?"

"Maybe tomorrow, okay? I want to try out something new tonight, and I haven't worked in my kitchen in a long time. I need to go shopping, too; I have some deliveries in a couple of days."

"Okay. But you let us know when that police officer is no longer outside your house. If need be, Dad and I will hire our own security."

"That's expensive, Mom."

"Would the money we saved be a comfort to us if something happened to you?"

"We'll talk about it later. I have some filing to do."

My mother's anxious face stayed with me even after she walked away.

When I got home I walked Mick, but only within sight of the police vehicle. Then I returned to my place and locked all the doors. I plugged in my iPod and clicked on one of my favorite playlists, a mix from the '70s to the present — my own version of Terry's jukebox. Dolly Parton started singing "Jolene" in a plaintive voice. I thought of Detective Grimaldi and her silky black hair.

I got out my big mixing bowl and started chopping apples. While walking my dog past Terry's big apple tree and smelling the fruit that had begun to rot sweetly into the ground, I'd had an idea for a sort of apple-cobbler bake. It would start with the traditional biscuit-mix bottom and a sprinkling of butter and brown sugar, but I'd decided to layer in some pecans and cranberries, as well as a touch of Angelo's Gourmet syrup, which had a rich autumnal taste. My hands got busy without me; I barely recalled making the dish and sliding it into the oven. I was lost in thought, but I wasn't even clear about what I was thinking. I was just floating there.

Then my doorbell rang.

I jumped; Mick rustled on the floor but didn't bark. I took a deep breath and walked to the front hallway, where I saw Parker's face through the small diamond-shaped window in the door.

For some reason I was sure he brought bad news, and my hand was suddenly so clammy that it slipped off the doorknob once before I could finally turn it.

"Hello," I said.

"Lilah. May I come in for a moment?"

He gave me that blue gaze of his and some moths of desire flew around in my stomach. "Sure."

We went, by tacit agreement, to the kitchen, and Parker sat down on the stool where he'd enjoyed the one dinner he'd eaten in this house. "How are you?"

"I've been better." I forced a quick smile. "What brings you here?"

He rubbed his right cheekbone with a

weary expression. "Well, good news, actually. We've made an arrest."

"What?"

"Hank Dixon was arrested this afternoon."

"Oh my God, Hank? Oh, poor Tammy. She was so sure of his innocence — I mean, *I* was sure, too. How do you know it was him?"

His face closed off a little. "I can't go into that. Suffice it to say that evidence was found in his home."

"What kind of evidence? You mean cyanide? Was that it?"

Parker said nothing. His shoes suddenly interested him.

I leaned against my refrigerator. "Hank Dixon. I can't believe it. He's the one who told my dad that he thought Bert Spielman was murdered. That he had wanted to hear what Bert had to say. It's so strange —"

Parker didn't look me in the eye. "In any case, you can breathe a sigh of relief, and we'll be terminating your police escort."

"Oh. Well — if you're sure. Then I guess I can go back to my old life." The reality of this dawned on me like a sudden burst of sunshine. "What a relief — thank you!" I said. I lunged forward and gave Parker a spontaneous hug. He had been sitting when I put my arms around him, but suddenly he was standing and I was even closer to him. I realized, moments later, that I'd let the hug last too long and that I'd allowed my nose to tuck itself into Parker's neck and smell the masculine scent of it, but I also realized that Parker hadn't seemed to notice because his own nose was buried in my hair.

Then his hands were busy on the clasp of my braid, and my hair spilled over my back and shoulders and Parker said, "Oh God," and I looked up in time to see his head bending toward me. It was not a gentle kiss. Parker's mouth was hard against mine and his hands tugged spasmodically on the tresses he had loosed; I pushed against him until he fell back onto his stool and I straddled his lap, my hands curling around his neck and sliding up into his lovely dark hair.

I probably never would have stopped kissing him, but he finally pushed me away — just slightly away — and smiled at me. "Lilah. I wanted to do that the first night I was here."

"Me, too."

"And now that the case is closed, I'm free to — pursue this. Which I want to do." His smile was such a rarity that I wanted to capture it somehow, the way you long to preserve a blooming flower.

His face grew solemn again in a moment, and I had a sudden realization. I backed up a little farther. "Except you don't think the case is really closed."

He sighed.

"You don't think Hank did it!"

"I can't really comment —"

"Oh, BS! So why did you arrest him if you think he's innocent?"

"I didn't." He looked regretful that he had spilled even that much.

I felt a burst of schadenfreude. "Oh, I get it. This was Grimaldi's collar."

"She had evidence. She was obligated to make the arrest."

"How did she know there was evidence? Wouldn't you need a search warrant unless there was some sort of — don't tell me someone called it in?"

"Lilah, we can't talk about this anymore."

"So Hank was framed, is what you're telling me."

I got an intense look from his blue eyes before he pulled me to him and kissed me again. Surprised, I melted back against him and realized just how comfortable it was, as though I'd been kissing Parker for years. This time I pulled away and attempted a glare. "You did that to make me be quiet."

"It worked. But also I really wanted to

kiss you."

We looked at each other for a minute, our faces close together. Then Parker sniffed the air around him.

"Whatever you're making seems to be done," Parker said. "Don't let it burn."

"Oh, shoot!" I yelled, climbing awkwardly off his lap and diving toward my oven mitts. I removed my dish, which I was tentatively calling "Harvest Apple Bake," with great care.

"That smells amazing," Parker said, coming up behind me.

"Would you be willing to taste it for me?" I asked. "It's a new recipe." I turned to see such a hungry look on his face that I felt a burst of pity. "Did you eat at all while you worked on this case?"

Parker shrugged. "It feels like I haven't eaten real food in years."

I sighed. "Sit down." I pushed him back to his stool and we both grinned a little. Clearly we already felt nostalgic about the stool. I went to the counter and scooped out some of the golden-brown apple casserole. "I'll let it cool for a minute. I don't want you burning your tongue on hot apples."

"No. I need my tongue intact," Parker said with a solemn expression.

"Yes, you do." I smiled at him, and his azure eyes seemed to glow like an actual light source in my kitchen. "Oh, your eyes, Jay."

"Remember the night I came here — the night of the vandalism — and you were wearing that — outfit?"

"Yes. Catwoman."

"That — I've been thinking about it a lot, Lilah. It was — flattering."

"Oh my."

With a smug smile, he leaned his elbows back on the breakfast bar and bumped the bottle of Angelo's Gourmet syrup. He picked it up, read it, and glared. "This guy. His name keeps popping up. But I really wish it hadn't come up in conjunction with yours."

"We were over a year ago. Why does it matter?"

"I don't know." He scowled as he set the bottle down.

I scooped some vanilla ice cream onto his apple cobbler and handed him the bowl. "Angelo's ingredients are good, and his Gourmet line is worth the money. Taste this."

He took a bite and rolled his eyes. "Okay, it's good."

"It's more than good, isn't it?"

"It's your gift, not his ingredients. But I don't just want to date you for your cooking. Although I would like you to cook for me sometimes. I'm a lonely bachelor with no culinary skills."

I sidled up to him. "You want to date me, Parker?"

He was almost finished. He'd taken about four huge bites. "I do," he said. He ate the last bite, put his dish down, and pulled me against him. Now his kisses tasted like apples and cinnamon.

I said, "Mmm," against his mouth and he growled a little. I put an inch between us and said, "Everyone kept asking me if I was dating you. I told them I barely knew you; I don't know why they all drew that conclusion."

"They probably noticed the way I look at you," Parker said. "I'm surprised you didn't."

"You always looked angry. Or disapproving. Or irritated."

He laughed. "You're a provocative person."

"I can be *very* provocative," I said, and he kissed me some more.

I pulled away with a new thought, though Parker's arms were locked behind my back. "Let's say Hank isn't guilty. Which, frankly,

I hope he is not. You officially have to remove my protecting officer, right?"

Parker nodded. "Yes. Tonight at midnight that protection ends."

"Ah."

He kissed me, gently this time, and stood up. "Which is why I have to go."

"What? Why?"

"Because I need to get home and grab some sleep. Because your protection ends at midnight, and your new assignment begins. Me."

"What? You're going to sit out there in a car?"

"Yup."

Now I wrapped my arms around him. "You can just guard me in here. I have a pull-out couch."

His eyebrows rose. Then he shook his head. "I don't want to rush things."

"Who said —"

"I'm not talking about you, I'm talking about me. I don't have a lot of self-control where you're concerned."

That made me laugh right out loud. "Really? You could have fooled me, Parker. Just yesterday I gave myself a lecture, saying that it was clearly never going to happen with you. You were just too cold and distant."

Parker gave me that stern look of his, with the addition of an ironic smile. "I was neither of those things."

"It felt that way."

"I was investigating a murder, Lilah. Maybe I still am."

He was in cop mode again, sexy and solemn. I lifted his right hand and kissed it. "Let me pack you some food, then."

CHAPTER NINETEEN

I thought I would toss and turn all night, worrying over Parker out in his car. To my surprise, I slept soundly and woke feeling refreshed. I looked out the window on Saturday morning and saw that his black Ford was already gone — he was probably at work. He had assured me he would be back, though.

I went downstairs with Mick and let him into the backyard. I checked my answering machine, which was empty, and let Mick back in for his breakfast, which he ate while I enjoyed the last of my apple cobbler (I had packed most of it for Parker). I tried not to think about Hank Dixon sitting in a jail cell, or Tammy Trent weeping in her office, surrounded by sympathetic animals. It didn't seem right; even as the angry ex-husband Hank hadn't struck me as a man with a motive. After all, he'd moved on, gotten engaged, bought a house.

Unless he had needed money? My father said Hank had gone over the asking price of four hundred thousand dollars. Had he needed Alice's life insurance bequest in order to do that?

I thought about it, running dish water into my sink. No. Even the money motive seemed too much like a plot from an episode of *Dateline.*

But assuming that Hank was not guilty, who else had a motive? Tammy, of course. Pet Grandy. Mike Sullivan?

Parker had said that there was evidence in Hank Dixon's house. If it had been planted there, then by whom?

I turned to Mick, who wore his wise expression as he sat in front of the refrigerator. "Mick, who would be able to get into Hank Dixon's house to leave evidence? Tammy, of course, because she had the key."

Mick nodded.

"And the Sullivans live right there, so there's a chance that at some point or other, Hank gave a key to one of them to do some house-sitting. One can't overlook the fact that the houses are contiguous, and there was a link between the Dixons and the Sullivans. A link Mike Sullivan does not want anyone to know about."

I thought about this, washing my bowl and

staring at the suds. Mike Sullivan did have a valid motive, assuming that he'd kill to save his marriage. But would he kill? Freckled, friendly Mike? When I had spoken to him on the lawn, the only thing his face had reflected had been regret. Was I terrible at reading faces? After all, I hadn't seen Angelo's betrayal until it had become embarrassingly obvious, nor had I clearly seen how much Parker liked me until Parker had yanked me against him and kissed me.

I smiled at the bowl in my hands. It was a beautiful bowl, blue as the grotto Serafina had told me about. I wondered if I could go there with Parker. The thought took my breath away: the two of us in a boat on an azure sea, Parker in a bright white shirt that exposed his suntanned arms, his warm hand in mine as we entered the cave where the light sparkled like sapphires or emeralds.

I sighed. "Oh, Mick. I've got it bad. But how could I run off to Italy with a handsome man and leave you behind? I would need someone to watch you, and not just anyone because you're my special —"

I dropped the bowl, and it broke. "Oh my God," I said. Mick edged closer to me. "Oh God." A dog walker. A dog walker would have access to the house — as Shelby did to

Hank Dixon's. He had probably given her the key. But what had Shelby said? That she shared the duty with other students, and with Miss Grandy.

My legs felt rubbery as I headed for my phone and dialed Pet's number. It rang twice, and then Pet's cheerful voice answered. "Hello?"

"Hey, Pet, it's Lilah." My voice sounded strange to me, but Pet didn't seem to notice.

"Hi, Lilah! What can I do for you on this bright Saturday morning?" She didn't seem to know about the arrest. Perhaps no one did. Perhaps it hadn't yet reached the papers or the news. Or perhaps that was why she was cheerful?

"Pet, I was planning a trip for the spring, and I was looking for a dog watcher. Are you the moderator of that group at the high school?"

I held my breath.

Pet laughed. "No, you want my sister. She's the animal lover, even more than I am. She devotes a lot of hours to that club, and the kids learn a lot from her."

"Which sister?"

"Harmonia. Our dog whisperer. Hang on, I'll get her."

"Uh, no — I'll talk to her in person when I get a chance. I have to run to work —

thanks, Pet."

I hung up before she could ask more. I sat down at my breakfast nook and Mick slid his big head into my hands. I petted him and worked it through. Harmonia also had access to Hank Dixon's house. But did Harmonia have a motive? It was ridiculous. How would Harmonia even get access to cyanide? Serafina had said that one either needed to possess it or have access to it through one's job — oh dear. I looked into Mick's honest face. Harmonia's boyfriend, the one Alice Dixon had teased her about, was a pharmacist at Rite-Aid. *A pharmacist.* Had the police, I wondered, already explored this connection?

But back to a motive. Why would Harmonia want to poison Pet's chili? Did she want to frame her sister? Or had she wanted to protect Pet by removing Alice and all her threats? Had Harmonia been trying to maintain the happy family dynamic? The three sisters and their platonic priest friend? The fun and happy evenings spent together, endangered by a jealous woman? What had Harmonia said to me at the homeless shelter? *It's nice to have everything back the way it was.* I had thought she meant the way it was before all of the tragedy. But perhaps she had meant something else — as in, the way it was before Alice ruined everything?

Or could it have been about animal rights? If Shelby and Jake had been fighting with Alice Dixon about Apollo, Harmonia would have been right there to hear it. And — "Oh no," I said to Mick, who looked truly worried now.

In the picture on the wall at the Grandy house, Harmonia had been the one pulling the sled the other way. Harmonia was the stubborn sister, the rebel, the renegade. She was also the youngest — pampered and loved. In the other photo, she had been holding a little black dog, and yet I had seen no sign of the dog at their house.

I picked up the phone again; this time I called Shelby. "Hello?" said a woman's voice.

"Rachel? This is Lilah Drake. I wonder if Shelby is there?"

"Oh, she's still sleeping, if you can believe it. These teens —"

"Yes, I see," I interrupted. "Well, I wonder if you can tell me — she had spoken to me about a little dog that once bit Alice Dixon, and the dog had to be sent away because Alice was calling for it to be put down."

"Oh, you mean Harmonia Grandy's dog? Titan? Such a funny name, because he was a tiny little miniature schnauzer. Yes, Shelby got all worked up over that story. I'm afraid Harmonia did rile up the kids sometimes, telling her tales of animal injustice."

"Huh. Yes, that would appeal to a teenager's righteous indignation. Well, that answers my question — thanks."

"Sure thing, Lilah. Have a great weekend."

"You, too." I hung up. Harmonia. But perhaps I was wrong. Perhaps, suddenly, all signs pointed to Harmonia because I was just asking questions that pointed to her. It didn't feel that way, though. I waited until I had taken my shower to see how strongly I still felt. I looked in the mirror and saw the suspicion in my own eyes. I returned to my kitchen and dialed Jay Parker.

"Parker," he answered.

"Jay."

"Hey, there. Did you sleep well?" His voice was soft and sexy, and it briefly distracted me from the huge accusation that lingered in my thoughts.

"I'm great, at least in the love department. I have a new boyfriend."

"Yeah? Is he a good guy?"

"He's wonderful. Very handsome and sexy."

"Hmm."

"Jay."

"What? Is something wrong?"

"I think it's Harmonia."

"What? You think what is Harmonia? You mean that Grandy sister?"

"I think she did it. Killed Alice Dixon. Killed Bert. Planted evidence in Hank's house. She had the key because she walked his dog. Did you know that?"

"No." I could hear him typing on his keyboard — perhaps the very things I was telling him. "What else?"

"A year or so ago, Harmonia's little dog bit Alice Dixon. Alice was infuriated and demanded that the dog be put down. Somehow Harmonia snuck it out of town so that Alice couldn't follow through on the threat."

"I don't know —"

"Apparently Harmonia's crazy about animal rights. And on the night of Alice's death, Harmonia found out that Alice was going to debark her husband's dog."

"Do what?"

"Slice his vocal cords so he couldn't bark anymore."

Parker typed more rapidly.

"And Alice had been threatening to report Father Schmidt to the archdiocese. The Grandys all love him — he's like a benevolent uncle to them all — and they have these happy weekend gatherings all the time. Alice was jealous of them, and the grapevine says that when Alice felt hurt or jealous, she looked to hurt people."

"How do you —"

"And Alice Dixon openly insulted Harmonia, said she was too old to have a boyfriend. I think — if Harmonia hated her, it could have been building for a long time. Oh, and Harmonia's boyfriend is a pharmacist. At Rite-Aid. I don't know if you investigated —"

"How did I not see this?" Parker hissed.

"Listen, you've been working so hard that you're half-dead, and besides you probably did see it and it would have come to you today, the way it did to me while I was doing the dishes, and — AGH!" I screamed in his ear.

"What is it? Lilah?"

Harmonia Grandy stood at my back door, smiling at me through the window. She looked utterly different from when she was flanked by her sisters. Larger, somehow, and stronger. More like an individual; her eyes were determined beneath her smile. I held up a finger to indicate that I'd be with her in a moment and turned away so that she wouldn't see my lips when I said, "Harmonia is at my door. She's at my *door,* Jay."

"Don't panic. And don't let her in. Just make an excuse. I'll be there in minutes."

360

He hung up in my ear. I was alone. Harmonia was tapping again, tapping, tapping on the window even though I'd already acknowledged her. It was frightening.

I moved to the door and spoke through the glass. "Hi, Harmonia. I'm just on my way out — I'll have to catch you later." I grabbed my jacket off a hook on my pantry door and pointed at it.

"I just need a second," Harmonia said, still smiling.

My hands shook. "I don't even have a second. My dog is sick, and I'm taking him to Dr. Trent. That was her on the phone. So." I grabbed Mick's leash and clipped it onto to him. "So I'm sorry I can't see you, but my dog is dying."

I couldn't even keep track of the lies that flowed out of my mouth; I was facing a murderer and I'd gone absolutely limp with fear. Never mind the fact that Mick stood smiling at Harmonia, obviously at his most hale and hearty.

Harmonia's smile disappeared, but she remained at the window. "I need to talk with you, Lilah," she said, her voice muffled by the glass in my storm window.

Then another face appeared beside her. Ellie. Oh no. My dear friend Ellie Parker, whose son was currently racing here to save our lives.

"Hi, Lilah," Ellie said, waving at me and then, in her polite way, introducing herself to Harmonia as they stood on my back stoop together. She either had the worst or the best timing — I couldn't decide.

"Lilah, may we come in?" Ellie said, sending me a curious glance through the window.

"Ellie, my dog is sick. Will you come to the vet with me? I'll meet you at the front. See you later, Harmonia."

Ellie's face registered surprise, then awareness, as she realized I did not want to admit the woman who stood with her on the stoop. She had just sent me a knowing glance when Harmonia's large hands wrapped around her throat. Ellie's eyes bulged in surprise and her own arthritic hands flew up to try to stop the pressure that Harmonia was exerting.

"Let me in, or I'll strangle her," Harmonia said. Oh, those shovel-like hands of Harmonia's! Damn heredity and her giant of a father.

I opened the door and pushed on the screen so that Harmonia could shove Ellie in. I shut the door but left it unlocked. Ellie, gasping, went to my sink and filled a glass with water, then drank it, looking at me with wide eyes.

"Harmonia, I've already called the police," I said. "I told them what you did and why, and they're on the way."

Her face was pale, her eyes measuring. "I don't believe you," she said. "You're just desperate, because you didn't expect me to show up here. And I wouldn't have, if you hadn't called Pet. Why did you want to know that? What made you even care if I was the moderator of the Animal Protection Club?"

If I kept her talking, nothing scary would happen. Parker would get here and hold a gun on Harmonia and take her out of my house.

"Because Shelby told me that you sometimes walked Hank Dixon's dog. Which meant you had access to his house and could plant the evidence that they used to arrest him."

Ellie gasped, then gulped some more water. Mick moved closer to me.

"What I'd like to know," I said, "is why you wrote on my house. Why you threatened me. I'm not your enemy, Harmonia. I never have been."

She said nothing.

"I assume that was you? Dressed as a monk? I'm sure I can get the police to ask around to see if you were wearing that particular costume that night."

Harmonia looked surprised. "Someone saw me? I never saw a soul."

"A very clever little someone who happened to pick up the scent of your paint in the darkness."

She shrugged. "That was nothing. I was just jealous. You were spending a lot of time with Pet, and she was acting as if she liked being with you more than she did her own sisters. I just wanted to scare you. It was just a distraction. Nothing to get all upset about."

Ellie and I exchanged a glance. Apparently we differed with Harmonia about what would make someone upset.

"And I suppose that was you the other night? Lurking around my house in the dark?"

"What?" She looked genuinely surprised; then again, I was clearly terrible at reading faces.

"Fine. You wanted to scare me on Halloween. Did you also want to *scare* Alice Dixon?"

Harmonia's eyes darted around the room. Then she took a little bag out of her pocket and went over to my stove. She picked up my teakettle, filled it with water, and turned on the heat. "Let's have some tea," she said.

That silenced me for a moment, and I exchanged a confused glance with Ellie. "Why Alice, Harmonia?"

She sighed. "She wasn't supposed to die. She was supposed to get sick, very sick. That's what my Internet research said. I didn't think I'd put in enough to kill her." She shrugged again, as if the light dosage cleansed her of a murder charge. "But if Alice got sick, I figured she'd give up on all her destructive little projects. And Bert — poor guy — he just got too close to the truth. Pet told me. It's not hard, to be honest, to poison someone. It's oddly easy."

"And you just figured if you left some cyanide in Hank Dixon's house and then called in an anonymous tip, then that would take care of everything, right?"

Harmonia giggled, and I felt a bolt of fear shoot through me. "It worked, didn't it? They went straight to his house, and he's in jail."

"And you're okay with sending an innocent man to jail?"

She shook her head, her face regretful. "That's the dilemma I'm in now. I like Hank — everyone likes Hank. He's a good man, a good parishioner. But obviously I don't want to go to jail, so we're just going to drink some tea and talk this out. Okay?"

She smiled at Ellie and me and I realized, looking at her slightly unfocused eyes, that Harmonia was not a rational person. Therefore, reasoning with her was not an option. I sent a warning look to Ellie and said, "That sounds good. I take two sugars in my tea."

Harmonia nodded. "You two sit down right there at the counter and I'll serve."

She lifted the little bag she'd brought with her and put it near my sugar bowl. Then she began opening drawers. "Where do you keep the teaspoons? Oh, here they are." She actually hummed while she worked. She had a pretty singing voice, which made the situation more surreal; Ellie stared at her, wide-eyed, seemingly reaching the same conclusion about Harmonia that I had just reached. It was amazing, really, that the woman thought she could poison both of us while we stood there watching, and that she would sing to us before our deaths.

"Yes, I like sugar in mine, too," Ellie said.

"Perfect," said Harmonia, her hands busy at the counter. She had found mugs and teabags and was now laying them all out, preparing them for the boiling water. "It will be ready in no time. So what should we talk about?"

Before I could say a word, Ellie lunged forward and cracked her water glass against the side of Harmonia's head. The glass broke, cutting Ellie's hand and Harmonia's ear. Harmonia screamed and grabbed the side of her head. Blood trickled onto the floor.

"I'll kill you!" Harmonia yelled. "I'll kill you both! And then I'll say you killed each other!"

She dove at Ellie and the two women began grappling. I dove low and pulled at Harmonia's legs, yanking her away from Ellie, and then I threw myself on top of her, trying to pin her hands, but not before Harmonia punched me in the eye.

"Ouch," I yelled. "Mick, help me out here!" I said.

Mick moved forward, menacing as a wolf, and placed his sharp dog teeth on either side of Harmonia's neck. He must have exerted pressure, because Harmonia went limp.

Parker burst in a moment later to find Harmonia on the floor, her hands bound behind her with Mick's leash and Mick still holding her by the throat. Ellie was running her bloody hand beneath some water at the faucet, and I was icing my black eye.

"Ladies," Parker said, ever polite.

■ ■ ■ ■

A whole slew of people came to escort Harmonia away, including Grimaldi, who looked relieved. Perhaps she, too, thought that Hank Dixon's arrest had seemed too convenient. Terry and Britt showed up, looking pale and bemused at the sight of all the police cars in their driveway. I assured them I was fine, and then they stood right outside my house like the guardians that they were, answering questions for the police and, eventually, the reporters. Finally, finally, they all left.

Parker stayed behind. He had wrapped his mother's hand in gauze and was now examining my eye, which had turned an interesting shade of yellow. "Poor thing," he said, kissing my eyebrow.

Ellie made a startled sound, then said, "Aha!"

I looked over and laughed at her triumphant expression. "I would have told you about us today when you came over, except a murderess was standing on my stoop and distracting me."

"Well, I'm glad to know it," Ellie said, her face smug.

Parker looked annoyed. "Yes, Mother,

your obvious plot to bring us together had the desired result."

I stared at him, then at Ellie. "You did, didn't you? You set us up! Having me come there with my delivery and then asking Jay to come at the same time — and then disappearing! Oh, Ellie, really!"

She smiled, not at all apologetic. "I knew you two would be the perfect couple. And I was right. No need to thank me."

I laughed and started to hug Parker, but he pulled away from me and walked to the door. He stood there looking out, his back to us. "What do you mean, you were making a delivery? You told me you cleaned my mother's house."

Ellie snorted. "Jacob Ellison Parker, would you take off the detective hat? How dare you grill your own girlfriend? In case you didn't realize it, someone tried to kill her today, and kill your mother!"

Jay turned back, his face blank. "Did you lie to me, Lilah? What were you . . ." He looked around my kitchen and then slapped his head. "Of course. I'm an idiot. You made the food. You delivered the food. And you couldn't tell me because —"

Ellie snorted. "Because I didn't want her to. Lilah has a thriving business making delicious food for people who would like their families to . . . think otherwise. I didn't want you and your brothers to know that I can't make it anymore. Not as often. Those big, heavy pans, and all that cutting. It hurts too much."

Jay's face looked pained, then regretful. "I'm sorry, Mom. Your secret is safe with me. I love your cooking, and I love Lilah's, too. Tom and Eric never have to know."

Ellie sniffed. "Lilah is a wizard. You're lucky to have her, you know."

"I know," Parker said, but his expression was still quizzical.

"Listen," I told him. "I'm not going to lie to you anymore. But this was your mother's secret to reveal, not mine. My whole business is based on discretion, Jay. That's why I felt so bad, every time you asked me, and every time I wanted to tell you —"

"Tell me what?"

His eyes narrowed, and I knew that I might be ruining everything, but better now than later, when I was even more in love. . . .

"I made the chili for Pet Grandy. The chili that Alice Dixon ate."

"*You* made it." Parker's eyes grew wide and his face reddened. Something moved in his jaw.

"Oh, here we go," Ellie said.

"You do realize, Lilah, that it wasn't for

you to decide whether that information was pertinent or not? It wasn't for you to claim 'discretion' when a woman had died eating your food! And you stood in front of me and lied, again and again! Even after I told you how much I hated it when people lied to the police. You still withheld that information."

"By then it was too late — you would have hated me."

"And why did that matter?"

"Because I liked you," I said.

Parker shook his head, his eyes wide. "It wasn't about you or me," he said. "It was about a dead woman and what was right."

"Jay, listen to yourself! Don't be sanctimonius," Ellie said, her voice stern. "You're being an ass. Leave the girl alone. Why are you being so hard on Lilah?"

His eyes were on mine. "Because I thought she was honest," he said. "And that's what I liked best about her."

"Jay," I said, hating the moisture that filled my eyes. "I don't know what to say."

"I have to go," he said. "I have reports to file." He opened the door and went outside, and my heart broke for the second time in my life.

"I can't seem to hold on to a guy," I said lightly. I turned to Ellie and burst into tears, and she pulled me into a warm hug.

"Honey, he's just pouting. It always did take him a while to get over a perceived injustice. You just have to give him time. He — he has a thing about honesty."

"I'm not a dishonest person," I said, sobbing into her ear.

"Don't cry, sweetheart. It will all work out. Didn't I tell you I thought you were the perfect couple?"

Mick rustled at our feet, and even though I couldn't see him, I knew he was nodding.

CHAPTER TWENTY

The next morning my whole family, including Serafina, crowded into my small kitchen and served me breakfast. Cam had pulled in a couple of extra chairs and we sat on either side of my breakfast nook. They all did an admirable job of ignoring my red, swollen eyes, and the fact that one of them was puffy and bruised.

"Listen to this," said Cam, reading from the *Pine Haven Gazette.* " 'Grandy was finally cornered at the home of local resident Lilah Drake, whom Grandy had been threatening at the time of her apprehension. "Ms. Drake was instrumental, not only in bringing Harmonia Grandy's suspicious activities to the attention of the police, but in clearing the name of the man who had been falsely arrested," said Detective Inspector Jacob Parker of the Pine Haven Police Department. "We cannot stress enough that Lilah Drake behaved heroically in a highly stressful circumstance." ' "

Cam looked at me triumphantly. "Check that out! Now the whole town will be asking about this heroic woman. And it certainly sounds to me like Jay Parker admires you immensely."

I shrugged, pushing my eggs around on my plate. Out of the corner of my eye I saw my mother make her concerned face to my father. "He has to say that in his official capacity. What's he going to do? Tell the whole town that he's disgusted by me?"

My mother got up and said, "Serafina, would you help me with these dishes? And Dan, maybe you can sweep Lilah's floor," she said to my father. "Lilah, honey, go in the living room with your brother and relax."

Here we go, I thought. My parents knew that Cameron had always been the most successful at drawing me out of my brief depressions, usually because he made me laugh. Cameron had almost single-handedly helped me to get over the Angelo slump, and my mother was placing the burden on him once again.

Cam came to my chair and practically dragged me out of it. "Come on, kid. Let's see what's on TV."

"Cam, you don't have to do this," I said.

"I just need some time."

We walked into the living room and Cam pushed me onto the couch. I lay there without moving. "Uh, yes, I do have to do it. Terry and Britt told me they tried to come out and see you last night, but they couldn't be heard over the loud strains of 'Some Enchanted Evening,' which you had playing on a loop."

"It's a great song. I was in *South Pacific* in high school, remember? I was Nellie Forbush."

Cam smiled. "I remember, Li. You were good. And that's a very romantic song."

I sighed. "It's about finding the right person and not letting him go. That's how I feel. He was the right person."

"There is no one right person," Cam said angrily. "If he doesn't appreciate you, then you move on."

"Really? So you could move on after Serafina?"

His shoulders slumped in defeat. "Okay. But, Lilah, the guy was too hard on you. You were stressed out. You saw a woman murdered in front of you. If you made some bad decisions, then he can get over it."

I sighed. "Cam, remember when I broke up with Angelo? Do you remember what I told you?"

"That he was an asshole?"

A watery laugh escaped me. "I told you that I couldn't ever trust someone who had lied to me. I said that since he hadn't told me the truth about another woman, I would never know if he was telling me the truth again. That's how Parker feels."

"It's not the same. You didn't sleep with some other guy and tell Parker you didn't."

"No. But what I'm saying is, we really *are* well suited, because I care about honesty, too. I'm an honest person, Cam. And now I've lied to the police, and to the one man who made me think life was pretty darn great."

"So what are you going to do now? Listen to show tunes and make yourself cry?"

"Yes."

"Lilah."

I said nothing. I hugged a pillow against myself and willed Cam to leave.

"Lilah." He put his face in front of mine, so close I could smell his breakfast. "Call him."

"No."

"Why not?"

"I have nothing to say. I lied. He knows it. That's it."

"You could say you miss him."

"I guess. It won't do any good. If he

wanted me, he'd be here."

Cam touched my black eye with a delicate finger. "You poor kid. You've been through so much this last month. But you know what? It's over now."

"Yes. It's over now," I said bleakly.

Cam sighed. "Lilah, call him or I will."

I laughed again. "What would you say? *My sister likes you and you need to come to her house?*"

My brother looked determined. "I'd say that thanks to him my sister had spent the night crying, and that he had better work it out with her before I decided to kick his ass."

"That sounds okay," I joked.

Cam pointed at the stairs. "Call him, Lilah. I'm not kidding."

"Fine." I went to the stairs and climbed up to my loft room, carefully shutting the door. Then I grabbed my cell, let out a deep sigh, and dialed Parker's home number. I got his voice mail, a fact for which I was intensely grateful. He said some terse words and then there was a beep.

"Hi, Jay, it's me. I just wanted to say — I'm sorry I let you down. And that I miss you. I miss cooking for you. And if you ever wanted to wander over some night and let me feed you again — maybe we could start over. I know how you feel, because I broke up with someone over the same principle. But I'm not a liar, and I'm telling the truth when I say I like you a lot, and I think you're pretty great at what you do. Anyway, this is the only time I'm going to call, so don't worry that I'll harass you. I just — anyway . . . Good-bye, Jay."

I hung up and turned on my iPod. Rossano Brazzi was singing "This Nearly Was Mine." Mick was scratching at my door, and I let him in. Normally he slept in his own basket, but now he jumped right up on my bed with me. "I'm too old for this, Mick. I'm acting like a lovesick teenager."

Mick nodded, and Rossano sang sweetly of the beautiful love he'd almost had.

When I went down about an hour later my family was gone; I was sure Cam had persuaded them to leave me alone.

My mother had made me a sandwich and left it under plastic wrap. There was a little note there from her, asking me to call her later and telling me to value myself.

I smiled and unwrapped the sandwich. It was delicious — ham and swiss on rye. I tore open a bag of potato chips and grabbed a Diet Coke, then took my food to the counter. When the phone rang, I jumped and shot potato chips across the room. Mick obligingly siphoned them up.

I answered on the third ring with a tentative hello.

"Hello, Lilah. It's Pet."

"Oh, Pet. I'm so sorry. What you must think of me."

"Of *you*? What are you talking about? My sister tried to kill you. I have been trying to get up the courage to call you and apologize for Harmonia — for our whole family — and to ask your forgiveness."

"Pet — don't cry."

"We should have seen it. We should have known. But how could we? She was our family member. Maybe we were too close to it. They said — she's going to need medication. That she has paranoid delusions."

"Oh my. I'm sorry, Pet."

"But maybe it will mean she'll get some help, rather than be sent to some prison far away. I don't know. What I know is that she killed people — two good people who I cared about — and she tried to kill you. I can't get over it — she knew you were my good friend, and yet she tried to kill you. And now she's ruined our friendship forever!"

"Pet, you're still my friend. And I'm sure you and I will still make chili together for years to come. Right?"

"I'm so glad to hear you say that, Lilah. You're such a good person. A truly good person, and that's why I'm so glad we're friends."

"Me, too, Pet. And I'm sorry about Harmonia. I know how hard it must be on your family."

"Father Schmidt is with us. He's helping us through. And he said that wherever Harmonia ends up, he'll be able to visit her as her personal chaplain. That brought us a lot of comfort, because she loves him so much. He'll help her to atone for what she's done — he'll help her to see the sin of it, and to be sorry."

"That's a good thing. Pet — can I ask you — the other night, I thought I saw you walking around near my house. Was that you?"

"Oh. Well, yes. I was going to talk to you, but then I saw a police car outside your house and it made me nervous. I didn't want them suspecting me of anything."

"What did you want?"

"It's funny to say now, but — I was thinking we could branch out and make something new. Always with the chili as a failsafe. But I wanted people to know that I could make other things. Even though I can't make anything at all."

I laughed, and Pet joined me. Our laughter was at least three parts relief.

"I'll talk to you soon, Pet. We'll think about those new recipes."

"Good-bye, Lilah. Thank you. And I'm sorry," said Perpetua Grandy.

I hung up and saw the light blinking on my answering machine; I had heard the call waiting beep while I spoke to Pet, but I obviously wasn't going to interrupt her to speak to another caller. Now I clicked a button and heard Parker's voice.

"Lilah. I just got your call. Thank you. It was good to hear from you. I hope you're doing okay and that black eye looks a little better today. I just wanted to say — I miss you, too. The other night, in your kitchen — we had a real connection. But I'm going to need a little time, just to work some things out inside myself. I hope you can understand that. There's a part of me that doesn't even understand it, but — hell, I'm leaving the worst message ever. Anyway, thanks for the invitation. Take care."

And a *click.*

I listened to it eight times, and then I grew sick of myself and my teenage mooning.

"Mick, let's go for a walk," I said.

A week later I had not heard from Parker. I

did not expect to hear from him ever again. I had started back into my routine: work at the real estate office in the day, deliveries to clandestine clients on nights and weekends. It was all fine, and I was fine. Life just didn't seem as pretty as it had before, but that was the reality of relationships.

In the evening I continued to listen to scratchy recordings of Rossano Brazzi singing about lost love. No one had ever sung those songs the way he did. Back in high school, when I was immersing myself in *South Pacific* as an earnest young thespian, I had listened to the movie sound track, starring soulful Rossano Brazzi and spunky Mitzi Gaynor, over and over. Although Brazzi played the role of a Frenchman, he was clearly an Italian. In the process of listening to the CD, I'd fallen in love with Brazzi's voice, and it remained my gauge for romance. Perhaps that's why I'd been attracted to Angelo — because with his Italian accent and good looks, he was my modern-day Brazzi, young again and ready to fall in love with me. Except that Angelo was real and flawed, and Brazzi had been playing out a fiction for my romantic soul.

Now I walked with Mick down a November-gray street, wet with recent rain. There's something lovely about November, despite its bare trees and sad gray skies. It is a reminder of the solemnities of life, and its starkness is as satisfying as stripped-down wood, as honest as a haiku. This weather, this season, made me want to be honest, as well. I faced the fact that I was twenty-seven and unlucky in love, but blessed with a good family, some solid talents, and a healthy enough constitution that I would probably live for many more decades. It was time for me to take control. I told Mick this as we walked, and he seemed to approve.

By the time we returned to Dickens Street and our beloved home, we were in a good place. I had "Blackbird," one of my dad's favorite Beatles tunes, floating melodically in my head. I liked it, especially the part about learning to fly with broken wings.

I took off Mick's leash and poured him some water, and he went to his basket by the fireplace.

The phone rang. I picked it up, said hello, and was greeted by the smooth, friendly voice of Esther Reynolds. Behind her I could hear a hubbub of voices and the clatter and clank of cutlery: the sounds of a busy kitchen.

"Hello, Lilah Drake! As promised, I am calling you in the midst of holiday chaos. I read about you in the paper, and I thought I'd better give you a few days to let things calm down. But now here I am, in desperate need of someone who knows what she's doing in a kitchen. So here's my question: are you still interested? If so, we're ready for you now."

I sat down at my kitchen table and looked around. Everything was neat and perfect. This was my milieu; the kitchen was the one place that I felt truly confident. I could be happy doing this forever. "I'm glad to hear from you," I said. A tree in my backyard undulated in the wind, shaking its branches at me.

"And your answer is?"

"I'm interested," I said. "And I can be there tomorrow morning."

I looked at Mick across the room, and he nodded.

RECIPES

PET'S CHILI
(Imagined by Lilah Drake)

Angelo's Gourmet Items:

1 8-ounce can Angelo's Gourmet tomato sauce

1 16-ounce can Angelo's Gourmet diced tomatoes

1/2 cup Angelo's Gourmet organic peanut butter

2 tablespoons Angelo's Gourmet chili sauce

1 15-ounce can pureed pumpkin

Other Items:

1 tablespoon butter

1 yellow onion, diced

1 green bell pepper, chopped

2 1/2 pounds lean ground beef

1 teaspoon cumin

2 teaspoons chili powder

1 teaspoon fresh oregano

2 teaspoons Hungarian paprika
1 16-ounce can dark red kidney beans
1 16-ounce can light red kidney beans

Heat a tablespoon of real butter in a Dutch oven; when it is melted, add diced onions and peppers. Enjoy the aroma, and allow the vegetables to soften. Add ground beef and break up into pieces; allow to cook evenly. When it is brown, remove all excess grease with a turkey baster.

Now your meat is even leaner. Pour in the rest of the wet ingredients; sprinkle dry ingredients on top, and mix thoroughly. A wonderful smell should permeate the air. The longer it cooks, the better it will smell. Serve after the ingredients have simmered together for at least a half hour.

Serving Ideas:
Consider having some "sprinkling" toppings in bowls on the table; that way people can help themselves according to their tastes. Some ideas for toppings include:
shredded cheese
sour cream
raw onions, diced
thinly sliced limes
diced tomatoes

avocado

bacon bits

corn bread croutons

Enjoy with friends. Chili is all about companionship.

LILAH'S "COMPANY'S COMING" SCONES
(Made for Britt and Terry)

3 cups flour

1/2 cup granulated sugar

5 teaspoons baking powder

1/4 teaspoon baking soda

1/4 teaspoon cinnamon

1/2 teaspoon salt

3/4 cup butter

1 egg

1 cup milk

1 teaspoon vanilla extract

Preheat the oven to 400 degrees. Lightly grease a baking sheet. (**Lilah's quick tip:** save butter wrappers in a box or bag in your fridge. When it's time to grease a pan, just slip one out and run it over the sheet — easy greasing with no mess!)

Combine all dry ingredients; gradually add softened butter. Finally, stir in the egg, milk, and vanilla extract. Mix until you have a stiff dough. Turn this out onto a floured surface and knead gently. Roll out the dough until it is about 1/2 inch thick. Then cut into eight even pieces and shape as you wish on a greased baking sheet. Bake for 15–20 minutes.

Options: add fruit or nuts to the recipe according to your taste, or sprinkle finished scones with cinnamon for a delicious breakfast bread!

Traditional sides: scones are traditionally served with strawberries or strawberry jam, clotted cream (or whipped cream), lemon curd, or butter.

LILAH'S FRENCH TOAST CASSEROLE
(Made for Toby Atwater)

1 loaf of soft French bread (or 10 soft rolls)
8 large eggs
2 cups half-and-half
1 cup milk
2 tablespoons sugar
1 tablespoon vanilla
1/4 teaspoon cinnamon
1/4 teaspoon nutmeg
Salt to taste

Streusel Topping (This Can Vary, But Here's One Option):

2 sticks (1 pound) butter
1 teaspoon almond extract
1 cup brown sugar
1 cup corn syrup
1 cup chopped pecans (or walnuts)
1/2 teaspoon cinnamon
1/2 teaspoon nutmeg
1/4 teaspoon cloves

For streusel: soften butter, then mix in the remaining ingredients until the topping has a crumbly consistency.

Meanwhile, slice bread into twenty slices (or separate ten rolls) and lay out in buttered baking dish.

Blend all of the ingredients and pour them over the slices of bread, making sure that the wet mixture gets under and in between the slices, and that all of the bread is saturated.

Cover the mixture with tinfoil and refrigerate overnight. In the morning, spread the streusel mixture on top of the saturated, chilled bread, and bake for 40 minutes at 350 degrees.

(As an alternative to the streusel topping, you can choose a fruit like raspberries or strawberries, and sprinkle them on before baking. Blueberries and apples are delicious options, as well.)

Serve with pats of butter and maple syrup.

Be ready for a delicious surprise to share with friends or family! Toby's five children love this recipe, but adults love it, too!

FIESTA BAKE
(Imagined by Lilah Drake)

Angelo's Gourmet Items:
1 16-ounce can Angelo's Gourmet tomato sauce
1 16-ounce can Angelo's Gourmet diced tomatoes
1 Angelo's Gourmet taco seasoning packet

Other Items:
1 white onion, diced
1 small green pepper, chopped
1 pound lean ground beef
1 16-ounce can kidney beans
1/4 cup water
1 teaspoon chili powder
1 1/3 cups uncooked instant rice
1 cup shredded cheddar cheese

Heat onion and pepper in a buttered pan;

add ground beef and cook until brown; drain excess grease. Mix beef mixture with tomato sauce, diced tomatoes, taco seasoning, kidney beans, water, chili powder, and rice. Pour into a baking pan.

Bake at 350 degrees for 20 minutes; pull out partway and sprinkle on cheddar cheese. Slide back into oven and bake for another 10 minutes.

Remove from oven and allow to cool for 10 more minutes.

Serve in individual bowls with dollops of sour cream on top and tortilla chips tucked around the sides — they are perfect for dipping and scooping!

LILAH'S BREAKFAST FRITTATA
(Variation Four: Frittata with Red Peppers, Onions, and Potatoes)

1 large onion, diced
6 to 8 small red potatoes (about 12 ounces), diced
2 red peppers, diced
Dash pepper
Dash fresh thyme
Dash fresh oregano
8 eggs, beaten
4 ounces crumbled feta

Preheat the oven to 400 degrees.

In a frying pan, sauté onion, potatoes, and red peppers. Add pepper, thyme, and oregano to taste. Mix until vegetables are of a desired consistency.

Add the eggs to the pan and mix in vegetables; pour into greased baking pan and sprinkle feta over the top of the mixture.

Bake for 10–15 minutes, until the eggs are completely set, look golden brown, and pull away from the sides of the pan.

Let the frittata cool. Then slice and serve with any of these elegant options:

sliced fruit
crusty bread
green salad
baked, oiled pita chips

Friends and family will ask for this delicious option again and again, and the magic of it is that it makes a good breakfast, lunch, or dinner!

ANGELO'S EGGPLANT PARMIGIANA
(Available at Cardelini's in Pine Haven, 444 Main Street)

1/2 cup bread crumbs (best from a dried loaf of Italian bread)
1 large eggplant, sliced
1 cup fresh shredded mozzarella
1 can Angelo's Gourmet diced tomatoes
1 can Angelo's Gourmet tomato sauce
1 teaspoon basil
1 teaspoon oregano
1 pinch garlic
Real Irish butter
Fresh grated parmesan cheese
Pepper

Preheat oven to 400 degrees.

Set aside your bread crumbs in a wide, shallow bowl.

Cut the eggplant into 10–12 slices, making sure they are at least 1/2 inch thick. Rub both sides of each slice with melted butter, then dip into bread crumbs.

Lay the slices on a baking sheet and bake for about nine minutes, or until tender; slide out the sheet and sprinkle the eggplant slices with fresh mozzarella. Bake one minute more, or until cheese is nicely browned and melted.

While they bake, combine the tomatoes, basil, oregano, garlic, and sauce in a pot. (You can substitute fresh diced tomatoes for the Angelo's tomatoes, but Angelo's are as good as fresh.) Cook tomato mixture until it is almost boiling, then lower heat and cook for five more minutes. Lay out four bowls and pour sauce mixture evenly among them. Take baked eggplant slices and distribute them into the four bowls (you should be able to serve three slices of eggplant to each diner). Sprinkle with parmesan and fresh pepper.

As an alternative, serve the eggplant and sauce on sliced loaves of fresh Italian bread. The eggplant parmigiana sandwich is a favorite at Cardelini's!

ABOUT THE AUTHOR

Julia Buckley is the author of the Teddy Thurber Mysteries and the Madeline Mann Mysteries. She's a member of the Mystery Writers of America, Sisters in Crime, and the Romance Writers of America, as well as the Chicago Writers Association. Julia has taught high school English for twenty-six years; she lives near Chicago with her husband, two sons, four cats, and one beagle. You can visit the author at juliabuckley.com.